"Mermaids shouldn't swim with sharks."

"I'm not—" Jassy didn't have time to finish the sentence. He'd dragged her into his arms, holding her tightly against his hard body, and one hand caught her chin, holding her face still.

"I'm a dangerous man, Jassy," Caleb muttered. "Haven't you realized that by now? I'm a danger to all you love and care about."

"Caleb..."

"Don't reason with me. Don't beg me, don't plead, don't bribe and, for God's sake, don't treat me like I have a conscience. I don't."

He was so close. His body was rock hard and hot against hers. She could smell the warmth of his skin, the whiskey he'd had before dinner, the night air surrounding them. "Of course, you do," she said.

"I guess I'm going to have to prove it." He pushed her back against the stucco wall, and his mouth covered hers with savage insistence....

ABOUT THE AUTHOR

Anne Stuart has a real appreciation for "steamy Southern lust," having lived in New England most of her life. Her husband, two children, three cats and a springer spaniel named Rags keep her busy when she's not writing.

Books by Anne Stuart
HARLEQUIN AMERICAN ROMANCE

Don't miss any of our special offers. Write to us at the following address for information on our newest releases.

Harlequin Reader Service
P.O. Box 1397, Buffalo, NY 14240
Canadian address: P.O. Box 603,
Fort Erie, Ont. L2A 5X3

ANNE STUART

HEAT LIGHTNING

Harlequin Books

TORONTO • NEW YORK • LONDON
AMSTERDAM • PARIS • SYDNEY • HAMBURG
STOCKHOLM • ATHENS • TOKYO • MILAN
MADRID • WARSAW • BUDAPEST • AUCKLAND

Published April 1992

ISBN 0-373-16434-3

HEAT LIGHTNING

Chapter One

The man was pure trouble. It didn't take much to see that, and Jassy Turner was a little more observant than most. It came from having to keep an eye out for details, for the little things that could turn triumph to disaster, turn a happy family evening into a screaming tangle, turn a successful fund-raising event into a debacle.

She'd worked hard that hot August day to make sure everything was just right at Belle Rive. The wide, manicured lawns leading down to the river were covered with brightly colored fair booths, with immaculately dressed men in their pale linen suits, with women in their floating summer tea dresses. The children tumbled around at their feet, grubby, noisy, bringing their own vitality to the stifling atmosphere. If it had been up to Jassy, the annual hospital fete, the fund-raising event that had been the Turners' pet project since the beginning of time, would have been for children only. Except that children couldn't dig deep into their pockets to keep the tiny little hospital going.

So while the lawns were covered with pony rides and games and even a carousel trucked in from Sarasota, the wide veranda was covered with long, linen-covered tables, and her mother, Claire, presided at the huge silver teapot, the trembling in her hands stilled by a discreet, purely medicinal, shot of vodka.

She'd known these people all her life, Jassy thought, moving through the crowd to the edge of the veranda, resting her hands on the wide stone railing. She'd never been away for longer than a few months, and she knew what every single one of them was thinking as the stranger made his way through the crowds, moving directly toward the veranda.

"My God, Jassy, who is that?" Mary-Louise Albertson hissed in her ear, her eyes bright with appreciation.

Jassy couldn't pretend to misunderstand. The noise from the children below covered up the sudden quiet on the veranda, but the forty or so people enjoying Miz Claire's tea managed an impressive buzz of conversation. And Jassy knew perfectly well at least half of them were discussing the sudden appearance of the stranger.

"I don't know," she replied, wishing she could turn away, unable to move. She brushed her hands down the length of her pale peach dress, and found they were cool and sweaty on this stifling hot day.

"He sure is a hell of a lot more man than I've seen around here in a long time," Mary-Louise said with a sigh. "The men around here were born wearing suits, I swear. I don't think I've seen that much chest since I saw a Patrick Swayze movie last year. The man is absolutely sinful, he's so good-looking."

"Patrick Swayze?" Jassy murmured.

"Him, too," Mary-Louise allowed. "But he's not here. The man who's heading directly toward us is in the flesh, and what wonderful flesh it is. My heavens, is that an earring he's wearing?"

"It is. I think you'd better forget him, Mary-Louise. Your mama won't allow you to keep company with a man wearing an earring,'' Jassy said with her first touch of humor.

"My mama wouldn't allow me to keep company with a man who wears shabby jeans, an old work shirt unbuttoned to the waist, and hair hanging down to his collar. However, my mama didn't raise no dumb chickies. What she doesn't know won't hurt her. I'm certainly not planning on making her privy to all my peccadillos.''

Jassy felt a real pang of dismay. "Mary-Louise, your divorce isn't even final yet...."

"I'm only going to play with him, Jassy. I'm not going to marry him. I've just got to figure out how I'm going to plan my attack.'' She drifted away, deep in thought. Jassy didn't even turn to watch her go.

He was halfway there now, and he'd stopped to talk to a little boy who was sobbing loud enough to be heard over the general din. At his feet was a smashed ice-cream cone, and the dark-haired child was crying with an enthusiasm found only in the young.

A moment later, after a short, earnest conversation with the stranger, the tears had miraculously stopped. In the next, a replacement ice-cream cone found its way into little Tommy Lee Philips's grubby fist. His mother was there, casting a wary eye at the stranger, and Jassy watched as he charmed the mother as effortlessly as he charmed the child.

Trouble, she thought again, acknowledging the little burning feeling in the pit of her stomach. And he's heading this way.

He wasn't particularly aware of her watching him. He had to know that almost everyone was watching his approach, either openly or covertly, and one pair of eyes wasn't going to mean any more than another.

Mary-Louise was right: he *was* more man than they'd seen in a long time. She was surrounded by southern gentlemen, all tall and immaculate in their white linen suits, Princeton basketball players and gentlemen farmers, her own brother, Harrison, included. The man coming up the lawn was cut from a different cloth.

He was tall, but not as tall as the men surrounding her, probably not much more than six feet. He wore scuffed leather boots, dusty, ripped jeans, and a work shirt open to his waist, exposing a great deal of bronzed, glistening chest. The men around her didn't sweat. Probably because they didn't do enough hard work to sweat, she thought with a trace of humor.

He was wearing dark glasses in the bright midafternoon sun, and they obscured half his face. His dark-blond hair was shoved back, and there really was a gold hoop in his left ear. A small one, but there nonetheless, and she could just imagine Harrison's contempt when the man finally had the nerve to reach them.

Except the man didn't seem to be lacking in nerve. His advance was steady, determined, his walk an inexplicable part of his presence. It wasn't a swagger—he was too sure of himself to need to swagger. It wasn't a stroll—he had too much intensity to stroll. It was a combination of both, a purposeful stride that allowed time for distractions like crying children, but moved inexorably onward.

He glanced her way when he reached the bottom step of the veranda. The polite murmur of the well-bred group crowded onto the wide stone terrace abated only slightly, and yet Jassy knew that every eye, every ear of the upper crust of Turner's Landing was concentrating on the rough stranger's presence.

Even behind the sunglasses the heat of his gaze was able to touch her. As it touched all the women present, impartial, seductive, an instinctive flirtation that meant absolutely nothing. If Mary-Louise wanted him she'd probably have no trouble getting him. But not for long.

"Jassy?" Her mother's cool, calm voice held not the slightest bit of slur. Thank heaven for small favors. Claire didn't usually do well on days like these.

Jassy forced herself to turn away from the stranger, moving to her mother's side with unhurried grace. "Do you want me to take over for you, Mama?"

"I do not. I'm doing just fine. I want you to tell me who that man is, and what he's doing here."

Even her mother's somewhat bleary eyesight was clear enough to detect trouble when it walked up her front lawn. "I don't know, Mama," she said. "Maybe he just heard about the tea?"

"Dressed like that?" Her mother sniffed with disapproval. "Things may have changed, but we don't have to get slack, dear. I refuse to pour tea for a man who's not wearing a tie."

"He's not wearing much of a shirt, either," Jassy murmured. "As a matter of fact, I don't think he's here for the fete, or the tea."

"Then what's he here for?" Her mother's voice was querulous, and Mary-Louise's mother cast a disapproving glance in their direction.

"I don't know. Mama, lower your voice. Mrs. Stevenson is watching us."

"Old biddy," Claire said. "She hoped I'd be indisposed this afternoon so she could play the grande dame. As long as I'm on this earth I'll be the one to pour at the hospital fete. Do you hear me, Jassy?"

"I hear you, Mama," Jassy said wearily. "So does everyone else." In point of fact, no one else was paying any attention to Claire and her daughter. That usual source of gossip was small potatoes compared to the man who'd mounted the wide stone steps and was moving without haste toward the group of people in the center.

Jassy edged away, toward the upcoming confrontation. She didn't know what she was expecting, or how she thought she might be able to stop it, but she knew she had to try.

She expected the stranger wouldn't be quite so devastating up close. She'd been wrong. The closer he got, the more overwhelming he seemed. He was a few feet away from her when he stopped, directly in front of her older brother, Harrison, lord of the manor, de facto king of Turner's Landing.

No one made any more polite pretense of conversation. The citizens of Turner's Landing were well-bred, but some things were even too much for their ingrained manners. The distant noise of shrieking children provided only a backdrop for the silence that enveloped Harrison Turner and the stranger.

Harrison, immaculate and polite as always, turned to the stranger, an uneasy expression in his brown eyes. "Can I help you?"

The stranger smiled. He had a wide, mobile mouth beneath the sunglasses, and the smile should have been charming, infectious. Indeed, the men surrounding Harrison managed uncertain smiles themselves. Jassy wasn't in the mood to smile. She stood there, behind Harrison, ready to do battle to protect her brother, if need be. He might not realize the stranger was trouble, yet. But she did.

"I'm Caleb Spenser," he said, his voice a smooth, easy drawl, roughened just slightly from cigarettes, like liquid honey laced with whiskey. "I've just bought the place down the road and I thought I'd stop by and make your acquaintance. Perhaps I picked an awkward time.''

Jassy could see Harrison's broad shoulders relax. "Now's a fine time," he said, his voice a hearty boom that signaled a return to a semblance of normalcy. "We're having a fund-raiser for our little hospital, and we're counting on all the local landowners to do their share. I'm Harrison Turner, by the way, and these are some of my friends and neighbors.'' He introduced the small group of men surrounding him, deliberately omitting Jassy at his shoulder.

Caleb Spenser's smile didn't change. Harrison seemed to take it at face value, an affable expression of goodwill. Jassy wasn't so sure. "I'll be more than happy to do my share,'' he said in that deep voice of his that sent flutters down half the female backbones on the veranda. Even hers, Jassy had to admit.

"Whereabouts did you buy?'' Harrison inquired, still sounding like the gentleman farmer talking to poor white trash. "I hadn't heard that any land was on the market.'' His condescending tone suggested that if he had, he would have been certain to have bought it himself, or at least made sure that whoever did purchase it passed his strict standards.

"An old place down by the swamp," the man said. "Used to be a bordello, I hear.''

Harrison's slightly rosy complexion paled. "The Moon Palace? You bought the Moon Palace? What in hell for?''

Caleb Spenser shrugged. "I kind of liked it. Besides, it's what I do. I buy run-down places, fix them up and sell them.''

"You won't find any buyers for the Moon Palace,'' Harrison said flatly. "This happens to be the one town in the whole damned state of Florida that hasn't been affected by the real estate boom. If you think you're gonna turn around and make a killing with some developer, you better think again, son. We're a tight-knit place, and we like things as they are.''

"I bet you do," Caleb murmured. "But things don't stay the same. I expect you've lived long enough to discover that." He pushed his sunglasses up to his forehead, and Jassy took a deep, involuntary breath, one loud enough to get his attention.

He had the most extraordinary eyes. They were a light, translucent, almost silvery gray, with just a touch of blue in them, like the shimmer of color on a frosty morning. They held just as much warmth. In the tanned planes of his face they made his smile seem the cynical thing that it was. If anyone had any doubt that Caleb Spenser was a man to contend with, all they had to do was look into those clear, cool eyes and they'd know better. Trouble, Jassy thought, as his eyes met hers beyond Harrison's shoulder. Real trouble.

"Do I know you?" Harrison demanded, unaware of the byplay going on behind him. "You look real familiar."

Jassy felt herself dismissed, as once more those mesmerizing eyes met her brother's, and Caleb Spenser's smile was not a pleasant sight. He looked like a shark at feeding time. "I've never been in Turner's Landing before," he said, not answering the question.

"But I'm sure I've seen you before."

Caleb Spenser shrugged. "Now that you mention it, you look familiar to me. I used to know someone who looked a lot like you. But his name was Billy Ray Smith, not Harrison Turner."

For a moment Jassy thought her brother was going to throw up. He looked at that cool, smiling intruder with a pale, sickly expression, and Jassy's worst fears were confirmed. She still didn't know how, or why. She only knew what.

"Sorry," Harrison managed, his voice strained. "I'm not in the habit of using aliases."

"I wouldn't have thought so, a fine gentleman like yourself," Spenser said easily, and most people would have thought he'd dropped the notion. Jassy knew otherwise. "Would you mind if I looked around, met a few people? I'm planning on being in these parts for a while, and I'd like to find out what kind of people I'll be dealing with."

Jassy couldn't stand it anymore. Her brother still looked tense and sick beside her as she stepped into the group. "You're not from around here, Mr. Spenser?" she inquired, pulling out all her charm.

"I'm from just about everyplace but here, Miss . . . ?"

"This is my baby sister, Jacinthe," Harrison said, suddenly protective.

Spenser nodded, getting the message. "As I was saying, I'm from about everyplace but the gulf coast of Florida. I've spent a lot of time in Louisiana, in Georgia, Tennessee, South Carolina. What time I've spent in Florida was mainly on the East Coast. Near a little town called St. Florence."

Once again she felt Harrison's turmoil, and she knew the obscure name of that town wasn't an accident.

"Well," she said brightly, "we're glad you're here now. We're very proud of our little town. Turner's Landing is one of the few undeveloped, unspoiled little towns in this part of Florida. I think you'll enjoy your stay here."

"Oh, I expect to, Miss Turner," he said. "I surely do." If the man had had a hat he would have tipped it. Instead he sort of nodded his head and drifted away, politely enough, but then he was gone. Jassy didn't move, watching as he drifted over toward the group of women by the railing who'd been watching him avidly, Mary-Louise included. Even from a distance she could see them preen and pout prettily.

She didn't blame them. She, who was usually immune to that type of flirtation, that type of man, had felt the intense charm he seemed to turn off and on automatically. She wouldn't be surprised to see Mary-Louise biting his ankles in another minute.

But then he was gone, leaving the women staring after him, hungry looks on their faces. She watched as he worked the crowd, moving from group to group with that same inexorable charm. Harrison stood beside her, watching in the same silence as the men around them turned to a polite discussion of the weather. Caleb Spenser was too close to be discussed, as everyone was longing to.

Claire even poured him a cup of tea. But then, Claire had never been much of a judge of character, starting with Jassy's father. She seemed to have forgotten her disapproval of his casual attire, and her face looked positively youthful as she looked up at Spenser from her thronelike position behind the huge silver teapot. Jassy could feel Harrison's outrage, and she turned, half expecting him to join Spenser and Claire. Half expecting him to pick the stranger up by the scruff of his neck and throw him off the terrace.

But Harrison had never been one to deal with things directly. Instead he turned on his heel, disappearing into the house without a word.

Jassy was torn. On the one hand, she wanted to go after her brother, to demand to know what was going on. It was more than clear to her that he'd known Caleb Spenser at some time in the past, and that association wasn't the slightest bit pleasant. He just as obviously didn't want people knowing about it.

But it wasn't an accident that Spenser had showed up there in a crowd of friends and family. And he'd known who he'd find when he reached the veranda—he'd headed straight toward Harrison. It wasn't an accident that he'd bought the old Moon Palace. The tumbledown building lay on a knoll by the edge of a swamp, and it had been vacant for the better part of twenty years. He'd have no use for it in a conventional sense. Even fixed up and spruced up, he'd be hard put to find buyers. It was too damp, too remote, and as Harrison had told him, Turner's Landing was on the back end of beyond. The place was unspoiled and undeveloped, not because of any great nobility on the landowners' parts, but because no one had offered enough money. No one had even been interested.

Jassy glanced behind her, at the closed screen door where Harrison had disappeared. His wife, Lila, for once was unaware of her husband's absence, as she did her social duties and kept up a conversation with the dragon-like Mrs. Stevenson. No one seemed to have noticed he was gone, and she was torn by her need to go after him, to confront him. And to stay and guard the terrace.

Harrison could wait. She wasn't going to abandon the battlefield until the enemy had left. And that's who Caleb Spenser was, for sure. The enemy.

She felt a sudden prickling at the back of her neck. She turned, and found he was standing in front of her, too close, crowding her. She could smell his skin, smell the dust and sweat and heat of him, and she wanted to step back, away. She held her ground.

"Mr. Spenser," she said politely.

"Just Spenser," he said. "Unlike most people around here, I'm not the Mister type."

"And what type are you?"

"Why don't you find out?" he said, soft enough so that even the ruthlessly eavesdropping Mary-Louise missed it.

She was used to this, Jassy reminded herself. She was used to macho men who had to flirt with anything in skirts in order to assert their masculinity. It was just that Caleb Spenser was much better at it than most.

"Are you flirting with me, Mr. Spenser?" she inquired coolly. "Because if you are, I may as well tell you you're wasting your time. You may have all the other women eating out of your hand, but I'm a lost cause. Anyone around here can tell you that. I don't flirt, and I don't respond to men like you."

"Men like me, Miz Turner? And just how do you define a man like me?"

"Trouble," she said flatly, without thinking.

He laughed then, throwing back his head, and his teeth were very white, very large in his wide mouth. Like a shark, she thought again. "You've got more brains than most of the people around here," he said.

"Remember that, Mr. Spenser. You aren't going to be able to charm me into thinking you're harmless."

"Oh, I wouldn't ever want you to think I'm harmless," he said softly. "That's half the fun."

"Mr. Spenser..."

"Spenser," he corrected softly. And then he was gone. Moving down the front steps and across the lawn with a graceful stride that wasn't the slightest bit leisurely. She watched him go, and she shivered in the humid August heat, suddenly chilled.

"Well, what did he say to you?" Mary-Louise demanded. "You were both looking pretty intense. I wouldn't have thought he'd be your kind of man."

"He's not," Jassy said absently. He was out of sight now, and it was hard to believe he'd ever been there, unsettling everyone. But he had.

"That's good. I told you, I saw him first."

"Actually," Jassy pointed out with a strained return to impartial good humor, "I noticed him first. But you've known me for almost all my thirty-one years, Mary-Louise. Do you think he's my type?"

Mary-Louise laughed. "Point well taken. What do you suppose he's doing here?"

"Didn't you hear? He bought the Moon Palace. He's planning to renovate it."

"For heaven's sake, why?"

"Maybe he's planning to run it."

Mary-Louise laughed. "Honey, that man doesn't look like a procurer. Besides, I don't think this depressed area can support a high-tone bordello. Not unless he was going to work it himself. I think he just might be worth paying for."

"Mary-Louise!" Jassy sounded just as scandalized as Mary-Louise wanted her to. "You're incorrigible."

"It's true," Mary-Louise said.

"What's true?"

"That I'm incorrigible. And that he'd be worth paying."

"Behave yourself," Jassy said. "I'm going in to check on Harrison. I don't want you climbing on the table and doing a striptease over the punch bowl while I'm gone."

"There'd be no point in it," Mary-Louise said cheerfully. "Mr. Spenser's already left." She glanced after him, sighing exaggeratedly. "What's wrong with Harrison, anyway? He was looking sick as a dog."

"He has a touch of the stomach flu," Jassy, who never lied, said smoothly. "I told him he should take it easy, but you know Harrison. A firm believer in his social duties."

"A firm believer in parties," Mary-Louise said with a note in her voice Jassy couldn't quite decipher. "Give him a kiss for me. I'll go rescue poor little Lila from my mother."

"She'd appreciate it. My sister-in-law has never known how to stand up to anyone, and your mother even puts the fear of God in me."

"And you're so tough," Mary-Louise said with light mockery.

"Yes, I'm so tough," Jassy murmured to herself as she headed through the French doors.

The house was still and quiet, slightly cooler than the thick heat on the terrace. They were due for a whopper of a thunderstorm. Overdue, in fact.

She found Harrison in the study, sitting behind his desk, a half-empty glass of very dark whiskey in his hand. He didn't bother to look up when she entered—he'd know she'd be the only one who'd dare come after him.

She wasn't one for drinking, but somehow the circumstances seemed to call for it. She poured herself a half an inch of bourbon in a glass, filled the rest with water, and moved to the chair beside the desk.

"Cheers," she said, holding her glass aloft.

Harrison glared at her morosely. "I'm in a mess of trouble, Jassy." It was an uncharacteristic admission. Usually Harrison would choke before admitting a weakness. The situation must be even worse than she thought.

"No," she said, taking a delicate sip and shuddering. "We're a family. If one of us is in trouble we all are. You want to tell me about it?"

Harrison glanced at her. He was a very handsome man—in truth, much better looking than the insolent stranger who'd invaded their afternoon tea party. His charm was also legion—the paternalistic variety that made most women trust him.

He shook his head. "I've got to think about it for a while. Come up with a plan. In the meantime, what you don't know won't hurt you."

"Harrison..."

"It's not women's business," Harrison said firmly. "You let me take care of it and don't worry your pretty little head about a thing."

It was moments like these that made Jassy long to pour her drink into his lap. She'd fought his condescension for years, and had finally given up, learning she could get her own way, run things pretty much as she liked, as long as her brother thought he was in charge. He wasn't very cheerful right now, but it would take more than the appearance of a dangerous stranger to make him take action.

It would be up to her in the long run. And if he wouldn't tell her why Caleb Spenser was here, there was only one way to find out. She'd ask Spenser herself.

She smiled at Harrison, resisting the impulse to pat his hand, just as she'd resisted the impulse to dump her drink. "All right, Harrison. You know best."

And Harrison, self-absorbed as always, believed her.

Chapter Two

Jacinthe Amalia Claire Turner was a thirty-one-year-old spinster of this parish. Or so she liked to think of herself. Devoted to good works and her family, she worked tirelessly on whatever seemed to call for her efficient good humor. She was on the hospital fund-raising board, as all Turners were, she tutored high school students, she drove the ambulance for the local rescue squad, organized the church auctions, worked on the volunteer fire department, and single-handedly ran the battered women's shelter in town. In her spare time she ran the huge, rambling house called Belle Rive, and her motley family besides.

She fully expected to get married eventually. She'd had more than her share of beaux—handsome, gentlemanly men who knew how to treat a lady. Kindly, friendly, moderately liberated men she'd known since childhood, and even though most of them had married and were busy raising families, there were still at least three suitable prospects waiting in the wings. The forerunner was Jim Roberts, the local veterinarian, a man too well-bred to ever make demands or to push her.

She was planning to wait, however. Lila and Harrison had been trying desperately for children for the three years they'd been married. They didn't need the added stress of a full-scale wedding and a possibly ensuing pregnancy. Jassy still had a few years leeway. As soon as Lila conceived she'd consider getting married. In the meantime, there was no hurry.

Harrison and Lila didn't need the added stress of Caleb Spenser's arrival in town, either, but it was several days before Jassy had time to deal with it. The cleanup from the fair was a major undertaking, one which she oversaw and pitched in with her usual calm energy. Then Lila needed someone to drive her down to Clearwater for the next round of tests, someone to hold her hand while she cried all the way home, someone to listen while she poured out her insecurities and fears. Lila had always been a clinging, frail girl, and she was terrified that Harrison would leave her when she couldn't provide him with a child. Harrison and his family had done everything to reassure her, but she still bordered on panic.

Then Claire went into a slump, refusing to leave her room, refusing to eat, refusing to do anything but sit in front of the television and sip delicately at her medicinal bottle. It took all Jassy's patience and determination to coax her back into civilization once more, and then there was a crisis down at the Women's Center. Tommy Lee Philips's father had once more taken his fists to Tommy's pretty mother, and the two of them had fled to the shelter for the third time that year. Jassy had the depressing feeling that it wouldn't be the last, but she was sympathetic, supportive and nonjudgmental. Faith Philips wouldn't leave Leroy and break the cycle of battering until she was ready to, and haranguing, lecturing and sermonizing wouldn't do any good but make her feel more miserable.

In the end, four days had passed before Jassy could put her hastily formed plan to work. During those four days, wherever she went, people talked about Spenser. About the huge order he'd placed at the lumber yard. About his charm with the ladies. About his secretive ways. And about the eventual fate of the Moon Palace.

She didn't bother telling anyone where she was going that steaming hot Thursday afternoon. For one thing, people seldom asked, unless they needed her for something, and she deliberately picked a time when everyone was well taken care of. Claire had gone out for a bridge game with Harriet Stevenson and her cronies, fortifying herself beforehand. Harrison was at work in the library, dealing with estate matters, and Lila, glutton for punishment that she was, had gone to visit a friend's new baby. She'd be in for a storm of weeping when she returned, and Jassy would need to be there to provide a shoulder. But in the meantime she had a few hours to herself, a few hours to see what she could learn about the stranger in their midst.

She took the old Jeep rather than her serviceable Ford. The roads leading to and from the old bordello were muddy and rutted, and four-wheel drive would come in handy. Besides, she didn't want to appear to be too much of a lady bountiful when she paid her social visit.

She put the basket on the seat beside her in the Jeep, then glanced down at her clothes, for the first time wondering whether she should have put a little more care into what she was wearing. It was too hot to wrap up, much as a small, insecure part of her wanted to. The oversize white shirt was buttoned up higher than the sultry weather required, the ankle-length cotton skirt was loose enough to let the air circulate. She probably should have worn boots rather than sandals. Water moccasins were known to frequent the swamps around Turner's Landing. One might have paid Spenser a visit.

It would probably be for the best if one had curled right up next to him. Harrison had been secretive, on edge, since the man's arrival, and the entire household mirrored his moods. Claire's recent bout stemmed directly from Harrison's snappiness, and Lila's crying jags seemed more frequent.

But she couldn't really wish ill on a stranger. Even if that stranger probably wished the Turners, Harrison in particular, a great deal of ill, she didn't want him dead. She just wanted him gone, out of their safe, comfortable life.

He wasn't going to budge, however, without a push. And while she didn't consider herself a pushy person, she did pride herself on being able to get people to do what she wanted with a minimum of fuss.

She didn't expect it to be easy. She didn't expect it to be fast. But she expected to win in the end, simply because she always did. And the well-being of her family mattered too much to her to even contemplate losing.

The Moon Palace was set a good five miles out of the small town of Turner's Landing, on the edge of Beeman Swamp. During the twenties, thirties and forties the randy young bucks of Turner's Landing had beaten a path to the door, learning the first lessons in the art of love. But the fifties had been a slowdown, and by the late sixties the place had closed down and been abandoned to the encroaching wilderness. Most people forgot it existed—the road led to nowhere but the Moon Palace, and the place was damp, mosquito-ridden and decaying. If people were looking for housing, they did better with one of the anonymous little boxes Harrison had built on a tract of land on the west side of town.

She pulled the Jeep to a stop beside an ancient, beat-up old pickup truck, turning off the engine. The place was still, silent, only the sound of a faint, lazy breeze riffling through the trees breaking the stillness. No sounds of saws or hammers, no sign of anyone working on the place.

It was a large, rambling building, conscientiously antebellum. She'd explored it when she was younger, with Mary-Louise trailing along behind her, and the two of them had giggled and made wild, anatomically inaccurate guesses as to what had gone on in those decaying bedrooms with the red flocked wallpaper stained with damp. The old house still had a sort of sexual mystery about it, with the huge live oaks looming over the front, dripping Spanish moss halfway down to the overgrown grounds. Jassy could tell herself the couplings that went on behind those doors were sad, financially inspired ones. But in truth, she could still feel some of the lazy, erotic energy of the place.

Reaching up, she made sure her thick brown hair was tucked securely back. Hair like hers was a trial and a blessing. It was much too thick and curly, and the humidity of late August made it an impossible mass to control. She had no choice but to pin it back, off her neck, if she wanted to survive the heat. She'd cut it short once, and ended up looking like a clown. Nowadays she just let it grow, pinning it back and ignoring the wisps of hair that escaped to curl around her face.

Grabbing her basket, she slid from the Jeep and approached the front door. It stood open, letting in mosquitoes and whatever critters felt the urge to frequent the Moon Palace, and Jassy hesitated before knocking on the peeling doorjamb.

Not a sound. The house was dank and dark inside, and she hesitated, too well-bred to simply walk into a stranger's house without an invitation. She checked her hair again, a nervous gesture she wasn't usually prone to make, and called out.

"Mr. Spenser?"

She heard a noise then, a rough scrabbling sound, and a dog appeared in the hallway. At least, she assumed it was a dog. He was absolutely huge, a motley shade of black and brown, and his ancestry was as mysterious as the old house. She could see Newfoundland in his size and the shape of his head, retriever in his coat and heaven knows what else in his sway back and short legs.

He opened his mouth, displaying an impressive set of canine teeth, and whoofed lightly. And then he padded forward, butting his huge head under her hand.

Jassy squatted down, scratching him lightly. "What a big, silly dog you are," she murmured affectionately. She loved animals, but Harrison was allergic to them, and she'd never owned a pet larger than a goldfish. "You're not much of a watchdog, I'll say that for you."

"He's not supposed to be." He was there, watching her, his eyes shadowed in the dark hall. "I can take care of my own."

Jassy looked up, swallowed convulsively, and rose. He was shirtless today in the still, moist air, and he hadn't bothered to shave. He should have looked derelict. Instead he simply looked . . . dangerous.

She picked up her basket and advanced, a determined, unwavering smile on her face. "I'm the local representative of the welcoming committee, Mr. Spenser. As your nearest neighbors we thought we ought to welcome you to Turner's Landing."

He didn't move, just let his eyes drift down over her body. "Who's we? Don't tell me your brother's decided I'll be an asset to the community?"

She considered lying, then thought better of it. She made it a habit not to lie—it was too easy to get caught. Besides, she had the unnerving feeling that this was a man who could see through lies. Who could see through almost any kind of falsehood.

"Actually he doesn't know I'm here," she said cheerfully. "But he knows I usually make an effort to welcome any newcomer, and if he didn't feel you were welcome I'm sure he would have said something. Do you think he doesn't want you here, Mr. Spenser?"

"Just Spenser," he said. "What's in your basket?"

She gripped it in both hands. "Answer my question and I'll answer yours."

His smile was slight, enough to make her wish she'd worn a turtleneck shirt in this vast, humid heat. "Games, Miss Turner? I think you'll find I'm not a good man to play games with."

"I don't tend to play games with men."

"Don't you? They can be fun. As long as you're prepared to face the consequences."

He was too much for her. She could feel the sweat forming at the small of her back, between her breasts, and she shifted the weight in her basket. "Red beans and rice," she said, answering his question. "Two loaves of fresh bread, a dozen chocolate chip cookies and a bottle of Miss Sadie's elderberry wine."

He reached over and lifted the red-checked cloth covering her offering. "Who's Miss Sadie?"

"Our cook, housekeeper, savior of our souls, warden. We wouldn't survive without her. Most of this is compliments of Miss Sadie."

"Give Miss Sadie my thanks. What isn't her doing?"

Trust him to pick up on that tiny slip. Once more she considered lying, and then thought better of it. Why should she lie? "The cookies, of course. Miss Sadie never could make enough to keep me happy, so I learned to cook early on."

"You have a sweet tooth, Miss Turner?"

"Please, you make me sound like some ancient southern belle. My name is Jassy." She kept her voice light, casual, trying to keep her mind from the opulent, decaying bedrooms upstairs and what she used to imagine went on in them.

"Jassy," he said, and she wished he hadn't. He took the basket from her hands and she stepped back, a little too quickly, then cursed her nervousness. "This is quite a friendly little town. More so than I would have imagined."

"We don't get too many strangers around here."

"So I gather. I would have thought that would make you more skittish."

He'd chosen that word deliberately. For one of the first times in her life she was feeling skittish, and the knowledge that he'd recognized that fact, commented on it, lashed her pride back into existence.

She straightened her back, pushing a hand through her escaping hair. "We have nothing to fear from strangers, Mr. Spenser."

His smile was small, secretive and unsettling, but he made no comment. "Would you like a tour of the place?" he said instead.

What she wanted was to get as far away from there as she could, as fast as she could go. But she'd come for a reason, and she wasn't about to leave empty-handed. "If I'm not interrupting your work," she said politely.

He shook his head. "Things are still in the planning stage. I haven't quite decided what I'm going to do with all this." He held out his arm for her, but she stayed back, finding there were limits, after all, to her pride and bravery.

"You lead the way," she said with only a tiny bit of breathlessness in her voice. "I'm afraid of snakes."

"The snakes are in the basement, Jassy," he said. "I wasn't planning on taking you down there." But he moved ahead anyway, and she followed him, watching the smooth strength in his tanned, bare back.

He must have started in the kitchen. This room, at least, was bare of rubbish and filth. The windows let in the greeny gray light reflecting off the swamp, but those windows were spotless, as was the sturdy oak table in the middle of the room, the old iron sink, the cracked linoleum floor with its cabbage rose pattern just discernible. He set the basket down on one narrow wooden counter, and Jassy noticed the other offerings.

There were pickles and jams, cakes and cookies, homemade wine and fine whiskey. She imagined the old-fashioned refrigerator that was humming busily was probably chock full of casserole dishes, all designed to feed the stranger. "I guess I wasn't the first to bring you a welcoming package," she said, moving past him to pick up a familiar-looking pickle jar. Mary-Louise prided herself on her spicy relish, doling it out like a miser at Christmas. She'd brought him three bottles of the precious stuff. Jassy could just guess what else she'd welcomed him with.

"Not the first," Spenser agreed. "But certainly the most interesting."

She turned to look at him, her earlier nervousness vanishing. "Why do you say that?"

"Oh, I've heard all about Miss Jassy Turner. The hardworking Jassy with her good deeds and her clean living. As far as I can tell, just about everyone who's come to visit has tried to warn me off you.''

''I can't imagine why.''

''Can't you?'' He shrugged. ''It's fairly obvious to me. The gentlemen who've come to visit, to check out the place and to bring me whiskey, have felt protective. They don't want the stranger to mess with their local saint. The women don't want the competition.''

''Full of yourself, aren't you, Mr. Spenser?'' she said coolly.

''Just realistic. This is too hard a life to let yourself be blinded by sentiment or the proper thing to think and say. But you wouldn't know about that, would you? I bet you spend all your time being proper.''

''I didn't come here to discuss my behavior.'' Her voice was sharp as she leaned against the counter, keeping her gaze in the vicinity of his stubbled chin. His shirtlessness bothered her. His entire body bothered her.

''Then why did you come here, Jassy?'' He moved closer, his voice dropping a notch. ''Did you want to check out the new talent like your friend Mary-Louise?''

Jassy didn't flinch. ''Not exactly.''

''Then why the Lady Bountiful act?''

''I want to know why my brother is frightened of you.''

She'd taken him by surprise. There was a hot, damp breeze coming in through the window, and it stirred the tendrils of hair that escaped her hairpins. It ruffled the hem of her skirt, it danced through his slicked-back blond hair. It slithered around them, between them, through them, as they faced each other in silence.

And then he shuttered those extraordinary light eyes of his, and withdrew. ''Ask him,'' he said, and she knew the subject was closed.

"I'll do that," she said. She glanced around her. "How about that tour?"

If she still surprised him he didn't let it show. He simply smiled, reaching out his long arms, and for one startled moment she thought he was going to pull her against his tanned, strong body. She didn't move, mesmerized, as he pulled open the refrigerator and grabbed two long-necked beer bottles. She'd been right—the old wire shelves were loaded down with casseroles. Including one of Mary-Louise's.

He shut the door again, opened both bottles and handed her one. "I didn't say I wanted a beer," she pointed out.

"I didn't ask." He tipped a goodly part of the bottle down his throat, and she watched him swallow, watched as drops of condensation from the dark brown bottle dripped onto his chest.

She took a hasty gulp of her own beer, letting the cool, peaty taste of it slide down her throat. It was a dark beer, stronger than the pale yellow stuff she was used to. She liked it.

He didn't try to take her arm again. He led the way, letting her pick her path through the rubble, the piled lumber, the barrels of trash and the broken floorboards. The red-flocked wallpaper was mildewed, stained, peeling off the walls on its own accord. The wide, curving stairs were missing banister rails, and one of the steps had a gaping hole in it leading down to the basement. And the snakes.

She followed him, quietly enough, as he led her through the empty bedrooms. One room was used to store furniture, an old Victorian bed frame, several marble dressers, an old chifforobe. The rooms had been swept free of rubbish, rat droppings and broken glass, but none of them were occupied.

"Where do you sleep?" she inquired artlessly as they reached the head of the stairs again.

He stopped a few steps down, so that his face was level with hers. He was too close, but this time she wasn't going to step back like a nervous ninny. "I didn't know you were interested." He'd finished his beer, leaving the empty bottle on the top stair. Hers was still half-full, and she had no intention of drinking any more. He addled her enough.

"I'm not . . ." she began, but he didn't let her finish.

"I guess you're not the clean-living saint everyone thinks you are. You're just as curious about forbidden fruit as the rest of them." He took the bottle from her hand, setting it down beside his, and she knew he was going to kiss her. The second time in her life she'd seen the man, and he was going to kiss her. And God, she wanted him to. She wanted to taste the beer and cigarettes on his mouth, she wanted to feel that naked, warm chest against hers.

She jerked away, nervously, before he'd even touched her. "I'd better be going," she said, moving past him with sudden clumsiness, kicking the two bottles so that they rolled and tumbled down the long flight of stairs, her own spraying beer all over the place. "I . . . I'm sorry," she said, rushing past him, half-expecting him to reach out and stop her.

He didn't. He simply stood near the top of the stairs and watched her run, a small, enigmatic smile on his face.

"You come back now, y'hear," he said, his voice mocking the typical southern farewell.

"Not if I can help it," she muttered under her breath, practically sprinting for the front door.

This time she didn't look for snakes as she ran across the overgrown patch of ground to the Jeep. It wasn't that she expected him to come after her. He hadn't put out a hand to stop her when she'd run like a frightened rabbit—he'd hardly be likely to come running after her into the murky afternoon heat.

She had to get out of there, before her brains melted into a little pool of sweat. The sheer sensuality of his presence, his subtle and not so subtle come-ons to her didn't have a thing to do with Jassy Turner. They probably didn't have much to do with whatever lay between him and Harrison. He flirted automatically, with whatever female was present. He probably would have been more than happy to take her to bed if she'd been willing, and it would have meant nothing more than the icy cold beer he'd just drunk. A pleasant way to satisfy a physical need and then forget about it.

He was the type of man she always steered clear of. The kind who let frustration reach their fists, and used those fists on whoever was too weak to hit back. She'd seen men like him every day, trying to get their battered wives back home to cook and clean and lie still for them. She never could understand why those women had gone in the first place.

Now she could.

She couldn't let him get to her like that. For all the danger he represented, the fact that she was just another in a long line of females was actually an advantage. He didn't see her as the enemy. He was still her best chance of finding out what Harrison was so frightened of.

She'd just need to be better prepared. Not go traipsing over to a place like the Moon Palace alone on a steamy afternoon. She should recognize dangers when she saw them. A place like the old bordello, reeking of ancient sex.

A man like Caleb Spenser, exuding his own powerful attractions. Next time she saw him it had better be on her own turf, with her defenses tight around her. Because the next time she might not get out in time.

Chapter Three

Caleb Spenser leaned against the open doorway, watching as his visitor disappeared down the twisty road leading away from the old bordello. A huge, shaggy head poked its way beneath his hand, and he stroked it with absent fingers. "What do you think of her, Dog?" he asked. "Not much like her brother, is she? Or am I wrong?"

Dog grinned his huge, doggy grin, panting in the humid heat, then flopped down at Spenser's feet, covering the toes of his scuffed boots and blocking the entrance-way. "You're not sure, are you?" Spenser said. "Well, neither am I. On the one hand, she might be just what she seems. A slightly nervous, slightly scattered lady who's out to protect her family from marauding strangers.

"On the other hand, she might know perfectly well why I'm here. She must be...let's see, late twenties? Early thirties? We'll compromise at thirty. That would have made her seventeen when it happened. Would the old man have told her? Probably not. You know these old suthun gennulmun, Dog. They don't confide in their womenfolk unless they have to.

"Junior's another matter, though. He's a sniveling coward. Just the sort to turn to his little sister and see whether she could bail him out of his troubles. Of course, he'd already gotten his Daddy to do just that, so there'd be no need to confide in little Jassy." He pushed away from the door, heading back into the house and picking up the fallen beer bottles. The smell of spilled beer didn't make much of a dent in the thick odor of mildew, rotting vegetation and general decay, and her horrified expression as they tumbled down the stairs had been worth it. He could almost believe her, except that he didn't believe anyone was that sweet and innocent anymore.

Dog got up and lumbered after him. "Yes, I know. Maybe I'm too hard on her. Maybe not. I expect she's really just like her friends. Like that hot-blooded creature who came out yesterday, loaded with pickle relish and chicken casseroles and come-hither glances."

Dog groaned, his paws tapping noisily on the old wood floors as they headed back out to the kitchen. "You don't need to tell me," Spenser said, setting the bottles down in the sink. "I was crazy to turn down all that ripe female flesh. Clearly the woman wasn't expecting it. But you know, when you get to my advanced age you get a little tired of being expected to provide stud service for any randy female who has an itch to scratch." He leaned back against the counter, surveying Mary-Louise's hot pickle relish, and he shook his head. "But you know, Dog, for Jassy Turner I might be willing to make an exception."

Dog woofed softly, shaking his big head toward his food dish in a meaningful gesture. "The thing I like best about you, Dog," Spenser said, opening the refrigerator door and staring inside, "is your conversational abilities. You don't always try to bore me with your problems, you're just content to hear mine. I appreciate that, Dog. As a matter of fact, to show how much I appreciate it, I'm going to give you a treat. I'm not really in the mood for

Mary-Louise Whatever-her-name-is's chicken casserole." He pulled it from the fridge. "It's your treat." And he set it down on the cracked linoleum with a thump.

Dog padded over to it, sniffing for a moment, and Spenser had the notion that Dog didn't care for Mary-Louise and her come-hither glances any more than he did. But food was food, and Dog had never been big on moral gestures.

"I wouldn't have minded Mary-Louise," Spenser continued, pulling out another beer, "if she hadn't found it necessary to cut out the competition first. I mean, the lady had curves in all the right places, a talented-looking mouth, and a man's got needs, right?"

Dog kept eating.

"But I didn't like her. I didn't like the way she had to tell me all about how boring and sexless Miss Jassy Turner was, or how sought-after Miss Mary-Louise was, and what a great favor she was doing me. If she was that sought-after, why was she sniffing around after me?"

Dog lifted his head, granted Spenser a quizzical expression, and then adjourned to his water dish. "Yeah, I know," Spenser said, levering himself up on the counter. "I have this knack. Women fall at my feet. It's come in handy over the years, you got to admit that. There were times when the two of us would have gone hungry if it hadn't been for sympathetic women and my pretty face. But things are better now. We don't have to worry about where the next meal comes from. And I don't have to take everything that's offered. I can pick and choose."

Dog went over and scratched at the kitchen door. Spenser had replaced the hinges yesterday, so that it no longer opened at the merest nudge, and Dog looked up with an aggrieved expression on his face. "All right, all right," Spenser said, getting down off the counter and opening the door. Dog bounded out with his usual enthusiasm, heading straight for his favorite live oak. Spenser leaned in the doorway, watching him. "I don't have time for recreation, anyway. I'm here for a reason, a very definite reason, and I'd do a hell of a lot better if I concentrated on it. Jassy Turner's a sister to that reason, which is why I'm going to concentrate on her. See whether that skittish look she gets in her eyes comes from fear or wanting. Or maybe both. See how she looks with that hair hanging down her back. See how she looks beneath those baggy clothes."

Dog finished his business and started back up the porch steps at a measured pace. "Yeah, I know," Spenser said. "I'm a class-A bastard. My daddy told me that from just about the day I was born, and I'm doing my level best to live up to it. I'm not going to let sentiment get in the way of what I've got planned for Harrison Turner. And I expect Jassy Turner will help me get what I want. Whether she's as straightforward and innocent as she seems, or just another version of Mary-Louise Whatsername. And it won't matter," he continued, shutting the door behind Dog, "if she is innocent. This life eats that kind of innocence alive. After I get through with her she'll learn not to be so trusting. I'll be doing her a favor, Dog."

Dog simply looked at him with an expression Spenser knew too well. "Maybe not," he said, draining his beer. "But whether I leave her alone or not, she's going to get hurt when her precious brother comes crashing down. If I know Harrison, he'll drag her with him." He reached into his back pocket for a battered pack of cigarettes. He didn't smoke much nowadays, but there were times when nothing else would do. "You know what I'm in the mood for tonight, Dog? Not casseroles or pickle relish or homemade wine or ancient bourbon. I think I'm gonna have me a meal of Miss Jassy Turner's chocolate chip cookies.''

Dog whoofed with approval, butting his head against Spenser's leg. "Okay, Dog," he said. "Some for you, too."

"WHERE THE HELL have you been?" Harrison was standing in the middle of the hallway, fuming, his tie pulled loose, his white linen suit rumpled, his dark hair awry.

Jassy had had the entire trip back in which to calm herself and put things into perspective. The rush of hot wind through her hair as she drove too fast back to Belle Rive had loosened the pins, and once she was well away from the Moon Palace and its new owner she'd undone another couple of buttons on her white shirt. By the time she'd parked the Jeep and mounted the front steps to the house she felt a lot more in control of both herself and the situation. She wasn't about to let Harrison in one of his moods rile her again.

"Out," she said briefly. "What's up?"

"Mother came home early from her bridge party. Claimed she was under the weather, but you and I know perfectly well that that witch, Harriet Stevenson, was probably serving sherry just to see how Mother could hold it. And Lila's been up in her room, crying loud enough to be heard all over the damn house, and Miss Sadie's saying she doesn't know what to cook for dinner, since Claire and Lila informed her they wouldn't be eating and you didn't see fit to tell her where you were going or when you'd be back, and I haven't been able to concentrate for a moment, what with all this fuss, and . . ." He suddenly let out a loud, incredulous sneeze, followed by another equally explosive one.

At least it silenced his tirade. Jassy immediately put first things first. "Have you been up to see Lila?"

"She refuses to talk to me. I told her she shouldn't go see Lorelei and the new baby, but would she listen? No siree. And she's been after me to have some more tests done, but that's ridiculous, since the doctors have said I'm perfectly fine, and the fault's got to be with her."

"Not fault, Harrison," Jassy reminded him gently.

"Well, I'm getting damn sick of it. If she'd just…" He sneezed again, violently. "If she'd just…" Another sneeze. "If she'd…"

Jassy put a hand on his arm. "Why don't you go up and see her? Don't lecture her, don't argue with her, just hold her. She needs that sometimes."

Harrison sneezed, looking aggrieved. "Have you been around animals, Jassy?"

She could think of one particular swamp rat she'd been far too close to, but she doubted whether Caleb Spenser could set off one of Harrison's allergic attacks, no matter how much Harrison disliked the man. And then she remembered the dog.

"Harrison, go see Lila, and I'll deal with Claire." She started toward the front stairs, twice as broad as the curving, damaged ones at the Moon Palace. This time, however, the man she was talking with reached out and grabbed her arm, not gently.

"Lila and Claire can wait," Harrison said, mopping his nose with a linen handkerchief. "You still haven't told me where you were."

"Do I need to report my activities to you, Harrison?" she asked quietly.

He looked intensely frustrated, that frustration complicated by still another bout of sneezing. "I worry about you, Jassy. I'm your older brother and responsible for you. This town isn't as safe and innocent as it appears. There are riffraff lurking about, and I wouldn't be doing my duty as head of the family if I didn't see to your well-being."

Jassy always hated it when Harrison tried to be paternal. He wasn't cut out for it, and she'd bailed him out of trouble too many times to play the subservient younger sister. However, she'd also learned over the years that life went on a lot more easily if she played the game. "I do appreciate it, Harrison. I am capable of seeing to my own well-being, but it's nice to know others care about me." She cast a meaningful glance down at her arm. There were times when Harrison didn't know his own strength, but she didn't want to offend him by pointing out that he was probably leaving bruises.

He released her. "I know you pride yourself on your self-sufficiency, Jassy, but you don't always know what's best for you. There are times when you simply must be guided by those older and wiser."

Jassy controlled her instinctive snort, still hoping she'd be able to get away without having to tell him where she'd been. "Yes, brother," she said mildly, starting to move past him, but his voice forestalled her.

"You still haven't told me, Jassy," he said, and his voice was low and strangely ominous. "Where were you?"

She couldn't lie. Indeed, there was no need to. She turned back with a limpid smile. "Visiting our new neighbor and taking him some of Miss Sadie's red beans and rice. Just one in a long line, I'm afraid. Most of the citizens of Turner's Landing seem to have made their way out to the Moon Palace in the last few days, if his larder is any way to judge it. I can't decide whether everyone's curious about the old bordello or the new owner. Probably a little bit of both."

She'd never seen such a lack of expression on her brother's face. He simply stared at her, blankly, his brown eyes distant, his face completely unreadable.

"I don't want you going out there again," he said, his voice flat and expressionless.

"I don't imagine I'll have any need to. I've brought him a basket of food, which, I might add, I told him was from all of us, and I welcomed him to the neighborhood."

"You told him *I* welcomed him to the neighborhood?"

"Well, I admit he found that a little difficult to believe," Jassy said.

"And did he say why?" There was no missing the underlying intensity beneath Harrison's oddly blank expression.

"No."

"Did you ask? Foolish of me, of course you did. And he refused to tell you?"

Jassy nodded. "He told me if I wanted to know why you were . . . didn't want him around, then I'd better ask you myself. So I'm asking you. Again. What has he got against you?"

That unnerving lack of expression vanished, leaving her brother looking like the old Harrison. Slightly shifty, infinitely charming, looking for the easy way out. "It's ancient history, Jassy. Something I'd almost forgotten, but apparently he hasn't. Don't worry about it. He'll make up his mind what he wants from me sooner or later, and we'll come to an agreement. He's just trying to extort money from us."

"How can he do that unless you've got something to hide?" she asked shrewdly.

"Everyone's got something to hide. Particularly Mr. Spenser. It all depends on just how desperately one wants to cover up, and how much one is willing to pay in order to do so. I haven't made up my mind how high I'll go, and he obviously hasn't made up his mind exactly what he wants."

"You'll pay him off?"

"In one way or another." He sneezed again, looking fretful. "You go and see Lila while I go pour myself a bourbon. This has been a hell of a day."

For me, too, Jassy wanted to say, but she bit her tongue. She'd gotten off lightly—Harrison was capable of making a major fuss if he set his mind to it, and while she didn't like to cave in, she found it much easier to get her own way if she went around it sideways, instead of confronting things headfirst. Some people might call if manipulation. She preferred to think of it as self-defense.

"All right," she said evenly. "Come up when you can." She climbed the stairs, resisting the impulse to rub her arm where his steely fingers had dug into the flesh, resisting the impulse to glance behind her. She knew he was standing there, watching her. And for the first time in her life, she had absolutely no idea what her usually transparent brother was thinking.

THE HEAT CONTINUED into the next day, with no relief in sight from the crippling humidity. Jassy pushed her hair off her neck, wishing the women's shelter could afford an air conditioner that worked. The one she had stuck in the window made a humming noise, and it sounded as if it was doing its job, but the air in the small, drab office was only marginally cooler than the blistering moist heat outside. On top of that, the damned machine ate electricity for breakfast, all without providing a lick of coolness.

However, it was even worse when she turned it off. The office became an oven, a hot box that turned her into a pool of sweat, made her stick to everything, including the old metal desk someone had donated.

She was going to have to go to Harrison for money to pay the electric bill. Maybe even see if he could make an additional donation, enough to get a new air conditioner. Or at least see if some life could be pumped into this tired old one. This might be the hottest August on record, but September tended to be almost as bad. She couldn't make it through another two or three months of living in a steam bath.

She hated having to ask Harrison, but donations had been down lately, due, no doubt, to the miserable economy and the generally depressed region. There were times when she almost hoped the developers would finally discover Turner's Landing, bringing in jobs and money and color and excitement.

She'd lose the peace and quiet she loved, she'd lose the clear waters and untouched swamplands. She'd lose the one parcel of Florida that hadn't been turned into a tourists' playground. But while a part of her loved Turner's Landing, its peace and solitude, another part recognized the fact that she'd lived there all her life. And she needed something more.

It was hard to weigh people's livelihoods against something as ephemeral as a piece of untouched swamp. She spent every day dealing with the fallout of poverty and hopelessness. How could she turn her back on a chance for renewed prosperity for the people she'd known all her life?

Fortunately it wasn't up to her to make the decision. She didn't own anything but a small patch of swampland with a tumbledown cabin, and no one was going to turn that section of soggy wilderness into a golf course.

No one had made any offers for any part of Turner's Landing, not since the big boom in the seventies when her father, the Colonel, had sent those land-hungry developers about their business. She'd always been deeply grateful he'd resisted temptation. She wasn't as certain Harrison was equally happy with that decision.

She might have a hard time getting money out of him. She'd already spent her monthly allotment on groceries for several families, and a bus ticket out of town for another. There was just so far her money could stretch, and Harrison had proved intractable when she'd tried for an increase.

Damn all southern men, her father included. He'd left her money, of course. He'd just left it entirely in Harrison's control, so that she had to go to him like a beggar looking for handouts.

It was good for her soul, she reminded herself. She spent a great deal of her time looking for handouts from the local citizenry, for the women's shelter, for the volunteer fire department and rescue squad, for the church. Pride was a waste of time.

Unfortunately, Harrison had never shown much sympathy for the women's shelter. He felt a Turner should concentrate on more ladylike activities, such as the hospital, and not the trash who beat each other with regularity. He probably felt the women deserved it, even if he never dared voice such an opinion within Jassy's hearing.

Well, she'd get the money out of him, and more besides. She hadn't gotten very far in this life by accepting defeat before she'd even tried.

She was accepting defeat for this office, however, she thought, pushing back from the desk and switching off her ancient electric typewriter. It was too hot and humid to concentrate. She'd take her paperwork back out to Belle Rive and try to accomplish something in the air-conditioned coolness of her bedroom. If anyone in Turner's Landing needed help they'd know where to find her.

She turned off the air conditioner, listening to it sputter and sigh to a damp stop. If Harrison proved intractable she could always sell something. Or hit up Claire.

The house was still and quiet when she returned home, parking her car in the shade of a live oak. Not that she would have expected otherwise—Harrison and Lila had gone to Clearwater for the weekend, and Claire was usually resting at that hour. She'd have the place pretty much to herself.

She heard the sound of voices from the front veranda as she started up the stairs. Claire's voice, sounding younger than it had in years, light with laughter. And Lila's, equally happy.

Jassy took an immediate turn, heading for the veranda. Something wonderful must have happened, for the two unhappy women of Belle Rive to sound so lively. Maybe Lila had finally conceived. Maybe there'd been a sudden windfall. Maybe...

Maybe Caleb Spenser had come to visit, she realized as she stopped still in the doorway, looking at the tableau set out in front of her. Claire was sitting at the table, her graying hair neatly coiffed, clasping a tall glass of iced tea, and smiling at their visitor with a complete lack of judgment. Lila was stretched out on the chaise, her long, quite spectacular legs displayed attractively, though Spenser was either too polite or too Machiavellian to notice. Probably the latter. The three of them looked dangerously cozy, and Jassy's sense of foreboding couldn't have been stronger.

"There you are, darling!" Claire greeted her, her eyes for once bright and lively. "We were afraid you were going to be chained to that old desk all day long."

"Then I would have missed this little tea party," she said, stepping out into the dappled sunlight, putting a nervous hand to her hair. The other women were dressed in flowing summer dresses, flowery, feminine. She was still dressed in her work clothes—wrinkled khaki pants and a wilted oversize shirt. She felt rumpled and grubby, and the fact that Caleb Spenser was seeing her in such a state didn't help matters.

"Ring for Miss Sadie," Lila said lazily. "She'll bring you a glass of tea."

Jassy wanted to rush upstairs, jump into the shower and throw on one of her own flowered summer dresses. But by then Spenser would be gone. Or if he hadn't, it would give him more time alone with the vulnerable members of her family, and she wasn't about to let that happen.

"Sounds wonderful," she said firmly, taking the seat between Spenser and Claire. "I'm parched."

"Take mine," Spenser said, his tone polite, only Jassy hearing the insinuation beneath the light words. "I've barely touched it."

It was a challenge, and she knew it. "Do you have a cold, Mr. Spenser?" she inquired, delaying.

"Nothing infectious," he said, his light eyes meeting hers. *I dare you,* they said.

She took the glass, feeling the cool sweat of it in her hot hands. "I'm very resistant anyway," she said, taking a deep swallow.

"I imagine you are," he murmured, watching her.

Suddenly she was reckless. The glass was so cool, and she was so damned hot. Her shirt was unfastened halfway down, exposing the upper part of her chest. She took the cold, damp glass and pressed it against her throat, slid it down between her breasts, closing her eyes as the delicious coolness washed over her. And then she opened her eyes again, to meet his. And she was hot all over again.

"Wasn't it nice of Mr. Spenser to visit us?" Claire cooed. "And Lila and I were feeling so bored, what with Harrison tearing off on some scheme."

"Very nice," Jassy murmured, staring at her hands.

"I had to come and thank you all for the basket of goodies," Spenser said. "I particularly liked the chocolate chip cookies."

She looked up then, straight into his challenging eyes. And then her backbone stiffened, and she pulled her generations of Turner sangfroid back around her. "I'm glad you came," she said. "I've been wanting to talk to you."

He smiled, that damnable, sexy smile that had half of Turner's Landing swooning, her mother and sister-in-law included. "Talk away," he offered. "I'll be glad to listen."

She was immune, she reminded herself. "We can talk in the library."

"We need privacy, Miss Jassy?"

"Not privacy, Mr. Spenser. It's a business proposition. Business bores Mother and Lila."

"It certainly does," Lila said lazily. "You two go off and talk your business, but you come back out here when you're done. It's too hot a day to do anything but sit around and drink iced tea."

"My pleasure, Miss Lila," Spenser said, rising.

Why did he seem so tall? Harrison was taller, broader, physically more intimidating. So why did Spenser seem to invade her space, overwhelm her being?

She led the way, telling herself he wasn't watching her hips in the baggy khakis, telling herself that even if he was, it didn't matter. She waited until he followed her into the library, Harrison's domain, and then she shut the door behind them, wondering how she was going to broach this.

She needn't have worried. Spenser's grin was quizzical. "So how much are you offering me to get out of town?"

Chapter Four

One thing she had to learn about Caleb Spenser, Jassy thought. To expect the unexpected. She did her best not to let her surprise show, moving past him into the room to gain herself some time.

"How much would it take?" she countered coolly.

"More than you have, sugar," he said lazily, sauntering over toward Harrison's broad walnut desk. It was covered with its customary neat little piles of paper, and with no shame whatsoever Spenser began glancing through them.

"How do you know?" She moved to stop him, then thought better of it. What would Harrison have to hide?

Spenser looked up, clearly having decided the desk held no secrets, and he smiled. "I know everything I need to know about the Turners. Particularly about their financial situation. I know, for instance, that you pump all your money into your various good works. I know that Harrison controls everyone's money, and you're all fools enough to trust him."

"Harrison's very good with investments."

"If you say so. Investing is like gambling, and I expect Harrison doesn't know diddly squat about either. He's the type who never knows when to fold or when to raise, and he'll always call at the wrong time."

"Harrison doesn't gamble," she said stiffly.

Spenser raised an eyebrow. "Is that so? You could have fooled me."

"And how do you happen to know so much about our financial situation?" she pushed on. "It's not any of your business."

"Now that's a moot point. I know everything I want to know. As a matter of fact, I was thinking of making a little donation to your pet project."

"Which one? I have a lot of charities."

"The women's shelter. It looks like that could use a little ready cash."

"Guilty conscience, Mr. Spenser?"

He looked startled for a moment, as he understood her meaning. And then he grinned. "No, honey. I don't have to beat women to get them to do what I want."

Jassy swallowed. Her reaction, and her pride. "We'd be more than happy to accept any donation you might care to make. I hadn't realized you were so wealthy."

"I'm not. I'm just a working man, wanting to do my best to make this life a little better for those less fortunate."

"Very pious."

"Yes, ma'am."

"But you clearly don't need work."

"What makes you think that?"

"Well, you've got the Moon Palace to keep you busy, and you have enough extra cash for charitable donations."

"I'm always interested in work. Did you have anything particular in mind, Miss Jassy? You want me to be your hired man?"

Why did everything he said sound like a come-on? At least today he was clothed, all that tanned, muscled flesh covered up by a fresh white shirt and linen pants. No tie or jacket, of course, and that gold hoop in his ear was ridiculous. How could anyone be taken seriously when they wore an earring?

Except that she needed to take him seriously, very seriously indeed. He was a dangerous man, and the worst mistake she could make would be to underestimate his danger.

"Just a little renovation job," she said, moving over to the window and looking out on the veranda. Claire and Lila were still sitting there, looking uncustomarily peaceful. "I have a piece of land and a cabin out in Rayder Swamp. It's not much, just one room and a veranda. I was thinking I'd like to see if it can't be fixed up, or at least kept from falling into the swamp."

"I didn't know you owned any land."

"Why should you? As a matter of fact, it was left to me by an old friend. He used to live there, up until he had to go into a nursing home five years back. When he died he left it to me. I don't usually get out there, and it seemed to be in pretty rough shape, but I thought it would be nice to have a place to escape to."

He moved closer, with that insinuating grace of his. "Now what would you need to escape from, Miss Jassy?"

Since the only response she could think of was, *you,* she kept her mouth shut. He moved closer still, coming up behind her as she stared out the window. She could feel the heat from his body on this hot, humid day, feel the faint stirring in her hair as he spoke. "And you'd like me to come out and have a look at it?"

She swallowed, reaching out to touch her tightly pinned hair. "If you're interested." She didn't dare turn around.

He was standing too close. If she turned, she'd be in his arms.

"Oh, I'm interested. I surely am. Just so long as you're not planning to take an ax to me and feed my remains to the gators." He'd stepped back, and she used that extra space to turn around and face him.

"You certainly have a lurid imagination, Mr. Spenser. Is that more of your guilty conscience?"

"We never established that I had any guilty conscience in the first place, sugar. When do you want to go out to the swamp?"

"As soon as you're able." She had no idea where Harrison had gone or how long he'd be away, but the sooner she got Caleb involved in renovating the old cabin, the better. Rayder Swamp was on the other side of Turner's Landing, and the cabin was well in there. He'd be gone from morning till night, if he decided to take the job, and the longer he was away from the little town the better.

She had no idea how she was going to pay for it. Rowdy's inheritance hadn't included much more than that piece of swamp and the cabin that sat on it, and Harrison watched her expenditures like a hawk, demanding accountings for anything above and beyond her childish allowance.

But she'd get it, someway or another. If worse came to worst she could leave Turner's Landing and get a job. Heaven knows, she'd been tempted often enough. Break the apron strings, leave Claire and Harrison and all the people who seemed to need so much from her and make her own life.

So far she hadn't been able to do it. Every time her family pushed her too far, seemed to be draining her dry, someone else would come to her, and she'd know she couldn't abandon them. She couldn't abandon Claire to

Harrison's tender mercies, she couldn't abandon Harrison to the house and Miss Sadie and his own reckless temper. Most of all, she wasn't sure she wanted to leave. This was home, and her brief sojourns in other places had left her restless and longing to come back.

She still had some jewelry she could sell. Some stocks that she could insist Harrison liquidate. She had resources, as hard as it seemed to find them.

"What about tonight?" Spenser said.

"Tonight?"

"What better time to check out the swamp than by moonlight? We can watch the swamp gasses."

"How enchanting," she said coolly. "But there won't be a moon tonight. And the moment the sun goes down the mosquitoes start playing for keeps. What about tomorrow morning?"

"Afraid you're going to get caught in the dark with me, Miss Jassy?"

"I'm not afraid of anything about you," she said flatly.

"You lie, Miss Jassy. Didn't your mama teach you to tell the truth?"

"You've met my mother, Mr. Spenser. You just spent the last half hour or so trying to charm her. Surely you must have guessed that she taught me to tell the truth when the circumstances merited it."

She wanted to slap him. Her palm itched with the need to do just that, she who never hit anyone in her life.

It was his smile that did it to her. She wouldn't have minded a big, smug grin. She wouldn't have minded a small, nasty little smirk. His smile was neither. It never reached his eyes, it simply curled the corners of his wide, mobile mouth and said, *I dare you.*

He was smiling at her now, that cool, double-dare smile, and she wanted to smack him as hard as she could.

"Tomorrow morning, Mr. Spenser. I'll come by and fetch you."

"I don't think you want to do that, Jassy. I sleep naked and I don't have an alarm clock. You might just show up at the wrong time." He moved toward the door. "I'll come by and get you."

"I don't think that would be a wise idea."

"Harrison's out of town till Monday, Jassy. He won't be here to threaten me with a shotgun."

Her eyes widened. "How did you know that?"

"That he'd threaten me with a shotgun?"

"I think we all know that, even if no one happens to know why," she said irritably.

"I know why."

"And you're not going to tell me, right?" He nodded his assent. "I mean how did you know Harrison was out of town till Monday?"

He opened the door, glancing back at her with that cool smile. "I could tell you I have mysterious, arcane sources. I've already told you that your family holds no secrets from me. But the answer is a lot more prosaic—Lila told me."

"It figures. That woman's tongue is hinged in the middle. It's a good thing Harrison doesn't trust any woman, or the family secrets would be public knowledge."

"Now that's real interesting, Jassy," Spenser said, pausing in the doorway. "What family secrets are you talking about? And does that mean your brother doesn't even trust you?"

"I'll see you tomorrow morning, Mr. Spenser," she said, smiling her own secret smile as she refused to answer him.

He closed the door behind him. She turned back to the window, watching him as he stepped out onto the veranda. He was different around her mother and Lila. There was no underlying threat in his manner, no hint of a ruthless sensuality bubbling beneath the surface. She could only see his back, but she watched the women's reactions to him. Lila's shy, flattered smile. Her mother's faded glow. And she wondered if she had the same besotted expression on her own face when she looked at him.

Reaching up, she touched her skin. She knew her features so well, knew what he'd be assessing every time he looked at her. They were regular, even, unremarkable. Hazel eyes that sometimes looked green. An average nose. Regular cheekbones, a wide mouth and a chin that somehow made her look vulnerable on odd occasions. He probably saw that chin and figured she was a chump.

But she wasn't. If Harrison wouldn't cooperate she was going to have to take matters into her own hands. She wasn't going to take an ax to Caleb and feed him to the gators. But she had every intention of keeping him so busy out on Rayder Swamp that her brother would forget his existence. At least long enough for her to find out what the hell was going on.

She waited until he left. Waited until he walked across the broad lawn, circling the house to the side driveway, where she could just see his battered old pickup truck. Waited until she heard the noisy rumble of its engine, and then he was gone. And then, and not until then, did she release her pent-up breath.

SHE'S A HELL OF A WOMAN, Spenser thought as he drove down the twisting, overgrown road to the Moon Palace. And part of what made her so delicious was the fact that she didn't realize it. She kept that tangled hair of hers pinned tightly back, but it kept trying to escape. She probably kept all her passions locked up just as tight. Were they trying to escape, too?

He'd thought about going after the wife. She was vulnerable, easy pickings, and a man was bound to be more territorial about a wife than a sister. But Lila Turner wasn't really to his taste. She was a little too skinny, a little too frilly, a little too wounded. She had that look in her pale blue eyes, like life had dealt her a hard blow. Hell, she didn't know the half of it.

Anyone married to Harrison Turner had more than their share of trouble. She just might not know it yet. And it wasn't up to him to set her straight. Or to add to her worries. Things were going to be tough enough for her when he got through with the Turners.

He'd even considered using Mrs. Turner, the Colonel's widow. But one look at the flushed cheeks, overbright eyes and slight tremor in her hands, and he knew she was already paying the price for her husband and son. Besides, he'd been around enough drunks in his life to feel both irritation and pity. Since he didn't have to live with her, he could let the pity rule.

That left sassy Miss Jassy. With her loose-fitting clothes and her tight-fitting smile, she was just the woman to provide him with the means to an end. The end of Harrison Turner's life of leisure. And he had every intention of enjoying that journey.

She thought she could outsmart him. She didn't realize she was dealing with someone who'd learned the hard way. Being the son of a preacher man should have taught him something, but then, she hadn't known his father. Buck knew early on that there was hell and damnation in his only son, and he did his best to beat it out of him. The only thing he managed was to beat more rage into his already angry son.

Prison hadn't helped much, either. Doing three years for killing a rich college boy wasn't conducive to a rosy view of life. When he got out he'd found he'd turned downright mean on occasion. And there were times when he wondered whether he'd ever come back.

He'd spent close to ten years looking for Harrison Turner. Now that he'd found him, he wasn't going to let him go, not for all the tears of all the sisters and wives and mothers. And if those sisters and wives and mothers got hurt along the way, that was just too damned bad.

At least Jassy Turner struck him as someone who could take care of herself. She was also the one most determined to protect her brother and the status quo. It stood to reason she'd be the way to get to Harrison. He found himself wondering whether there really was a sleeping tiger beneath her cool, patrician face and clear, steady gaze. He intended to use their trip to the swamp to find out.

Dog was lying on the front stoop when he drove in, a disgruntled expression in his canine face. Spenser could see why. Mary-Louise Albertson's Mustang convertible was parked haphazardly in the thickening shadows. Dog had the good taste not to like the lady. Spenser didn't care much for her, either, but she certainly was persistent. Maybe she had her own hidden agenda that went beyond a hunger for a new male body. Maybe he'd wait to see what she had to say before chucking her out.

She was sitting on the stairs, waiting for him. She was wearing one of those frilly summer dresses, but hers was strapless, and her abundant breasts spilled over the top of it. Her blond hair was awry, her feet were bare, and her solid gold bangle bracelets clinked as she raised the bottle to her lips. He recognized the brand of bourbon from where he stood. He recognized that it was half-gone.

"Well, there you are, sugar," she purred. "I was wondering where you were. And you look mighty fine. I didn't know you could clean up so nice."

She was drunk, all right. But she wasn't as drunk as she was pretending, a fact that interested Spenser a lot more than her cleavage. She was here for a reason, and he was more than willing to play along.

"I was off visiting your best friend," he said, taking the bottle from her and tipping some down his throat. A better brand that he usually drank, but then, he didn't have the sophisticated palate that came along with old southern money.

"Jassy? Why would you want to visit her for? She's not your type."

"Why not? I like to think of all women as my type." He leaned against the wall, watching her out of hooded eyes.

"Not Jassy. She's too straitlaced for a wild one like you. Who'd know that better than me? She's what you'd call a semi-virgin. Tried sex once and didn't care for it. You need a real woman. Like me."

"What makes you think she tried sex once?"

"Spenser, honey, I'm her best friend. I know all about the night she spent with Jimmy Pageant, and I know what she's thought about every man who's sniffed around her ever since. She's not interested."

"What does she think about me?" he asked lazily.

Mary-Louise pouted. "You're not seriously thinking about sleeping with her? It would be a waste of time. Even if you managed to get her into bed she'd be no fun at all. You need someone with experience. Enthusiasm. Imagination." She leaned forward, her breasts plumping out of the top of the dress. "Leave Jassy to her charities and her good deeds. Leave her to the indigent mothers whose husbands beat them up every Friday, leave her to church auctions and family teas. Take me.''

"Take you where, Mary-Louise?"

She brightened, some of the phony drunkenness vanishing. "Well, now that you mention it, New Orleans would be nice this time of year. Or even up north, away from this stinking humidity. I don't know how people can bear living in it. Let's go away, Spenser. Somewhere far away from here and the boring people who live here.''

He took another slug of the bourbon, then set it back on the stair beside her. "Did Harrison put you up to this?"

She stared at him, too bad an actress to fake it. "What the hell kind of question is that?" she demanded in a screechy voice.

"You're sleeping with him, aren't you? Isn't that part of why Lila's looking so downright miserable? He must have sent you down here to see whether you could lure me out of town. How did he think that would solve anything? Sooner or later I'd come back, after I'd enjoyed your luscious body, and then he'd have to deal with me. That's the problem with Harrison—he never did think very far ahead. He should have known I'd come after him, sooner or later. That I'd find him, track him down, no matter where he chose to hide.''

"I don't know what you're talking about," Mary-Louise said with a trace of desperation in her voice. She rose on unsteady feet, leaning toward him. "I just thought you and I might have something special together.''

"There's nothing special about what you have in mind, Mary-Louise. Enjoyable, certainly, but it's been going on in this house since it was built.''

It took her a second. "Are you calling me a whore?" she demanded with lofty dignity.

"Yes, ma'am. You're ready to use your body to do what Harrison tells you to do. Where I come from that's called whoring."

"Well," she said, putting all her huffiness in that one word. She brushed past him, heading toward the front door in her bare feet. Dog moved out of the way, growling low, and if the front door weren't being planed and sanded on a couple of sawhorses she would have slammed it. She stopped, turning around with an accusing glare, and he braced himself for a noble speech.

"You're wrong about one thing, Spenser," she said. "It wasn't just because Harrison told me to."

He listened to the sound of her Mustang as it roared to life, glancing down at the whiskey bottle on the step. He'd hate like hell to have to do the gentlemanly thing and drive her home, but he wasn't going to send a drunk out on the road. He took another tentative slug, noticing for the first time that it was almost half water. She'd been no drunker than Claire Turner on a pilfered glass of sherry.

Even in her temper she was driving a straight line as she tore down the road. He reached down and scratched Dog's huge head. "I'm a fool and a half, aren't I, Dog? She's a good-looking woman, not too skinny, and she was more than willing. Why the hell didn't I take what was offered? That bed is mighty big, and it's been too damned long. Hell, I could have closed my eyes and pretended she was Jassy Turner."

Dog drooled, sinking his head down on his paws. "Yeah, I know," Spenser said. "Why settle for imitation when I can have the real thing? But the real thing is going to be a peck of trouble. I'd do much better to concentrate on the wife and forget about the sister. I don't really want the wife."

Dog woofed softly in the gathering dusk. "Still," Spenser said, "there's no reason why I can't enjoy myself while I take care of Harrison. And there's no reason why I have to make it easy. Maybe once I get Miss Jassy to let her hair down I won't be that interested."

Dog gave him a look of canine incredulity. "All right, maybe she'd be the most fascinating woman since Mata Hari. That, or Saint Joan. Either way, it doesn't matter. I'm going to screw her brother, and if I get the chance to screw her in the process then that's just gravy. And don't look at me like that. You're too softhearted. She's a Turner. She doesn't deserve any sympathy."

Dog rose, haughty and disapproving, and lumbered toward the back of the house, his huge shoulders and haunches expressing his disdain, his long, looping tail not even wagging. "Stupid dog," Spenser muttered to himself, sinking onto the stairs and taking another slug of the watered-down whiskey. "What does he expect me to be? A decent human being? It's too damned late for that."

And from somewhere in the kitchen he heard a low, mournful howl.

Chapter Five

Most of the Turners loved Belle Rive with a deep, possessive passion. Jassy could never see why. It wasn't as if it were the family mansion, lived in for generations. Her father, the Colonel, had bought it from a horse breeder who'd dabbled a bit too improvidently before the Second World War. After generations of genteel poverty the Turners were back on their feet again, thanks to the Colonel's acute business sense and astounding good luck. Jassy couldn't remember when things hadn't been as comfortable, but her mother could, and every now and then she could see a worried expression in Claire's faded blue eyes as she looked around her precious elegance.

For Jassy, the house was a little too stiff. A little too conscientiously gracious, with its chintz-covered furniture, its expensive antiques, most of which actually did belong to the Turners of old. The carefully manicured grounds were soothing to the eyes and pleasing to walk through, but a part of her preferred the wildness of the surrounding swamps.

She'd tried to make inroads on her room but she hadn't gotten very far. At least she'd been able to replace the pale peach walls with a stark white, and throw out the chintz priscillas with their matching draped dressing table. The huge tester bed was comfortable enough, though when she was young she would have sold her soul for a bunk bed. And she banished the rest of the overstuffed furniture, including the de rigueur chaise, to the attics, stripped the rugs off the cypress floors, and found some measure of peace in the uncluttered stillness of the room.

The bathroom she shared with Lila was pink. Pink shower curtain, pink lace curtains, pink wall-to-wall carpeting, even a pink toilet seat. She bore it with good grace. As long as she had her retreat, she could stand anything.

Her room, however, wasn't inviolate. The French doors led out to a communal veranda, Lila could and did wander through the bathroom into her room anytime she pleased, and everyone knew where to find her. If the cabin out in Rayder Swamp could be made habitable she'd be out of reach, with no one to answer to but herself.

She didn't fool herself into thinking she was some sort of martyr. There were a number of very good reasons why she seemed to have taken on the well-being of everyone she'd ever met.

For one thing, she was good at it. Good at organizing, at soothing, at coming up with creative alternatives and facing up to an intractable bureaucracy. She could make things happen when they needed to. And they often needed to.

For another, she had the time. She had no regular job, no husband, no children, no lover. No excuses, if someone needed her.

And the most telling reason of all. She liked it. She liked to feel needed. She liked to accomplish things, to solve problems, to take care of the wounded and sorrowing. Even if her own life was emotionally arid, she could bring a little rain to the parched souls of others.

But it had been a long time since she'd been able to say no. A long time since she'd been able to curl up in a little ball and think only of herself. To read a favorite book, wrapped in a comforter. To drink herb tea and watch old movies on television, to wax her legs and pluck her eyebrows. She needed a retreat, and Rowdy's old cabin would provide just that, as long as she wasn't overly frightened of snakes and gators and mosquitoes. And, having lived near the Gulf coast of Florida all her life, she wasn't.

Tonight wasn't bad, though, she thought, wandering barefoot through the perfect rooms of Belle Rive. Lila had gone out with a couple of girlfriends to see the new Kevin Costner movie, Claire had retired early as usual, and Miss Sadie and her husband were tucked up safe in their quarters. She had no one to make demands—she could wander through the place as she pleased, sipping on Harrison's very best cream sherry and thinking about winter.

She had real doubts as to whether that season would ever come. The humidity was so thick around Turner's Landing that it was hard to breathe, and even the night didn't bring much respite. Tonight for example, she thought, stepping out on the deserted veranda that overlooked the broad front lawn, the temperature couldn't have dropped more than five degrees, and the hot wind riffling through her hair only made her feel restless. Oddly anxious. Longing for something she couldn't even begin to name.

She leaned her arms on the railing, staring out over the empty lawn. For a moment she could almost imagine Caleb Spenser, moving toward the house through the crowds of people, inexorable, determined, handsome as sin and twice as mean. She'd known he was trouble the moment she saw him. Now she knew he was more than that. He was disaster, pure and simple. He threatened everything she held dear, she knew that with instincts as sure as death and taxes. He didn't threaten only Harrison. He was a danger to all of them.

So why did she keep thinking about his bare chest? His mouth? His long, hard-looking hands? His mesmerizing eyes?

She shook her head, slapping at the hungry mosquito feeding on her upper arm. She was tired, that was it. She'd been doing too much for too many people, and it had made her foolish, vulnerable, prey to fancies that had nothing to do with what she really wanted or needed in this lifetime. She would have been much better off joining Lila for the Kevin Costner movie. Except that Caleb Spenser would even put Kevin Costner to shame.

And she was going to be spending hours with him tomorrow. It took at least half an hour to drive as close to the cabin as they could. That meant half an hour shut up in the front seat of his pickup. Talking about the weather, probably. And half an hour back. Alone. With him.

She took another sip of her sherry, shaking her wet tangle of hair back away from her face. She'd taken a shower, hoping to wash away some of the fretful malaise that was dogging her. It hadn't done any good. The heat, the sultriness of the night air only added to the inexplicable sense of longing. But she refused to recognize what she was longing for.

She glanced up at the house. Claire's light was on. She usually fell asleep with all the lights blazing, her reading glasses slipping down her nose, an unread book propped against her chest. Jassy always checked her.

The doctors kept prescribing sedatives, sleeping pills, tranquilizers. She kept dosing herself with secreted bottles of vodka. Jassy was half-afraid she'd wake up some morning and find her mother dead from some lethal, accidental combination.

So every night she checked, unable to sleep unless she were certain her mother was safe. Harrison told her she worried too much, that she was imagining a problem where none existed. That Claire's mostly discreet tippling was harmless. She only wished she could be convinced.

Lightning speared across the sky, a jagged streak of white slicing the roiling purple. The thunder was distant, far too distant to be anything more than nature's cruel taunt. Just more heat lightning, flash and fire, signifying nothing. She would have given ten years off her life for a cool, cleansing downpour.

She turned and headed back inside, rubbing her arms briskly, almost imagining a chill where none existed. She needed her sleep. Tomorrow was going to tax all her emotional and mental reserves. Caleb Spenser was no boy. He was all male, all threat, all overpowering presence. She would need her wits about her if she was going to win. And she had no intention of losing. The stakes were simply too high.

Her room was just as hot and sticky as the rest of the house, but it felt cooler, with its uncluttered walls and bare floors, when she entered after turning Claire's light off. Stripping off her clothes, she pulled on a skimpy silk chemise and climbed up onto the high bed, grimacing in the darkness. She would have slept nude were it not for Lila's habit of walking in unannounced. Jassy wasn't particularly modest, but she hated the idea of being vulnerable. At least the whisper-thin silk felt almost as light as nothing at all.

She lay back against the feather pillows, staring at the canopy over her head. Some night she'd like to sleep out under the stars. Drag her mattress out onto the veranda,

let the warm breezes blow over her, even let the mosquitoes feed on her. Sometime, before she grew too old to
care, she was going to do that. And let the warm night air
caress her.

She turned over on her stomach, punching the pillow,
snorting at her own fanciful notions. What in heaven's
name had gotten into her recently? Must be an early mid-
life crisis. Didn't women go through traumas when they
reached thirty? Must be hormones.

But she knew it wasn't. She closed her eyes, trying to
shut out all conscious thought, trying to see nothing but
cold water and rain clouds. But she knew what had gotten her into such a turmoil.

Caleb Spenser.

"DARLING," Lila said artlessly as she poured herself a cup
of coffee, "you look like you have the world's worst
hangover."

Claire dropped her cup with a loud clatter, splashing
coffee on the white tablecloth. It was after nine the next
morning, and for once the three Turner women were together at the breakfast table.

Jassy and Lila tactfully ignored her. "It's no wonder,"
Jassy said, aware of her mother's barely concealed sigh of
relief as she realized Lila was talking to her daughter. "I
don't know that I slept more than three hours last night.
If this weather doesn't break soon I think I'll go mad."

"That lightning," Lila said. "I see it flash outside, and
I think it's got to mean something, and it doesn't. Just
heat lightning, promising relief, giving nothing. I wish I'd
gone with Harrison after all."

"Exactly where did Harrison go?" Jassy asked, slath-
ering butter on one of Miss Sadie's fresh biscuits. "I

thought you two were going to Clearwater to visit the Stillmans."

"Something came up at the last minute," Lila said, that worried expression back in her fine blue eyes.

"Like what?" Jassy persisted.

"Oh, you know your brother. He never likes to bother me with the details of his business. He says I haven't got the head for it, and you know, he's right. It was something more important, whatever it was. I think he's gone over to St. Florence on the East Coast. I can't imagine why—I don't know of a thing that ever came out of St. Florence."

Except Caleb Spenser, Jassy thought. It was no surprise. Harrison had been too riled by Spenser's appearance to be able to concentrate on anything else. She knew perfectly well his abrupt disappearance had something to do with the stranger in their midst. She just didn't know what.

"Harrison had a friend who lived just outside of St. Florence." Claire spoke up in her absent voice. "A nice young boy he went to Princeton with. Sherman, his name was. Sherman Delano."

"Maybe he went to visit him," Jassy suggested, reaching for another biscuit when she knew perfectly well she should reach for the grapefruit instead. Lila, who beat and coerced her lithe body into shape, frowned at her disapprovingly. Jassy reached for the butter.

"I doubt that," Claire said, leaning back in her chair. As usual she'd barely touched a bite of food. "He was murdered."

"Murdered?" Lila echoed, immediately fascinated. "You're kidding!"

"It's perfectly true. Someone stabbed him in a gambling game. They caught the man. Or boy, I think it was.

I don't know whether he was executed or just put away for life.''

"How awful for his parents," Jássy said.

"Whose parents? Sherman's or the killer's?" Lila asked with an uncharacteristic tartness.

"Both, I suspect. Did Harrison know both of them, Mama?"

"I couldn't say. I do know that Harrison was quite upset at the time. Of course, this was quite a while ago. Maybe ten, fifteen years ago." Claire took a discreet sip of her coffee. "I hadn't thought of Sherman in such a long time."

"Why would Harrison suddenly remember him?" Jassy swallowed the biscuit, controlling her urge to reach for another.

"What makes you think he has? After all, St. Florence isn't that small a town. There must be other things there. Besides, Sherman lived outside the town, and I think his parents moved away after he was killed. Still, I imagine it must be hard for Harrison. He's bound to think of Sherman while he's there."

"What did you say his name was again, Mama?" Jassy asked innocently, pouring herself an unwanted cup of coffee so that she wouldn't have to meet anyone's eyes.

"Sherman Delano. Some distant relative of the northern Delanos, I suppose, though I never asked."

"Maybe he was related to the northern Shermans," Jassy suggested with a touch of mischief.

"I doubt that," Claire said haughtily. "That wouldn't have gone over too well in the south, and Florida is, after all, a southern state."

"Yes, ma'am," Jassy said meekly, meeting Lila's amused gaze.

"So what are your plans for the day, Jassy?" Lila asked, tactfully changing the subject. Claire had come from old Georgia stock, and for her the Civil War was only a few generations old.

"I'm taking Caleb Spenser out to Rowdy's cabin."

Her words couldn't have had a greater effect if she'd dropped a water balloon on the damask-covered tablecloth. "I beg your pardon?" Claire said.

"You're *what?*" Lila shrieked at the same time.

Jassy sipped at her cold coffee, trying to look innocent. "Whatever's wrong with that? You know I've been wanting to fix up the place. Caleb's a carpenter. I need some carpentry work done. It all seems perfectly logical to me."

"Caleb?" Lila echoed. "I thought he wanted to be called Spenser."

"So he said. I, however, plan to call him Caleb. It has a nice, biblical ring to it. Maybe it'll remind him of his Christian duty."

"That man's a pagan if ever I've seen one," Claire said with a discreet snort.

"I didn't think he was just a carpenter," Lila said. "I got the impression he was more of a contractor and developer. I mean, just any carpenter couldn't come in and buy the Moon Palace, no matter how tumbledown it was."

"They couldn't have been asking that much."

"Seventy-five thousand, Eldon Reynolds told me yesterday. And he paid it. In cash."

Suddenly Jassy began to feel queasy. The butter and cold black coffee weren't sitting too well on a stomach that had already survived a restless night of intermittent sleep. "Cash?" she echoed.

"I wouldn't have believed it, but Eldon's sister works for Junior MacCoy in his real estate office, and she saw it. A whole mess of hundred-dollar bills, she told him. Gives a person thought, doesn't it? Do you suppose it's . . . drug money?" Her eyes were huge at the very idea.

"I suppose it's possible. Somehow he doesn't seem that type. Don't drug dealers drive better cars?" Jassy said, still troubled.

"And wear better clothes," Lila agreed. "And they don't look so . . . healthy." She let out a lascivious sigh. "That boy looks extremely healthy."

"The two of you are being absurd," Claire said in her most reproving voice. "The man isn't a drug dealer, he's simply a hardworking businessman. Though why someone who has seventy-five thousand dollars in cash to toss around would be interested in a little pick-up carpentry work on that tumbledown cabin in the swamp is beyond me."

"Beyond me, too," Jassy murmured. "Maybe I should call and tell him I've changed my mind."

"Has he got a telephone?"

"I don't think so."

"That settles that. Besides, I think that was his disreputable pickup truck that just drove up our driveway. You're too late."

Jassy sighed. "I guess it's out of my hands, then. If he's willing to take the job then why should I argue?" She pushed back from the table, wishing she felt as confident as she sounded.

"You gonna invite him in for coffee?" Lila asked, putting an anxious hand to her perfect coif of stylish blond hair. "I'm not in any shape to receive callers."

Jassy knew perfectly well that Lila's vanity was automatic. Unlike most of the young women in Turner's

Landing, her reaction to Caleb Spenser was instinctive and impersonal. She flirted with everyone, it was part of her charm, but it had nothing to do with her emotions. She was deeply, truly in love with Harrison, and all the handsome outlaws riding into town wouldn't make a lick of difference.

"I thought we'd take right off. I had Miss Sadie pack us a picnic basket if we get hungry. It's a bit of a hike out there."

"You're going like that?" Lila shrieked.

Jassy looked down at her clothes. She'd gone through seven changes of clothing, and when, not if, Lila made herself at home in Jassy's room she'd discover the other six choices lying discarded on the bed. She'd finally settled on the least conspicuous outfit she could find—an old faded pair of jeans, scuffed boots, an oversize white shirt in deference to the heat, with a thin silk camisole underneath. She'd braided and pinned her hair back, and she looked practical, no-nonsense, down to earth. As far removed from the fluttering debs of Turner's Landing as could be found.

"Yes, I'm going like this. Did you think I was going to wear a tea dress and heels to a swamp?"

"What about a little makeup, dear?" Claire murmured. "And couldn't you do something with your hair?"

"It's hot. It's more than hot, it's an oven around here, and Rayder Swamp will be a steam bath. Makeup would melt right off my face, and my hair's already a mass of frizz. I'm going out for business, Mama, not seduction."

"A girl should always keep her future in mind," Claire murmured absently.

"Claire!" Lila said, astonished. "You're not thinking that Jassy should keep company with Mr. Spenser? He's not really our kind."

Nothing was more calculated to make Jassy's hackles rise than her family's instinctive snobbery. Setting her hands on the table, she leaned toward Lila. "Well, honey," she said flatly, "neither am I." And she turned and headed for the door.

Caleb was there, a shameless eavesdropper, a faint smile curving his mouth. "Morning, ladies," he said.

Lila blushed a deep, unflattering red, one that mottled her fine chest and clashed with her peach robe. "Good morning, Mr. Spenser," she said, struggling for her usual ladylike demeanor. "Beastly hot day, isn't it?"

"Hell on wheels, Miz Lila," Spenser said. "You ready to romp in the swamp, Jassy?"

This time it was Lila's turn to drop her coffee cup in shock. Jassy, however, was more than ready for him. Since the moment she saw him lounging in the doorway like a lean and hungry tomcat waiting to pounce on a fat, juicy little mouse, her resolve and her backbone had stiffened. "I believe this was more in the line of a job interview, Mr. Spenser."

"It's whatever you want to make it, Miz Turner." He mocked her use of "mister."

She had to learn not to underestimate him. Lila's artless disclosure of just how much ready cash he had on hand had set Jassy's few preconceived notions about the man into an uproar. Obviously he didn't need the job of fixing up Rowdy's cabin. Just as obviously, he was prepared to take it. Or at least prepared to accompany her out there to check it out. And she knew damned well it wasn't because he needed the work.

So why was it? What went on behind those clear, unnerving gray eyes, that wicked smile, that lounging, graceful posture? And did she have any reason to be as frightened as Harrison so clearly was?

"I'm ready to go. Unless you'd like some coffee first?" She gestured toward the table.

"No, ma'am. I've been up since five this morning. I've had more than my share of caffeine. At least for now. Nice seeing you ladies," he said to the two Turner matrons.

"And you, Mr. Spenser," Claire replied with her customary graciousness. And Jassy wondered how far into the day Claire would make it without resorting to her medicinal bottle.

He trailed behind her as she headed back toward the hallway, not too close, but she was acutely aware of him. He caught up with her by the door, and there was just a hint of mockery in his drawling voice.

"That was real nice, the way you took up for me back there," he said.

"What do you mean by that?"

"You know perfectly well what I mean by that, don't pretend otherwise. I didn't think you were the kind to play games like your sister-in-law and your friends."

"Well, you're wrong. I've been taught the same games as everyone. I may like to handle things a little more directly, but I'm just as capable of avoiding what I want to avoid as anyone else."

"Yes, ma'am," Caleb murmured. "So am I."

"There's a hamper over there. I thought we might like a thermos of coffee and some sandwiches. It's a long ride out to Rayder Swamp and back."

"Does that mean we might not get back before nightfall?"

"Not a chance," she said flatly.

"I just thought I'd ask. I didn't want to get my hopes up." She hated that smile of his, that damnable, double-dare grin. At that moment there wasn't anything she wouldn't do to wipe it off his handsome face.

"Tell me something, Mr. Spenser."

"Sure thing, Miz Turner," he said.

Here goes, she thought, holding her breath, knowing the danger she was stepping into. Or at least guessing at it. "Did you happen to know a boy named Sherman Delano?"

He didn't move for a moment, and his clear, winter-colored eyes were blank. "What makes you ask me that?" He finally spoke, his voice even. Deceptively so.

"He lived around St. Florence. You mentioned you'd spent some time in that area, and I wondered if you'd ever met him." She tried to look as innocent as possible, but underneath her calm exterior her heart was beating way too fast. She'd stepped into currents she hadn't expected.

"I met him," Caleb said flatly. "Are we going out to Rayder Swamp or are we going to spend all morning jawing?"

She wanted to push, just a little bit further. She prided herself on being fearless, able to face down just about anything. She could stand up to abusive husbands, three-alarm fires, the horrifying results of a car accident and her family, all without flinching.

But something told her that there were times when it was much better to just drop something, then pick it up at a more opportune time. Now was definitely not the time to quiz Caleb Spenser about a murdered young man.

"We're going to Rayder Swamp," she said. "That is, if you're still interested."

This time she was almost happy to see his mocking smile break the eerie stillness of his face. "Believe me, ma'am," he said, opening the door to the pickup for her, "I'm extremely interested. You might almost say obsessed."

And Jassy, in the smothering heat of the late-morning sun, felt a little chill race across her skin.

Chapter Six

Caleb kept his eyes on the road, humming lightly beneath his breath as they bounced and jounced over the rutted surface that led to Rayder Swamp. The Everglades were much farther south than this particular stretch of the Gulf Coast, but one couldn't tell that by the swamps that were in abundance around Turner's Landing. That might account for the surprisingly undeveloped state of the area. That, or someone might have made a big mistake. One they hadn't lived to regret.

Jassy Turner was curled up on her side of the bench seat, clinging to the door handle, and he couldn't be sure whether she was holding on because of the rough ride, or to be ready to jump if he scared her. It would be easy enough to find out. She was one tough lady, despite the occasionally vulnerable look in her warm hazel eyes, and he imagined there were few things on this earth that frightened her. He also knew perfectly well that he was one of the chosen few.

He'd thought about that when he was driving over to the Turner's antebellum mansion. He wasn't given to much brooding about women, and there was certainly more than enough distraction around Turner's Landing that he didn't have to concentrate on anyone as problematic as Jacinthe Turner. But he was having a hard time getting her out of his mind. It might have been the fact that she was so intimately related to the object of his vengeance. Or it might have been the fact that she stood up to him, when he clearly made her intensely uneasy.

Or maybe it was simply that he was a sucker for greeny brown eyes, and a soft mouth, and the kind of body he suspected lurked beneath her deliberately baggy clothes.

It didn't really matter, since anything he did to involve her would rebound on Harrison, making revenge all that sweeter. If he brought down Harrison's baby sister along with the man himself, it would only add to Harrison's crushing burden of guilt. Not that the man had seemed in the slightest bit afflicted by regrets over the past. But no one could watch their safe little life destroyed without remorse.

It would make everything that much more devastating to leave Harrison with a publicly drunken mother, a cuckolding wife, a broken-hearted sister, bankruptcy and a jail term. He could hardly ask for a more complete revenge, though he liked to call it justice.

And he could break Jassy's heart; he knew he could. For all her matter-of-fact manner, her cool gaze and touch-me-not attitude, he suspected that she could break as easily as a china figurine. When touched by the right man.

"So why do you want to fix up an old cabin?" He broke the silence, and she jumped, nervously, clutching the door handle before forcing herself to release it. "Why don't you just sell it?"

"Because it's mine."

"Do you hold on to everything you own, Jassy? I'd think you'd start to run out of space."

"I hold on to what's important. Don't you?"

"No."

She looked up at him, startled, and he could see her shoulders relax slightly beneath the oversize shirt. "What do you mean?"

"I mean I don't hold on to anything. I travel light. I go from job to job. I buy places, fix them up, and sell them as soon as someone makes an offer. I rarely get to finish the job before someone wants to come in and do it their way. And they're willing to pay me good money for that privilege."

"Doesn't it give you a sense of unfinished business? A lack of completion?"

"Honey, I live and breathe unfinished business. I got used to leaving things hanging years ago. Nowadays I concentrate on tying up the loose ends that matter, and let the rest go to hell."

"Is my brother one of the loose ends that matter?"

"Ask him."

She let out a little sigh of exasperation, and he waited for another question, but she surprised him by dropping it. "So if you don't hold on to things that matter, where did your dog come from?"

Caleb stretched, rolling down the window even farther to let the thick, damp air billow through. "He showed up at a construction site one day, a frayed rope wrapped around his neck. He looked hungry, so I fed him. He's been following me ever since." He didn't bother mentioning the marks of abuse on the dog, the fear in Dog's huge black eyes, the time it had taken to coax a snapping, edgy, overgrown puppy into the relatively peaceful oaf that lounged around the Moon Palace nowadays.

"What's his name?"

"Dog." He drummed his fingers on the steering wheel. "I figured I didn't have any right to name him. If I named him I own him, and I don't figure on being that beholden to any living creature. But we get along well enough, and he listens to me complain. Dog and this old truck are about the only constants in my life.''

She glanced at the bleached, cracked dashboard, the broken speedometer, the overflowing ashtray and the toolbox at her feet. ''I bet you've got a sports car stashed away someplace. If you could afford to pay cash for the Moon Palace you can afford a better vehicle than this.''

''Someone told you about that, did they? I should have known—this town is small enough that only the important secrets are kept. I do appreciate your taking the time to ask about me, though. Did you find out anything exciting?''

''Not what I wanted to know. So *do* you?''

''Do I what?''

''Have a Corvette stashed someplace like Tampa or St. Pete?''

''Think you're pretty smart, don't you? As a matter of fact, I used to own a Mercedes. I sold it when I discovered it wasn't really my style. This truck is all the transportation I want or need. Don't let her shabby looks fool you. Beneath that rusty hood is the sweetest V-8 engine this side of Daytona. She can go from zero to sixty in a matter of seconds, and the air conditioner, when I choose to use it, works great.''

She looked over at him. He could see a faint sheen of perspiration on her upper lip, and just above the top button of her shirt. ''Then why don't you choose to use it?''

''Maybe I like to see you sweat.''

She reached over and shoved the button marked Air with a defiant glare, retreating back to her corner. He pushed it off. She reached for it again, and he caught her wrist in a grip that was just hard enough for her to realize he was serious. Not enough to hurt her.

She backed off, and he released her. "Typical," she said.

"Typical what? I don't like back-seat drivers messing with my instrumentation."

"You're a bully, just like the kind of men I hear about at the women's shelter. You're a typical male using brute force to get what you want. You're not above hurting someone if they get in your way."

He waited until his first anger had abated. "You're right," he said flatly. "I don't mind hurting someone if they get in my way. And I'll use force to get what I want. But unlike your pet charity, I don't use my fists on helpless women when I've had too much to drink or I'm in a bad mood, or for any other reason. I don't beat on women. There's a difference, subtle, I grant you, but there's a difference."

"Not as far as I'm concerned," she said, her face stubborn beneath the thick tangle of dark hair.

"Then maybe I'm just going to have to educate you about those differences," he drawled.

He got the reaction he wanted. She was almost too easy, sometimes, the way she'd react to the things he said and did. Except that she immediately erected her defenses, and that shocked expression vanished from her hazel eyes, leaving her stern and determined. "We'll see about that," she said.

"Uh-huh."

The shabby cab of the old pickup lapsed into silence, and Caleb considered flicking on the radio. He would have, if he'd known what would be most likely to irritate her, but chances are she'd like the same kind of music he did. Besides, he liked listening to her breathe.

The old narrow road grew steadily worse, bumpier, more overgrown, until it ended in a vast slime-covered expanse of water. He could probably drive through it, but he was too fond of his truck to risk it. He stopped the truck and turned off the engine.

"Where do we go from here?"

Jassy was already out of the truck. "We're lucky it's been so dry. Normally we'd have to use Rowdy's old boat, but right now we can make it on foot."

"I take it the cabin's smack dab in the center of the swamp?" Caleb was resigned, reaching for his tools.

"Hardly. I doubt we could reach the center of the swamp, even with a boat, it's so overgrown. It's just a little ways in—far enough to keep out visitors, close enough to be reachable."

"You want to keep out visitors? I thought you were out to save the world." He slammed the door shut behind him and immediately slapped away a hungry mosquito.

"You can't save the world all the time," she said without looking back, taking off on a narrow path of dry land. "Even a saint like me needs time off."

He paused for a moment, watching her move farther into the swamp. A saint wouldn't have such an unconsciously seductive grace about her. A saint wouldn't have the very definite effect she had on him. It was a good thing she wasn't a saint. He'd have a hard time keeping his hands off her if she was. And he had no intention of behaving himself. She was just too damned enticing, whether she knew it or not.

The hike to the cabin was a lengthy one. The ground was wet and soft beneath his boots, and he could tell that its sojourn out of water had been brief. One good rainstorm and it would be flooded once more. They climbed over downed cypress trunks, mangrove roots, pushed

Spanish moss out of their hair as they moved doggedly farther into the murky depths of Rayder Swamp. The sun didn't penetrate very far into the overhung green depths. The humidity, so omnipresent around Turner's Landing, was even thicker here, so he could practically see the oozing green of the air around him. He unbuttoned a couple of buttons on his chambray work shirt, and wondered how Miss Jassy Turner was surviving under that tent of a shirt.

His first glance at Rowdy's cabin was a daunting one. A ramshackle little building, it was half sunk in the mud. The tar-paper siding was ripped and peeling, the roof looked about to collapse, and the windows were cracked with some of them missing altogether. Jassy turned when she reached the sagging little porch that ran the length of it, looking at him with such innocent pride that he almost grabbed her there and then. She reminded him of Dog when that canine had managed some particularly impressive feat. Proud and anxious at the same time. Clearly she loved her tar-paper shack. And just as clearly, to his professional eyes, there was no saving it.

"I know it's falling apart," she said, letting her hand touch the railing in an unconscious caress. "And I don't have a whole lot of money to put into it. I just don't want it to get into any greater disrepair. If you could see what it would take to shore it up for a while, keep it from falling into the swamp until I can fix it up right."

It was already falling into the swamp. It wouldn't take much more than a strong wind to finish the job. That, or a push from him.

But for some reason he wasn't ready to douse that light shining in Jassy's eyes. For the first time she was looking at him without wariness, her delight and anxiety over her tumbledown piece of real estate wiping out all other considerations.

He needed to make use of that temporary trust. Right now she'd forgotten he was the enemy, and that she'd gotten him out there for nefarious purposes of her own. It hadn't taken much to guess those purposes—she obviously hoped she could keep him out of Turner's Landing and Harrison Turner's way while he worked on this place, giving her enough time to find out what was going on.

Since she was part and parcel of what was going on, he'd been perfectly willing to comply. Any time spent with her, away from Harrison Turner, was not necessarily time wasted. There were several means to his particular ends, and Jassy Turner was one of the most attractive ones.

But he could see without coming closer that Rowdy's cabin wasn't going to provide him with much of an excuse to work on her. He was going to have to take full advantage of today, and trust in Jassy's coming up with another excuse when this one fell through. Knowing her determination to take care of her worthless older brother, he had no doubt whatsoever that she'd manage to do just that.

She set the picnic basket on the porch and busied herself with the fancy lock. "You know, half the windows are broken on the place," he drawled, stepping onto the narrow porch with her and feeling the old rotten boards sag beneath his feet. "If someone wanted to get in they wouldn't bother with the locked door."

She pushed the door open, propping it a bit as it sagged on a broken hinge. "It's the principle of the thing. There are people around here who know that if someone bothers to lock a place, it belongs to them. If I didn't lock it, they'd consider it public domain." She disappeared into the darkness, and he followed her, gingerly, uncertain whether he was going to go crashing through the floorboards into the swampy muck below.

After the green murky light of the swamp, the shadowed interior of Rowdy's cabin wasn't much darker. It was a tiny place, not more than eight by ten feet, and sparsely furnished. An old table, a stool and a sagging cot comprised most of the furnishings, along with an old bureau stacked with rusting tin cans. An old wood cookstove stood in the corner, equally rusty, its stovepipe dismantled.

Caleb glanced around him. "So what do you use this place for? Meetings with your lovers?" He was teasing her, but she took the question with her usual seriousness.

"I don't have lovers," she said. "And if I did, I'd hardly bring them to a place that only had a cot, would I?"

He strolled over to the cot and sat down on it. It had less give than the aging floorboards. "It can be managed," he drawled.

"I'm sure it can," she said tartly. "Are you hungry?"

He looked up at her. "Uh-hunh." He smiled a lazy smile, wondering what it was going to take to get her on that narrow cot, lying beneath him. Whether that was what she'd had in mind all along. All she had to do was move a tiny bit closer and he'd catch her hand, pull her down to meet his hungry mouth, and...

"I'll get the food," she said breathlessly, whirling away before he could move. And he watched her go, telling himself the regret he was feeling wasn't as strong as acid. Telling himself his time would come. And so would she.

She sat on the floor, well out of reach, as they finished the coffee and half a dozen honey-laced biscuits. She still had every button but one done up on her shirt, and he wondered what she was wearing underneath. He wondered whether he was going to find out.

Finally he pushed himself off the cot, grimacing as he felt the sponginess of the floorboards beneath his booted feet. "I'd better check this place out," he said. "Take a few measurements. I wouldn't be real hopeful if I were you."

She looked up at him like a wounded fawn, and for some reason he felt more guilty about her ridiculous cabin than about what he had planned for her brother. "What do you mean?"

"It's falling apart. I think it might have been left too long to save it."

"But surely..."

"I can't tell until I check it out," he forestalled her pleading, trying to ignore the vulnerable eyes. "It'll take me about an hour to make sure. Do you want to stay put or come back and get me?"

"It'd take me longer than that to go anywhere. I've brought a book." She held up a paperback, and he noticed with real amusement that it was a florid-covered romance. Miss Jassy had more vulnerabilities than she realized.

But he decided not to tease her. He simply nodded, heading out to the porch where he'd left his tools, and began taking stock of the tumbledown cabin.

FOR A MOMENT Jassy didn't move from her spot on the cabin floor. She could see him from where she was, watch him as he stripped off his shirt in the hot, humid air, reaching for his tape measure with unconscious grace. For a moment she simply stared, bemused at the honey-colored tan that covered his body, the wiry muscles. She'd kept her eyes away from his body the time she'd visited him, made uneasy by all that bare flesh. For the moment she could look her fill, without him being aware of it.

She'd seen naked chests before. There was no reason for her particular fascination with this one naked chest. Except that she wasn't usually alone with them.

And having seen so many, she could tell that Caleb Spenser had a particularly nice one. A flat stomach, not too much hair, and the understated muscles that didn't bulge and lump all over the place, but nevertheless were more than sufficient for getting the job done. She wondered what his skin would feel like. Warm, smooth, hot?

He turned sideways, and for the first time she saw the scar. It wasn't that large, and it was no wonder she'd missed it before in her determined effort to keep her gaze at shoulder level or above. It was a nasty slash of whiteness in the bronzed skin, just beneath his ribs, and she knew with unquestioning instincts that it came from a knife.

She closed her eyes, but the vision remained. She'd thought watching him would have blunted some of her fascination. It only fed it. Moving away from temptation, she climbed onto the cot, still warm where he'd lounged. She picked up the book, determined to concentrate on boardroom and bedroom politics and ignore the sounds of him moving around outside. She could hear the lazy buzzing of a bee, far enough away that she didn't need to worry. The quiet sound of the water moving slowly around their tiny spit of land. The soughing sigh of the wind through the cypress trees overhead. She closed her eyes, for one short moment, and she was asleep.

When she opened her eyes the cabin was dark. And then she realized that the murky light from the front door was blocked by the man sitting on the cot beside her, his face shadowed in the darkness.

"What time is it?" she asked, her voice rusty from sleep.

"A little after three. You looked so peaceful lying there—I didn't have the heart to wake you."

She hadn't thought he had a heart at all, but she didn't say it aloud. "I didn't sleep well last night," she murmured instead.

"Didn't you? I never have any trouble sleeping."

"The result of a clean conscience, no doubt," Jassy said tartly, struggling to sit up.

"No doubt," he said, not moving, simply watching her, holding himself as still as an alligator waiting for its prey to make a foolish move.

Jassy felt sudden coolness against her skin, and she looked down to see that her shirt was unbuttoned, exposing the maroon silk camisole she'd worn beneath it. She yanked the open edges of her shirt together, telling herself that the shaking in her hands came from rage that he would touch her while she slept.

She didn't even need to accuse him. He simply shrugged. "You looked so hot, buttoned up like a nun. I thought you'd sleep better if you had a little ventilation."

"You're lucky I didn't wake up and start screaming."

"No one would have heard you." His voice was very gentle, but it in no way blunted the effect his words had on her. She told herself they were a threat, of the most basic sort. But he made no move to touch her.

Instead he rose, moving away from her, tucking his hands into the pockets of his tight jeans. He'd put his shirt back on, but he hadn't bothered to button it or tuck it in, and the effect was still completely disturbing. "This place is hopeless," he said, a deliberate change of subject. "But I suspect you already knew that."

Her fears forgotten, Jassy leaped off the cot and followed him. "I didn't suspect any such thing. And nothing's hopeless. Surely there's something we can do. Shore up the place, put a few new beams in..."

He stepped out onto the porch, and she followed him, using all her self-control not to catch his arm and plead with him. Touching him would not be a good idea. Not at all.

"Let me give you a little lesson in construction, Jassy. This place is built on cypress pilings sunk into the muck. Those pilings have lasted a long time, but they're rotten through and through. Normally the next step would be to jack up the house and put new pilings in. But in this swampy area there's nothing to rest the jacks on, and if there were, the rotten timber in the house would crumble from the weight. All this place needs is one good blow and it'll tumble back into the swamp."

"But..."

"All you can do," he continued ruthlessly, "is to tear it down and build something completely new."

For a moment she didn't say a word. "I can't afford to do that."

"I know."

The Turners didn't seem to have any secrets from him, financial or otherwise, and lying wouldn't get her anywhere.

"So that's that," she said tonelessly.

"If I were you, I wouldn't even come out here again. The place is downright dangerous. The roof won't stand a good soaking rain, and if the water level rises the whole thing might collapse." He picked up his toolbox.

"Thanks for your concern. If you send a bill for your time out here..."

"Consultations are free," he said, and there was a trace of irritation in his usually slow, deep voice. "Would you stop looking like I kicked your dog? I'm sorry this place is in such a state, but there's not a damned thing I can do about it. You'd be better off putting the money into a bus ticket and getting the hell out of town."

She looked at him with astonishment, but he already seemed to be regretting his hasty words. "Why should I get out of town?" she asked in a calm enough voice.

"Forget I said it."

"I don't forget things. Why should I leave town?"

"You might be happier if you did." He moved closer to her, and she could feel the heat from him in the hot afternoon air. Overhead she could hear the distant rumble of thunder. Another false promise from the sky, and she'd had too many false promises.

He looked down at her, his light eyes no longer cool and calculating, but suddenly hot. He put his hands on her, resting on her shoulders, and they were strong, heavy, and she knew they were going to pull her close, closer, until she rested against his chest and her mouth met his. And she'd go, willingly, open her mouth to his willingly, and they'd go back into that room and see whether the cot was really too small.

She had to stop it, while she still could. She squirmed, and his fingers tightened, just briefly, before releasing her. At the same time he released his pent-up breath. "Let's get out of here," he said in a neutral voice, as if the momentary flash of something between them had never existed. "Maybe for once that thunder means business."

But she didn't trust him. If he changed his mind, reached for her again, she wouldn't back away. Her only defense was words. "It's not going to rain," she said, picking up the picnic basket and locking the door behind them. She could feel his eyes on her, watching, waiting, and she said the only thing she could think of to throw him off.

"Where did you get that scar?"

He was silent, and she turned to look at him, uncertain whether he had heard. "Which scar?" he asked finally, and if she'd thought she'd thrown him off balance she could see she'd underestimated him.

"The one under your ribs. It looks like it came from a knife."

"Very observant, Miss Jassy. I didn't know you were watching so closely."

Her turn to flush. "I just happened to notice it."

"Sure," he said. "And you're right. It's from a knife. A couple more inches and I wouldn't be here right now."

"Lucky for me," she said dourly. "How'd you get it?"

"You are nosy today, aren't you?" he murmured. "You aren't going to be happy with the answer."

"I assume it was in some fight."

"You assume correctly. I got it when I was in the state penitentiary."

She swallowed, the thick, hot air choking her. "What were you in jail for?" she asked, then wished she hadn't.

Caleb Spenser smiled. "Why, for murdering your brother's friend, Sherman Delano. Didn't you guess?"

Chapter Seven

It didn't make for a comfortable ride back toward Turner's Landing. For once in her life Jassy was simply too shocked to ask questions. The more she turned it over in her brain the more she knew she shouldn't have been so surprised. There was something going on—something that involved her brother, Caleb Spenser and a long-ago murder. She just hadn't guessed how bad it was.

Neither of them said a word until they had driven out of the roughest part of the swamp. There was a great deal of difference in their moods. While Jassy struggled with the shocking information he'd so casually imparted, he seemed more concerned with the state of the roads. He was humming something lightly, under his breath, and his expression was deliberately bland and guileless. He'd set out to shock her on purpose, she knew that full well.

Finally she couldn't stand the silence any longer, that damnable humming that was making her want to commit murder herself. "Mother said the man who killed Delano was executed."

At least he stopped humming. He glanced over at her, an amused expression on his face. "Honey, your mama doesn't know diddly. I got seven years for manslaughter, and I served three of them, with time off because I was such a good boy."

"You needn't seem so lighthearted about it. Murder's a serious business."

"I've lived with it for a long time, Jassy. It no longer has the power to surprise me."

She glanced at him, caught by something in his voice. "Surprise you? You were surprised that you killed a man?"

"You could say so."

"Does Harrison know you killed Sherman Delano? Of course he must. That's why he's so frightened of you, he knows you're a killer."

"Now, Jassy, do I look like a cold-blooded killer to you?" he said, the epitome of reason. Except that she wasn't buying it.

"You look like you're capable of anything you set your mind to." She shivered in the thick, humid air, remembering that she'd almost kissed him, minutes ago. Realizing that she still wanted to. "Does Harrison have anything to do with...with..."

"With the killing? Why don't you ask him?"

"I'm asking you."

"And I'm not answering." He pulled onto the paved highway, stepping down on the accelerator, and Jassy realized he hadn't exaggerated the old truck's potential. It shot forward with the smoothness of a brand-new sports car, and instinctively she reached for the door handle. "I have to stop by my place before I drop you off. I need to see whether the lumber company has finally made the delivery they've been promising. If they haven't, I need to go kick some butt after I leave you home."

"My brother has part ownership in the lumber company," she said, then could have kicked herself. "And I'd prefer to go straight home."

"I'm sure you would. But I'm the driver, and I'm going by way of the Moon Palace. If you've got a problem you can walk."

"I guess they didn't teach you manners in prison," she said, half-shocked at her boldness.

He grinned then, amused rather than irritated. "Well, if they tried, it's worn off by now. I got out more than ten years ago."

"But Mama said Sherman was only killed ten years ago."

"Honey, your mama is a lush. Everyone knows that, no matter how hard you all try to cover up for her. You'd best not take her word for anything. Sherman Delano died on November 23, 1979. Southern justice moved swiftly, for once, and I was neatly convicted and serving time within six months."

"Harrison was in school up north back then," Jassy said slowly. "He couldn't have been anywhere around when Delano was killed."

"Thanksgiving break," was all Caleb said.

"Are you telling me my brother had something to do with it?" she asked sharply.

"Ask him."

"Stop saying that, damn you. You can't just drop hints and then clam up like some sphinx."

"Honey," he said, pulling to a stop in front of the decaying old building. "I can do anything I damn please."

Dog bounded out of the front door, a huge, quivering mass of canine delight. Caleb was already out of the truck, rubbing Dog's head with his large strong hands and crooning to him before heading on into the house. Dog looked over at her, still sitting in the truck, then turned to look back at his master disappearing through the front door. He let out a mournful little whimper, torn between two human delights, and Jassy took pity on him, climbing down from the rusty old pickup and approaching him.

Dog whoofed in joy, prancing over to her and slobbering all over her hands, batting his huge head against her hip before rolling over on his back to have his shaggy tummy scratched. She squatted down beside him. "You're ridiculous, Dog, you know that? I think you need a name, though, and an owner who's going to take more responsibility."

"I take enough," Caleb said from above her.

She leaped up, startled, but he was so close she rammed into him. He put out his hands to steady her, and she looked at them, at him, and the breath left her body. She didn't move, and neither did he, and this time he was going to kiss her, and if he didn't, she was going to kiss him. It didn't matter, as long as his mouth was on hers and his body was touching hers and his arms were . . .

"Whoof." Dog jumped up, placing his huge paws on Caleb's chest and slurping him happily, knocking him back away from Jassy before it could happen.

Jassy didn't wait for regret, or another chance. She ran back to the truck, jumping onto the seat, and fastening the frayed seat belt around her like a chastity belt.

"I'm going to turn you into alligator food," Caleb informed Dog, scratching his head. "I thought you were more sophisticated than that." He climbed back into the truck, swinging his long legs in first, and glanced over her way.

"Did the lumber get delivered?" she asked in an effort to forestall conversation about anything more intimate.

"No. Got any suggestions?"

"Can you work on this place if they won't deliver?"

"Yes and no. I can have the lumber trucked in from outside, which I certainly will. It'll mean a couple of days' delay, but I'm sure I can find ways to keep me busy while I'm waiting."

Jassy swallowed. "I'll have a word with Ed down at the yard. I'm sure your lumber will be delivered by tomorrow."

"I should have come to you first."

"I understand threats better."

"I'm not threatening you."

"Aren't you? It seems to me that you're threatening my brother, for whatever misguided reason, and anything or anyone that threatens my brother threatens me."

"Such family loyalty." The shadows were getting longer on the old narrow road, and the constant rumble of thunder only added to her sudden sense of unease.

"Most people can understand family loyalty," she said stiffly.

"Not me. I got away from my family as soon as I was old enough to run, and I haven't been back. Not that there's anyone to go back to now. But I learned early on you look out for yourself and yourself alone. Your family will stab you in the back if it suits them."

"Your family, maybe. Not mine."

"You really don't think Harrison would throw you to the wolves to save his own worthless hide?"

"Of course not," she said, shocked.

Caleb laughed, but there was no humor in the sound. "I wish you didn't have to find out otherwise. But I expect you will. As long as I'm here."

"Then why don't you leave?"

"Not a chance. I've got unfinished business to take care of. As soon as that's done, I'll be gone."

"I can't wait," she said stiffly.

He didn't bother replying. The wind had picked up, thrashing the trees about overhead, and the rumble of thunder was growing louder. Jassy cranked down the window, peering out, when suddenly Caleb's hand reached out and caught her forearm, yanking her away.

"What . . . ?" she started to protest.

"Get down on the floor," he ordered her.

"Are you out of your mind? Why should I . . . ?"

"Don't argue with me, just get down. We've got trouble." He shoved her, hard enough so that she had no choice but to duck down, and she did so, muttering imprecations about abusive men.

And then the truck came to an abrupt halt, and Caleb's hand came down on her head, keeping her down as he leaned out his window.

"Can I do anything for you boys?" he asked, slow and affable, the tension in the hand on Jassy's head at odds with the ease in his voice.

"That depends." It was a voice Jassy didn't recognize, and she knew everyone who lived within twenty miles of Turner's Landing. "We're looking for a troublemaker, name of Caleb Spenser. Ever heard tell of him?"

"Maybe," Caleb drawled. "What do you want with him?"

"Why, we thought we might learn him a lesson or two. Such as not to cause trouble for peaceful, law-abiding folks. Such as, maybe he'd better git back to where he come from, if he wants to stay in one piece." She heard another noise, an ominous sound somewhere between a slap and a thud. The kind of sound a board would make if it were being slapped against a waiting hand.

"Maybe Caleb Spenser doesn't take to learning too well," Caleb said. The engine was still running in the truck, and Jassy crouched there, wondering why in heaven's name he didn't just drive through them.

"Then maybe we're going to have to be real thorough in teaching him," another stranger's voice spoke.

"Tell you what, boys," Caleb said easily. "You want to have a go at me, and it doesn't look like I'm going to have much to say about it. So why don't you let me pull the truck off the road and we'll see about it."

"He's gonna drive away, Jesse," the first stranger warned. "Don't let 'im."

"Don't be a fool, Willard. That truck can't get around this here tree. Not until we decide to move it. As a matter of fact, I kind of like that truck. She's sort of beat-up, but that's a sweet-purring engine."

"Leave the truck alone," Caleb said flatly. "And you'll have an easier time with me."

"Hell, we don't want an easier time with you. There are three of us, and only one of you. And I want to know why you're so durn protective of that truck."

It happened so fast she barely realized what was going on. The passenger door was slung open, and meaty hands reached in, hauling her out into the gathering dusk. Hurtful hands, and she fought instinctively, biting down hard on the nearest wrist.

One of them howled with rage, shoving her away from him and backhanding her across the face. "Damned bitch bit me," he moaned. "I guess I'm gonna have to learn her a lesson, too...."

The sound of a gunshot brought them to a curious standstill. Jassy looked up from her position on the hard ground, aching all over, staring at Caleb in shock. He stood in the open doorway of the truck, a very large, very nasty-looking gun in his capable-looking hands. "Now, I'm not a believer in violence," he said amiably, "but I think I've had plenty of provocation. Why don't you just run along now, while I'm still in the mood to let you go? Not you, there...." The gun pointed at the man who'd hit Jassy. "You stay put. Your friends can find you later."

The other two jumped into the old pickup parked on the other side of the fallen tree blocking the old road, and a moment later they roared off into the gathering darkness, leaving their comrade behind.

Caleb jumped down from the truck, the gun held loosely in his hand, and he strode over to Jassy. "You all right?" he asked, running a critical eye over her.

She managed to climb to her feet, brushing the dirt from her clothes. Her face throbbed, her heart was pounding, and her hands were cold and damp and shaking. She wanted to cry, she wanted to scream. Instead she nodded. "I'm fine."

He smiled at her then, a look of particular sweetness with none of his dare-you quality, and she had the sudden thought that he knew everything that had gone through her head, up to and including bursting into tears. "Good girl," he said. "Now you just stay out of the way while I let Willard try to teach me that lesson he was talking about."

"You're pretty tough when you're the one with the gun," Willard sneered. He was a huge, hulking brute, several inches taller than Caleb and outweighing him by a considerable amount of poundage, at least half of which was muscle. Jassy knew for certain she'd never seen him or his friends around Turner's Landing before.

"The gun bother you, Willard?" Caleb said gently. "Then I'll ask Miss Turner to hold it for me. That way if by any remote chance you happen to best me, she can still blow your ugly face off if you come anywhere near her."

"Miss Turner?" Willard echoed, suddenly looking uneasy.

"The name ring a bell, Willard?" Caleb asked. "Maybe whoever hired you happens to have the same one. How's he going to like hearing that you slapped his sister? I don't think he's going to be pleased."

"I don't know what you're talking about," Willard said sullenly, watching out of beady little eyes as Caleb placed the gun in Jassy's unwilling hands. The metal was warm from Caleb's grip and from its recent firing. Jassy knew about guns, knew and hated them. But she also had no great confidence in Caleb's ability to best someone who was bigger and probably meaner than he was. She set the firing mechanism, holding the gun in capable, steady hands.

"You know, Willard," Caleb said in a low, almost seductive voice, "it strikes me that I'm not the only one who needs to be taught a lesson. I think you need to learn not to hit women, not unless they're tough enough to take you on. Now, Miss Turner's plenty tough, and if it came to a battle of wills she'd win, hands down. But she's just not as big as you are, and not as strong, and I don't believe she's into physical violence." The two of them were circling around each other like wary dogs. "However," Caleb added with his dare-you smile, "I am."

With a roar Willard charged at him, and Jassy let cowardice overcome her, shutting her eyes for a moment, unable to watch Caleb being pounded to a pulp. And then she opened them, to see Willard lying flat on his back like a landed fish, gasping and groaning in agony, struggling and failing to get to his feet.

Caleb stood over him, an enigmatic expression on his face. "Not so tough, are you, Willard?" he said in a soft voice, one that barely carried to Jassy's ears. "This one's for the lady." And to Jassy's horror he brought his boot down on Willard's right hand, hard.

Willard's shriek of pain echoed through the night, but Caleb had already turned away, taking the gun out of Jassy's limp hands. "Shall we go?" he asked in a pleasant voice.

She looked up at him, shell-shocked. The violence of the last few minutes hung in the air like a sour perfume, and now that she no longer held the gun she found she was shaking. "What did you do to him?"

If he noticed her reaction he didn't mention it, simply putting an impersonal hand under her arm and escorting her to the old truck. "Broke his hand," he said. "Stay in the truck while I move that old tree out of the way."

"You can't just leave him there...."

"His friends haven't gone far. They'll be back to get him."

"But..."

"It'll give him time to meditate on the error of his ways. Unless you'd rather have me shoot him and be done with it?"

"No!" she shrieked, and then realized he didn't mean it. She leaned back against the bench seat of the truck, shivering. "Just take me home."

The tree they'd dragged across the road was an old oak, fallen years ago but still heavy. Caleb pulled it out of the way with seemingly little effort, not even glancing at the man writhing on the ground as he headed back for the truck. There wasn't a mark on Caleb, Jassy thought, touching her own cheek with a rueful hand.

"We should go to the police," she said, forcing her weakness away.

"Why?"

"Because those men were lying in wait for you. They were planning to beat you up. You need to report it, have them arrested for assault...."

"I think after what I did to Willard the shoe might be on the other foot. After all, they didn't manage to touch me. Willard's not in very good shape." He started the truck, flicking on the lights against the gathering gloom and driving very carefully around Willard's writhing body.

"Someone hired those men...."

"I don't think you want that someone found," he pointed out. "It doesn't take much to guess who has it in for me. I thought your family loyalty came above all things."

"I'm willing to bet you have a lot more enemies than my brother," she said with a certain amount of shrewdness. "And even if he did hire them, he shouldn't have. Taking care of my brother includes stopping him from doing jackass things."

They were coming to the fork in the road. Belle Rive was to the left, the tiny town of Turner's Landing, complete with sheriff's office, was to the right. He slowed the truck on the deserted road. "Take your pick," he said, as if her decision meant absolutely nothing to him.

Perhaps it didn't. "Take me home," she said finally. "I'll call Clayton Sykes from there."

He nodded, turning left, and they drove on in silence for a while, the rush of hot moist air blowing through the windows, soothing Jassy's bruised cheek. He'd hit her on the right side of her face—if there was any mark she kept it averted from Caleb's too observant eyes.

"We've got one little problem," he said as they started up the long, curving driveway that led to the front entrance of Belle Rive.

"What's that?"

"A convicted felon doesn't have the right to own a handgun. Particularly a concealed, loaded one in a vehicle."

She looked at him. "Gun? I didn't see anyone with a gun there."

He smiled at her, and then his eyes narrowed, and he pulled the truck to a stop halfway up the driveway, with the lights of the big house visible in the distance, and she knew he'd seen her face.

He reached out to touch her cheekbone, very lightly, but she flinched anyway. "I should have killed him," he said in a flat, emotionless voice, and once more she believed him.

She tried to pull away, but his other hand reached up and caught her neck, gently, his thumb tracing gentle patterns on her exposed throat, while he pushed the tumbled hair away from her bruised face. "You're going to have a mark there tomorrow," he said. "You'd better lie down with an ice pack the moment you get inside."

"After I call the sheriff." Her voice came out strangled. She wanted to tell him to take his hands off her, but if he did she thought she'd die. He was looking at her out of those clear, light eyes, and he was close, much too close.

"What are you going to tell your family?"

"The truth."

"Even Harrison?"

"Particularly Harrison. I still refuse to believe he's responsible for those men, but just in case he is, he needs to see what a stupid move like that can bring about."

Caleb's smile was wry, self-deprecating. "I don't think he's going to learn his lesson, Jassy." His fingers were lightly stroking her face, whisper soft against her hairline, soothing her, as his thumb danced across her sensitive throat.

She pulled all her resolution around her. "I think you'd better drive me home," she whispered, wetting her lips in sudden nervousness.

"I know I'd better," he said. "There's just a little something I have to do first. I've been putting it off for too long." And his mouth dropped down on hers, cutting off the light.

She'd expected something more forceful. Strength and violence, demanding a response. She could have fought that. Instead his lips feathered across hers, a gentle wooing, clinging for a moment, traveling on, across her cheekbone to brush gently against her abraded cheek before returning to her lips.

She'd drawn in her breath at the first touch of his mouth, steeling herself to fight him, but there was no defiance in her. He nibbled at her mouth, softly, teasingly, coaxing her lips apart in a lazy seduction that had her moaning deep in the back of her throat, half longing for the fierce demand she'd been prepared to resist.

He knew women too well. He pulled away, leaving her dazed, aching, longing for more, and his old smile was back in place. He didn't say a word as he started up the truck again, pulling up to the front of the house and leaving the engine in neutral. His voice was neutral, too.

"You want me to come in with you?" he asked. "Looks like Harrison's come home."

He'd noticed Harrison's late model Buick before Jassy had. "Maybe I'd better deal with this on my own," she said, her voice husky.

"Suit yourself. You know I'd prefer to come in."

"Please . . ."

He nodded. "If you call the sheriff . . ."

"*When* I call the sheriff," she corrected him.

"Tell him I'll be at home if he has any questions."

"I'll do that." She opened the door, sliding out before he could touch her again. She had no idea whether he'd planned to, and no idea how she'd react if he did. She was better off not knowing. "Those men won't be waiting for you, will they?" she asked, suddenly worried.

"I doubt it. Willard's going to need to see a doctor real bad, and the other two were cowards. They weren't told to kill me, otherwise they would have had guns of their own. I expect I'll be just fine. Don't worry about me, Jassy. I always come out okay."

"I'm not worried," she denied. "I just don't want my brother brought up on charges of murder."

Caleb's laugh was chilling in the hot evening air. "I don't think that's going to be up to you, sugar." And before she could say anything more, he drove away, speeding down the driveway with all the power his deceptively ancient truck could offer.

Chapter Eight

"What in God's name happened to you?" Lila was standing in the hallway. Her face was blotchy and red from tears, but for once Jassy couldn't summon forth her usual concern.

"I got hit," she said flatly. "I gather Harrison's back?"

"I can't believe it!" Lila said in a carrying voice. "That man actually hit you? Harrison's going to kill him."

"Who am I going to kill?" Harrison appeared in the doorway, dwarfing the generous proportions. He had a drink in his hand, and a sullen, belligerent expression on his handsome face.

"Look at your sister," Lila said shrilly.

"I'm looking." He set the drink down. "We're calling Clayton Sykes. That boy's butt is going to be in a sling before he knows what's happening. He's gonna go back to jail so fast he won't know what's happening to him. Unless the people of Turner's Landing find out what he did to you and get to him first."

Jassy took all this in quite calmly. "I was just about to call Clayton," she agreed. "Though why the two of you idiots think it was Caleb Spenser is beyond me. I got mauled by one of the gorillas who was after Caleb. The man defended my honor."

"Spenser doesn't know what the word means."

"Maybe not. But he doesn't stand around and let women get hit without doing something about it."

"Who hit you, Jassy? And where's Spenser now?" Lila asked, coming toward her and putting her arms around her, her own troubles temporarily forgotten.

"We were coming back from the swamp when three good old boys stopped the truck. They'd dragged a tree trunk across the road and were waiting in ambush. Caleb made me hide on the floor while he tried to deal with them, but they found me." She shrugged. "One of them hit me. Caleb scared the other two off and beat the hell out of the one who'd touched me."

"Whereabouts did this happen?" Harrison was looking remote, and if she didn't know better she would have thought he was half-drunk.

"Right before the old Wilson place." Too late she realized just what she was saying.

"That's on the road from the Moon Palace. I thought you said you were coming from the swamp," Harrison said.

"We stopped at the Moon Palace on the way back. Caleb had to check on a few things."

"I'll just bet he did. You don't have a lick of sense, do you, Jassy? Women like you are easy prey for a con man like Spenser. All he has to do is crook his finger and you're flat on your back for him...."

"Harrison!" Lila said, shocked.

"I never thought to see the day that my own little sister was a disloyal tramp! The man's trash, a worthless, no-good jailbird who's come here to cause trouble, and you lift your skirts like you're not better than you should be. It's a good thing Papa isn't alive to see this day, it's a good thing Mama's indisposed...."

"Mama isn't indisposed, she's drunk," Jassy said tartly, having had enough of this. "And it's none of your damned business, but I didn't sleep with Caleb Spenser. He was going to do some work for me on Rowdy's cabin, and we were checking it out. He was a perfect gentleman at all times." Or almost, she thought, remembering the heated expression in his clear, light eyes.

"That's another thing. Why the hell did you hire him to work for you, when there are any number of unemployed carpenters hanging around the general store in town, just begging for work?"

"Because I wanted to find out what the hell is going on between the two of you. You won't tell me a damned thing, I thought maybe I could get it out of him."

Harrison was suddenly very still. "And did he tell you?"

"Not a blessed thing."

There was no missing the faint sheen of relief in Harrison's dark eyes. "What about the cabin? Is he going to work for you? Try and resurrect that old relic?"

Harrison had done nothing but lie to her. For the first time in her life she had no compunction about lying right back to him. "We're still in the negotiation stage."

"Damn it, Jassy, I want that man out of this county!"

"You can't make him leave. And siccing out-of-town thugs on him doesn't help matters."

"What are you saying, Jassy?" Lila demanded. "You couldn't think Harrison had anything to do with those men."

"Couldn't I? Where else would they come from?"

If Harrison was responsible he was more than adept at hiding it. "A man like Spenser would have hundreds of enemies. I'm not the only one he has it in for."

"You're the only one around here."

"I wouldn't count on that, little sister. I don't think you're any too safe from him, either."

That hit a nerve, one she couldn't quite disguise. She didn't trust her brother, but she sure as hell didn't trust Caleb Spenser, either. She had no idea what he wanted in Turner's Landing, either from her brother or from her, but she had no doubts whatsoever that he'd ride right over her if she got in his way.

"I'm not worried about him," she said coolly. "Right now all I want is a telephone. I've got to call Clayton and see if he can find out where those men went. They shouldn't be too hard to find. The one named Willard needed a doctor."

"Don't bother Clayton with that nonsense, Jassy," Harrison said, picking his drink up again. "He won't be able to find them. You know Clayton—he couldn't find his own backside. Those men will be out of the county by now. They were probably just troublemakers from wherever Spenser came from, out for a little revenge. I doubt anyone's going to hear from them again."

"I'm still going to report them."

"Why don't you let Spenser take care of that?"

"He doesn't care whether they're reported or not."

"Then why should you?" Harrison asked in a reasonable tone. "I think what you need is a nice stiff drink, an ice pack for your face and a good night's sleep. We don't need to get involved in that man's business. He's nothing but trash, and the sooner he's gone, the better."

"The drink and the ice pack sound fine. But I'm calling Clayton."

"Suit yourself. But don't drag me into it. I'm not interested in Mr. Spenser's troubles," Harrison said.

"You're not interested when a man hits your sister?" she countered.

He glanced toward her bruised cheek, then shifted away uneasily. "It wouldn't have happened if I'd been around. I would have put my foot down and refused to allow you to go out with that man this morning."

"Harrison, I'm thirty-one years old. I'll go where and with whom I please."

"Not while you're living under my protection." He drained his glass, and there was no mistaking the belligerence in his stance.

"I'm going upstairs," Lila said faintly, an unwilling witness to the sibling argument. "I've got a headache."

"You do that, my dear," Harrison said, and Jassy remembered Lila's pale, tear-streaked face when she'd first arrived home. She must have interrupted them in the midst of some battle, only to provide her own fuel to the fire.

"I'll come up with you and make sure you're settled."

Lila's blue eyes took on an odd, startled expression. One that almost looked like fear, though Jassy knew perfectly well that Lila had no cause to fear her brother. "Thank you," she said, in a small, quiet voice, starting upstairs.

"Wait a minute, Harrison," Jassy said as her brother moved past her.

"What now?" His tone was aggrieved.

"What's wrong with Lila?"

"What's always wrong with Lila?" he countered, as his wife disappeared on the upper landing. "She's fussing about children again. She's badgering me to take those stupid tests. There's nothing wrong with me, and she knows it. She's just clutching at straws."

"Can't you humor her?"

"Hell, no! You don't understand what it means to be a man, Jassy. We have pride. We have dignity. We don't want our intimate functions messed with by some damned quack."

"But your wife can go through all sorts of painful tests...."

"She's the one who's so all-fired set on having babies," he said in a sulky tone.

Jassy just stared at him. At the handsome, sullen face, the belligerent set to his broad shoulders, and she wondered if, after thirty-one years, she really knew him at all. "I'm calling Clayton," she said.

"Give him my best." Harrison started up the stairs, but her voice called after him.

"Just one thing, brother mine. How did you know Caleb Spenser had spent time in jail?"

Harrison turned and looked at her, the contempt on his face plain. "How did you, Jassy?" And without another word he continued up the stairs.

THERE WAS NO SIGN of Willard or his friends when Caleb drove back down the old road to the bordello, but then, he hadn't expected there to be. They were long gone, at least for now. He had little doubt either, they or a reasonable facsimile, would be showing up later. Harrison wasn't going to give up on him, any more than he was going to let Harrison slip away from the justice he so richly deserved.

It was fully dark by the time he pulled up outside the old house, and Dog was waiting for him, howling plaintively, a reproachful expression in his huge dark eyes.

"Yeah, I know, you didn't want me leaving you," Caleb said, cuffing him playfully as he strode through the darkness to the house. "But I need you to play watchdog, you know that. No one in their right mind will mess with my things if you're around, for all that Jassy Turner thinks you're just a sweet, overgrown puppy.''

Dog woofed cheerfully, as if in agreement. "Yeah, I can't say much for her judgment. She can't see the wolf in you, and she probably thinks I'm not nearly as dangerous as people think. She's wrong in both cases, dead wrong.''

Dog looked aggrieved, his nails clacking on the worn wooden floor as he followed Caleb into the sparse kitchen. "I know. You wouldn't hurt her. You've fallen for her, you big stupid canine, and if it came to choosing between her and me you'd probably forget all I've ever done for you and pick her. She has that ability. A talent for making people forget what they should be remembering. Things like anger, justice, revenge. It sure would be nice just to wrap her around me and forget about why I'm here. But I can't do that. And don't you expect me to, either.''

Dog wandered over to his empty dish and sank down with a disapproving sigh. "I know you think I ought to let her be. Hell, you probably think I ought to forget about the whole damned thing. But I can't. Not after three years of my life were ripped away by that sniveling coward and his old man. Not after spending the next ten years trying to track him down. I just can't let go of it. Even if I wanted to. And I don't. You hear me, Dog? I don't want to let go.'' He opened the refrigerator, pulled out a beer for himself and a pot of leftover stew for Dog. He dumped it down on the linoleum, but Dog only looked up at him out of reproachful eyes.

"Don't look at me that way. I'm not listening to you.'' He opened the beer, tilting back a goodly swallow down his throat, then running the cold bottle against his forehead. "You know what I need, Dog? I need a woman.

Maybe that'll take my mind off Jassy Turner. Maybe I'll just go look up Miss Mary-Louise Albertson. She's certainly been more than willing."

Dog growled, low in his throat.

"I didn't say I was going to bring her back here. I just thought maybe I could take the edge off my mood. A couple of hours between the sheets with Mary-Louise might make me see things a little more clearly. Even if I'd rather be between the sheets with Jassy."

Dog let out a little bark of enthusiastic agreement. "Pervert," Caleb said cheerfully. "Don't think you're going to get to watch. When I bring Jassy back here we're not going to want any distractions. You're going to stay outside and guard the place."

Dog sighed, nibbling at the congealed beef stew. "*If* I bring her back here. I'd be much better off leaving Jassy Turner strictly alone. She's the most distracting woman I've met in a long time." He strode past Dog's disapproving figure, into the back room that served as his headquarters, bedroom, office, what have you. He laughed at the thought of what prim and proper Miss Jassy Turner would say if she saw where he slept.

The old billiard table was one of the few sturdy pieces of furniture left in the old place. He'd considered sleeping in one of those oversize, red-flocked bedrooms upstairs, but while the wooden frames of the old beds were still in worthwhile shape, the springs and mattresses had rusted and sagged their way into oblivion, and he sure as hell wasn't going to spread his sleeping bag on the floor. One of the first things he'd done after he'd bought the place was head down to Clearwater and bring back a queen-size mattress to throw on top of it. Pool tables were made of slate, and this one was as heavy as hell. He liked a hard bed, and the pool table gave him that. He just wondered how Miss Jassy would feel stretched across it, looking up at him.

He climbed up on it, leaning back, his half-empty beer in one hand as he unbuttoned his shirt to the warm night breezes blowing through the house. The thunder had died away long ago, the promise of a cooling rain unfulfilled. He could feel the tension thrumming through him, frustration, edginess, all boiling away in the pit of his stomach. He wasn't going after Mary-Louise—at least not now. He wasn't in the mood for dealing with all the little games you had to play to get someone into bed.

Something had to happen, and happen soon, before he exploded. The confrontation tonight with Willard had only heightened his tension, set his nerve endings on edge, so that he wanted to smash his fist into someone's face.

It had to rain. Or Harrison had to make one false move. He couldn't get him yet, and indeed, he didn't want to. He wanted the man to sweat. To suffer. To know that retribution was waiting for him, ready to pounce when he least expected it. To know that his comfortable little life was going to dissolve into ruin, and there was nothing he could do to stop it.

He heard one distant rumble of thunder, and he drained his beer, dropping it over the side of the bed and letting it clank onto the bare wood floors. Closing his eyes, he thought of all the people who'd made love under the shabby roof of the old place. He tried to think of Mary-Louise and the smug promise in her ripe mouth. But instead, all he could think of was Jassy Turner, of the trembling softness of her lips beneath his, the way she tried to look so cold and starched up, and the way her breasts looked beneath that thin silk camisole. He groaned out loud in the dimly-lit room, and Dog replied from the kitchen with a commiserating whine.

"Life's a bitch, Dog," Caleb muttered. "I just wish to hell I knew of a way to get my cake and eat it, too. I want Harrison Turner strung up and I want Jassy Turner spread out, and I don't think I'm gonna manage both. But I'll tell you one thing, you mangy, flea-ridden critter. I sure as hell am going to try."

And Dog, wagging his ponderous tail in agreement, sank onto the floor beneath the billiard table, feeling more secure in that moment than Caleb had ever felt in his entire life.

IT WASN'T ANY HOTTER in the stifling office at the women's center than it had been two days earlier, it just felt that way. The air conditioner was groaning like an arthritic old lady climbing stairs, the plastic chair was sticking to Jassy's thighs through the loose cotton skirt and her state of mind was a match for the day.

Clayton Sykes had been everything that Harrison had warned her. Supremely uninterested, unwilling to take a statement, condescending and smugly superior, he'd suggested that she was exaggerating the whole incident. No one else in town had noticed three strangers, and in a place as small as Turner's Landing, someone would have said something. If Caleb Spenser had anything to complain about, maybe he'd better be the one to file the complaint. Otherwise, Miss Jassy ought to pour herself a stiff drink and get a good night's sleep.

Jassy had slammed down the phone on him. She was getting tired of men telling her she should have a stiff drink. If that was the way men had always treated her mama when she was younger then it was no wonder that Claire was in her current state.

Damn Caleb Spenser. She'd worked so hard at making excuses for her mother, refusing to see what Claire had become. With a couple of blunt sentences Caleb had ripped that comfortable veil away, and she saw her mother as she really was.

Worry about Claire hadn't improved her state of mind that day. Nor did the sight of her bruised cheekbone. She'd pulled her hair loosely around her face, trying to cover some of the telltale mark, but when Lizzie Grady and Faith Philips came by midday they'd taken one look at her poor excuse at subterfuge and given her commiserating looks.

They hadn't said anything, and Jassy hadn't bothered coming up with excuses, such as running into a door. Both women knew far too well what kind of mark a man's fist left on a woman's face, and they thought they recognized another victim.

Her only success that day had been in dealing with Ed down at the lumberyard. She'd explained to him in short, succinct sentences that he'd best get Spenser's load of lumber delivered to him that morning, or the uncomfortable situation out at the Moon Palace was bound to get a great deal more uncomfortable. Ed had always been a reasonable man, and he was fonder of Jassy than her brother, and to her surprise he'd agreed without more than a token protest. He'd never cared for the way Harrison tried to run the town, and the Turner investment in Ed's lumberyard wasn't as high as it was in some of the other town industries.

But the rest of the day had gone from bad to worse, until the air conditioner had finally let out a long, gasping wheeze and settled into an ominous silence. Jassy had stared up at it in dismay, her lower lip quivering at this final insult of fate, when she realized that someone was lounging in the open door. The person she most and least wanted to see.

"You look like you're in a rare mood," Caleb drawled. "Things not going too well?"

"You could say so." She put her hands in her lap. She wanted to push her hair out of her face, she wanted to cover the mark on her cheek, she wanted to wet her lips and pull her loose shirt around her. She forced herself to sit utterly, completely still.

Caleb pushed away from the door frame. "I wanted to thank you for talking to the folks down at the lumberyard. My delivery was on my doorstep at eight-thirty this morning."

"That didn't take long." She'd talked to Ed at just after eight. He must have gone right out and made the arrangements.

"Dog scared the hell out of them, though, showing up like they did. I guess I'm going to have to have a telephone put in, much as I hate the damned things." He pushed his dark blond hair away from his face, and his gold hoop glinted in the afternoon light. "Dog doesn't like unannounced visitors."

"Don't be ridiculous. Dog is nothing more than a gentle old pussycat."

"That's when he likes someone. You have his seal of approval, for some reason." He shut the door behind him, and the place suddenly seemed ten times smaller and a hundred times hotter. "So what did the sheriff say when you called him?"

He didn't ask whether she'd bothered calling. At least he knew her well enough to realize she'd follow through with what she said she'd do. "He told me not to worry my pretty little head about it," she said, her voice rich with disgust.

He didn't look surprised. "I told you it was a waste of time. What did he say after you told him where to stick it?"

"I didn't. I just hung up on him."

"I guess you save the bulk of your hostility for me."

"I don't feel hostile toward you," she said hotly, lifting her head.

His eyes focused on her cheekbone, narrowed, and she could feel the warmth of his gaze. "Maybe I should have killed him," Caleb said softly.

"Clayton?" Jassy asked, momentarily confused.

"Willard. Does it hurt much?"

She shook her head, giving up any attempt at camouflage. "As a matter of fact, it has its advantages. The women around here don't seem to think I'm that much of an elitist do-gooder with a man's bruise on my face. At least now they figure I know what I'm talking about."

He smiled briefly, that brief upturning of his mouth signifying his disagreement. "You don't know anything about the kind of lives most people live," he said. "You've been protected all your life."

She wished she could dispute him, but she knew it was true. She'd been wrapped in cotton wool from the day she was born, and if she weren't so determined she'd be just as helpless and dependent as Lila and Claire were.

But she was determined, and she wasn't going to spend her life locked in the safety of Belle Rive. Away from men like Caleb Spenser. "Was there anything else, Mr. Spenser?" she asked coolly, deciding to put this conversation on a more businesslike note.

He grinned, leaning back in his chair and stretching his long legs out in front of him. "As a matter of fact, there were several things. We haven't finished discussing the condition of the place out in Rayder Swamp."

That jarred her out of her self-possession. "I thought you said it was hopeless."

"Not necessarily. There are a couple of things I could try. If you're willing."

"I'd need an estimate. I told you, I'm not sure how much money..."

"It'll depend on whether it works. If it doesn't, there'll be no charge. If it does, I'll charge you what's fair."

"And I'm supposed to trust you?" she asked.

"Yes, ma'am. You're supposed to trust me." He leaned forward, across the desk, and she wanted to reach out and touch his hands, feel the strength in them, the rough, hardworking texture of his skin.

She nodded, not committing herself. She'd be a fool and a half to trust him in any way. And yet she knew she did, on some basic level that she didn't even understand. "All right," she said. "Do what you can. What else?"

"What else what?"

"What else did you want to see me about?"

He glanced around him. "It doesn't look like you're so damned busy that you can't spare a few minutes in socializing. The wife-beating business must be a little slow these days."

"It's no joking matter."

"Honey, life's a joking matter. If you take it too seriously you'll wind up dead or drunk or crazy."

There was no way she could refute it. "What do you want from me?" she asked in a low voice.

He just looked at her for a moment, and she could see into his mind so clearly that it shocked her. And then he smiled. "We'll get to that part later," he said mildly. "In the meantime, I want an invitation to dinner."

"I beg your pardon?"

"I want you to ask me up to the big house for dinner. Your brother's been slinking around like a polecat with a guilty conscience. Don't you think it would be better if he just faced me like a man?"

"Not with women present," she muttered.

"I'm not going to lay a finger on him." He gave her what he obviously thought was his most disarming smile. She didn't believe him for a minute. "Maybe he'll find that I'm not the threat he imagines me to be."

"And maybe all hell will break loose."

"Maybe," he allowed. "But if it does, it's bound to happen sooner or later. You want to put it off, dreading it? Or do you want to see what happens when you push things?"

She had to be crazy. But the tension in the house kept escalating, until there were times when she thought she might scream. Caleb was right, all hell might break out. But she'd had enough of heat lightning. It was time to risk a real storm, one that would wipe away the tension and shadows and half-truths. It was time for rain.

Chapter Nine

"So what made you invite Mr. Spenser for dinner?" Lila stood in the open bedroom door, her blue eyes surveying Jassy with critical approval. "I thought you considered him to be dangerous."

"I do." She poked herself with the mascara she used to darken her naturally thick eyelashes, cursed, and wiped away the excess. "I figured it would be better to keep an eye on him. Besides, Harrison isn't accomplishing anything by trying to avoid him. The sooner he faces up to Caleb, the sooner we'll get past the feeling we're walking on eggs."

Lila looked doubtful. "I'm not certain Harrison is ready to face him. Don't you think it might have been better if you'd asked him before inviting Mr. Spenser into the family home?"

"You mean because he's not 'our kind'?"

"I never should have said that," Lila said.

"You're right." Jassy sat back and surveyed her appearance with uneasy satisfaction. She'd loosened the thick cloud of hair, fastening it at the back of her neck with an antique silver barrette, and she'd even gone to the trouble of putting on makeup. Clothing now lay strewn all across her bed, a fact that hadn't escaped Lila's too-observant eyes, and her final choice, a plain beige linen sheath, had to be the worst one. She'd rejected a Belle France dress that made her look like a virginal schoolgirl, another navy outfit that made her look like a spinster. Everything else was too small, too big, too short or too long. She'd finally thrown in the towel and picked her most innocuous dress. She'd just as soon fade into the woodwork when Caleb Spenser turned those mesmerizing eyes her way.

Not that he'd be looking at her. She had every certainty that he'd be concentrating on Harrison, and not Harrison's little sister. Which was just as well. He wouldn't expect her to be much protection. It was always better to be underestimated.

"Not that it isn't true," Lila persevered, coming into the room and dropping onto the littered bed. She was dressed in something flowery and frilly, her attributes displayed by the low-cut neckline, her long, silk-covered legs stretched out. "He isn't our kind, and you know it. Call me a snob if you like, but I've learned that it's better if like marries like. Even if there are problems, disagreements, at least you have a shared heritage, background..."

Jassy swiveled around to stare at Lila. "Are you and Harrison having problems?"

Lila flushed. "Of course not. You know I absolutely worship your brother. The only problem in our relationship is my barrenness. I'm just grateful he's so patient with me. It's no wonder that sometimes he gets a little...upset. After all, I have been obsessing about it, and a man like Harrison needs distractions after the problems of the day, not new problems."

"Upset?" Jassy repeated softly.

Lila jumped up from the bed, busying herself sorting through the discarded clothes. "I can't imagine why you've chosen to wear that old thing. Half these clothes look better on you. Not that I approve of Mr. Spenser, but if you've decided you're attracted to him you ought to at least make an effort. The makeup's good, but you could use more eye shadow. I have a delicious shade of nile green that would really bring out the color of your eyes, and it looks terrible with my blue eyes. And you could let me do something with your hair, instead of just bundling it back there. After all, you are a lady, whether you accept that fact or not, and Mr. Spenser ought to be reminded of that fact and not think you're just a social chippie like . . ."

"Like who?" Jassy asked, having listened to Lila's nervous babbling with an uneasy fascination.

"Like your friend Mary-Louise," Lila said defiantly.

"Mary-Louise's great-grandfather was a general of the Confederacy," Jassy pointed out, wondering where in heaven's name all this sudden antipathy came from. As far as she knew, Lila and Mary-Louise had always been cordial, if not terribly close.

"Well, there's trash somewhere in her bloodlines," Lila said flatly, dropping the folded clothes back onto the bed with a complete disregard for her careful neatness. "Her mother ought to keep a better eye on her if she doesn't want the family name dragged in the mud."

"Mary-Louise is thirty-two years old. That's a little long in the tooth for her mother to be keeping watch over her. And she's no longer a Stevenson, so Blanche doesn't need to worry about the family name. Not that there'd be any controlling Mary-Louise. She's always done exactly as she's wanted to do, and the devil with everyone else. That's one of the things I've most admired about her."

"Admired about her?" Lila shrieked. "Her blatant disregard of honor and decency and other people's feelings?"

"No," Jassy said, rising. "But her refusal to kowtow to foolish opinions when something really matters." She crossed the room to Lila, putting her hands on her shoulders. "What's got you so upset, Lila? I know it can't be Mary-Louise, or Caleb Spenser for that matter. Why are you so wound up?" The thin shoulders beneath Jassy's hands felt like iron from the tension thrumming through her body.

Lila shook her head, managing a totally unconvincing smile. "Nothing," she said. "I'm just a little high-strung nowadays. This damnable weather." She glared out the French doors to the darkening night beyond. "If only it would rain."

"The same problems will be here, whether it rains or not," Jassy pointed out.

Lila squirmed away from Jassy's touch. "Yes, but I might be able to deal with them a little more rationally. We'd better get downstairs, don't you think? We don't want Harrison and Spenser meeting up without a referee, do we? They may end up killing each other."

Jassy closed her eyes for a moment, remembering Caleb's merciless expression. If he killed one man, he could surely kill another. If only she knew why he'd want to. What he had against her brother. Maybe Harrison testified against him. No, that was unlikely. She would have heard about it.

Far more likely that he could have testified in Caleb's favor, and had simply taken off. Hadn't Caleb said something about knowing Harrison under another name? And why had he waited ten years to confront Harrison? Unless it had taken him that long to find him.

If only one of those damned men would simply answer a straight question! If she didn't start getting some answers soon she was going to have to take matters into her own hands. Trials were a matter of public record. She could go over to St. Florence and check old newspapers from thirteen years ago. She could hire a private detective, if there was any way she could come up with some ready cash. But she wasn't going to sit around any longer and be patted on the head and told to be a good girl and not ask questions.

"We'd better get downstairs," she agreed, pausing a moment to glance at her reflection in the mirror. She looked as though she had no curves at all in that beige dress. No color, either; nothing but legs that were too long and hair that was too frizzy. "You keep Harrison in line, I'll control Caleb."

Lila shook her head. "If only it were that simple." And she left the room before Jassy could ask her to explain.

Obviously she meant Jassy controlling Caleb. Though she couldn't rid herself of the feeling that there was something going on between Harrison and Lila. Lila's struggles to conceive were bad enough, but there was something else happening, something dark and troublesome, something that might or might not have to do with Caleb Spenser's precipitate arrival in Turner's Landing.

If Lila resented Caleb's presence at Belle Rive, you certainly couldn't tell it to look at her, Jassy thought critically a few moments later when she walked into the living room. Caleb had already arrived, and he was seated next to Lila on the sofa, flirting with her quite blatantly, and Lila was flirting back, her soft voice trilling with laughter, and her big blue eyes batting at him fatuously.

For a moment Jassy paused in the doorway, taking in the scene. Caleb had dressed for the occasion, wearing a freshly ironed striped shirt, the sleeves rolled up to reveal his strong forearms, his dark blond hair slicked back away from his face, the gold hoop in his ear glinting in the light. He looked like a pirate, Jassy thought. A dangerous marauder, out to pillage the countryside. And there was no one to stop him. Certainly not the two gullible women in her family.

Claire was sitting in the chair next to Caleb, a tall glass of iced, amber-colored liquid in her pale hand. Jassy frowned at it, wondering if she dared to say anything, when the happy trio finally noticed her arrival.

"Jassy," Claire said with uncustomary brightness, "we wondered what was keeping you. Would you like a glass of iced tea, or something stronger?"

Iced tea, she thought, relaxing a bit as Caleb rose to his feet with an insolent grace that took most of the politeness out of the gesture. At least Claire wasn't drinking tonight. And curse Caleb for making her see exactly what she didn't want to see. How far her mother's drinking had gone.

"Tea would be fine," she murmured. "Sorry I'm late."

"It was worth the wait," Caleb said with mocking gallantry that she didn't believe for a moment. "You look very... dignified."

She had to bite back her instinctive, shocking retort. Instead she gave him a sickly sweet smile. "Compliments *do* go to my head," she murmured, moving to the heavy silver tray of drinks and pouring herself a tall glass of tea. Given the circumstances she would have been much happier with a whiskey and water, but she decided the least she could do was join Claire in abstinence. Besides, she'd need all her wits about her to chart their way through the dangerous waters that surrounded them that night. "I can't imagine what's keeping Harrison. He knows we serve dinner at seven, and he's usually home well before then.''

"Maybe he heard he had guests," Caleb murmured.

Jassy sat down across the room from the three of them, crossing her legs and swinging one foot gently. "Perhaps. My brother's not a coward, Mr. Spenser."

Caleb sat down again, closer to Lila this time. Lila didn't move away. "I never said he was," he said, in the tone of voice that conveyed quite clearly that Harrison's cowardice was a given.

"Jassy, darling, you're sounding awfully cantankerous," Claire said in a reproving tone of voice.

"It's this weather," Caleb drawled. "Miz Lila and I were just discussing how this heat and humidity can make one want to commit murder."

She looked him in the eyes, and her message was clear. Of all people, he should know what it was like to commit murder. He smiled then, just a faint quirk of his mouth that deepened the groove in his cheek as he acknowledged her silent message and she felt herself relax. After all, how bad could things get? Caleb Spenser was a reasonable man. Her brother was civilized. They weren't going to kill each other.

If she expected the evening to be awkward she hadn't counted on one very salient point. The other three members of their mismatched dinner party were adept at acceptable social behavior. Claire could keep any conversation going, and put anyone at ease, as long as she herself was in a comparatively sober state. It didn't take much to charm Lila out of her snobbish misgivings, and she flirted as naturally as she breathed. It had been too long since she'd been given a chance to exert her inborn feminine wiles, and she was having a glorious time of it, batting her eyes at Caleb and giggling at each one of his sallies.

As for Caleb, he was a past master at manipulation. As before, he had both women eating out of his hand, forgetting their initial mistrust. His charm was as natural as Lila's, though he put it to more constructive use.

The only one spared was Jassy. She sat across from them, nursing her iced tea, watching him wrap the two other Turner women around his little finger, and she wondered why he didn't bother with her. Why he'd simply glance over at her now and then, an odd expression in his eyes, before turning back to her mother and sister-in-law. Did he think she was already so completely smitten that he didn't have to bother? Or conversely, did he consider her such a tough nut to crack that he couldn't waste his time?

Except there was something faintly conspiratorial in the covert looks he'd cast her every now and then. As if he knew perfectly well that she saw through his charming act, and even preferred that she did. As if the two of them shared a secret, one that might make the others appear foolish, but never cruelly so.

It was an unsettling, intimate feeling, one she was powerless to break. And she wondered whether she'd been right in the first place. That he'd simply known that he had her, come hell or high water, and could concentrate his energies on the unknown quantities.

"I think we'd best go in to dinner," Claire finally announced. "I don't know where Harrison is, but we can't wait any longer or Miss Sadie will put us all on bread and water. I'm sure he'll turn up sooner or later."

Caleb rose swiftly, offering Claire his arm with all the flourish of a southern gentleman of old. "Does he do this often?'' he murmured, and Claire didn't even notice that the question was none of his business.

"Oh, Harrison is always busy. We learn to work around his schedule. Sometimes he doesn't get home till midnight...."

The sound of mingled laughter drifted in from the front hall, and Jassy felt the adrenaline shoot through her. She couldn't just wait for the confrontation—the long delay in Harrison's appearance had strung her nerves so tightly they felt as if they might snap.

"Here he is now," she said brightly. "You go on in to dinner and I'll let him know we have a guest."

Caleb reached out a restraining hand, a frown on his face, but she skirted him effortlessly, ignoring him. She practically raced to the front hall, half-afraid he'd try to stop her, but when she glanced behind her she saw the three of them had gone in to dinner.

Harrison wasn't alone. Mary-Louise was with him, laughing, her full-lipped mouth curved in delicious humor. "We wondered what was keeping you," Jassy said, pausing in the doorway.

Harrison looked up. He had his arm around Mary-Louise's shoulders, and he looked more relaxed than he had in weeks. He frowned at her implied question, but before he could say anything, Mary-Louise spoke up.

"Your brother was kind enough to give me a hand with my finances," she said smoothly. "You know what a cotton-headed creature I am. The divorce settlement makes no sense to me whatsoever, and Harrison spent several hours explaining it all to me. Then of course the dear man insisted I come to dinner, so here we are."

"Here you are," Jassy echoed dully. Mary-Louise had a financial mind of steel. She knew down to the penny the details of her divorce settlement, and had fought for them more intently than her barracuda of a lawyer.

She was also one of the most fastidious of women. She seldom had a hair out of place, a shiny nose, a smudge of lipstick around her full mouth.

Her hair was perfect, her nose freshly powdered, her lipstick new and creamy. And her blouse was buttoned wrong.

Suddenly it all made sense. Lila's antipathy and barely controlled hysteria. Jassy looked at the two of them, and contempt filled her.

She smiled grimly, not showing a sign of it. "We are always glad to see you, Mary-Louise. As a matter of fact, we have another guest tonight and we've just gone in to dinner. I'll have Miss Sadie set another place. Come along." She turned back to the dining room.

"Who's here?" Harrison demanded, following behind her.

"A surprise," Jassy said, not pausing.

The only problem with leading those two in, she thought, was that she couldn't appreciate the full effect of Harrison's expression when he saw Caleb Spenser sitting at his table with his mother and wife. She could only see Caleb's expression, distant, unreadable, a faint smile of satisfaction on his mouth as Harrison stopped abruptly behind her.

She took the seat next to him, glancing up at her brother. Harrison was statue-still in the doorway, all color drained from his face, his brown eyes bulging faintly. By his side, Mary-Louise looked more troubled than she had any right to be.

The silence was thick and angry as the undercurrents of emotion swept through them. Lila's cheerful flirtatiousness had died an abrupt death when Mary-Louise sauntered into the room. The hatred that flowed between the two men was as tangible and as raw as the swamp, though a lot swifter moving. Jassy herself was feeling ready to scream, and more than anything she wanted to break the mood, to make some smart comment about one big happy family.

Fortunately Claire's years of breeding came through before Jassy could precipitate a showdown between any of the warring groups of people. "There you are, Harrison. We waited as long as we could, but you know how evil-tempered Miss Sadie gets. And Mary-Louise, how lovely to see you, dear. Take the seat beside me, and Harrison will set a new place. I gather the two of you must have met Mr. Spenser. I thought it would be nice to invite him to dinner. I have no reliance on any bachelor being able to provide himself with a decent meal. I'm sure the ladies of this town have done their best, but it's nice to eat with other people, use fine china, drink wine." The last sounded wistful, but Claire sailed on, blithely ignoring the tension in the room. "Maybe you could open the French doors while you're at it, Harrison. It's beastly hot, as always. Harrison?"

Harrison hadn't moved, and for a moment Jassy wondered whether he'd do what he obviously wanted. Lunge across the damask- and china-covered table and go for Caleb's throat.

In truth, she wouldn't have blamed him. Caleb had that damnable, taunting smile on his face as he looked at Harrison, the others around them, including Jassy, forgotten. She held her breath, waiting, and then swallowed her sigh of relief as Harrison moved toward the window to do his mother's bidding.

The remaining place at the table was directly opposite Spenser. Harrison sat down, looking across at his nemesis, and for the moment his expression was completely unreadable. "Spenser," he said in a dull monotone, by way of a greeting.

Caleb's smile didn't change. "Harrison," he replied, just as circumspect, and Jassy was reminded of two wary dogs, circling each other, hackles rising, waiting for the other one to attack.

"So tell me, Mr. Spenser," Claire said, still firmly in charge of the social amenities, "how's the work going on the old Moon Palace?"

"Just fine, Miz Turner. Now that my lumber order has been delivered I should be able to make some progress."

"You had trouble getting your deliveries?" Harrison asked in a silken voice.

"Until Jassy kindly helped out. All she had to do was make a phone call and the lumber arrived."

Harrison didn't even bother to look at her, but Jassy could feel his anger nonetheless, and knew he'd be dealing with her later. When his main object was out of the way. "Seems like a mighty big job for one man," he said, leaning back in his chair, seemingly at ease. Except that Jassy could see the faint quiver in the slightly pouchy skin beneath his left eye, and she knew that relaxation was all sham. "And I still can't imagine why you'd want to do it. The Moon Palace is at the end of a dirt road—I can't imagine why anyone would want to live there."

"Some people prefer seclusion," Caleb drawled, taking a sip of wine. "And I'm not doing it alone. My crew is arriving tonight."

Harrison paled slightly, and he picked up his heavy silver fork, tapping it against the thick damask cloth. "Crew?" he echoed. "How many men?"

"Just two at this point. The rest of my men are busy on a job up in Mobile. They'll come down here later to finish up."

"I didn't realize you were such an entrepreneur, Mr. Spenser," Lila said with a toss of her head. The flirtation was back, this time with a harder edge, and she shot a defiant glance at her husband.

Harrison was too absorbed to notice, though Jassy had the feeling that Lila would be called to account later, just as she would be.

Caleb smiled at her, and Jassy noticed with sudden irritation that there was a different quality to the smile he gave her sister-in-law. As if he realized, beneath her silliness and vanity and snobbery, that she was sweeter and more vulnerable than the lot of them. "I've had a certain amount of success, Miz Lila," he said. "I pick places no one's interested in, and hire people no one's interested in. The combination is good for everyone—any success is unexpected."

"What do you mean, people no one's interested in?" Mary-Louise spoke up, and Harrison cast her a quelling frown.

The feral edge was back in Caleb's smile, and Jassy didn't know whether she was pleased or not. "All my workers are ex-convicts, Mrs. Albertson. Forgotten men and women who just need a second chance."

"You're bringing jailbirds to town?" Claire demanded faintly, disapproval wiping out some of her calm demeanor.

"They're all fully rehabilitated," he said. "Bo and Ray wouldn't hurt a fly. Unless that fly were causing an undue amount of trouble. I imagine you heard about the little mess Jassy and I got into last night."

All eyes turned to Jassy, to the bruise on her cheek she'd tried to cover with makeup, and she squirmed.

"We heard," Harrison drawled. "I just figured you must have done it yourself. With a mouth like that girl has on her it's amazing she hasn't been smacked before."

"Harrison!" Claire said, shocked.

Jassy didn't say a word, too busy observing the others. The dangerous way Caleb's eyes narrowed. The pale chalkiness of Lila's complexion. And the covert smugness in Mary-Louise's big blue eyes.

Caleb leaned back, a slight, contemptuous smile on his face, as something passed between the two men that neither of them understood. "I don't hurt women, Harrison," he said. "I save my violence for those who deserve it."

The look the two men shared was steady, implacable and chilling, and the silence that filled the room was broken only by the distant sound of thunder. And then Caleb broke the moment deliberately, leaving Harrison with no choice but to stare down at his plate.

"Anyway, Miz Turner," he said, turning to Claire, "I wouldn't worry about having ex-cons around. Why, I've been here a week and I haven't caused a lick of trouble. Have I?"

And there was no answering his innocent, engaging smile.

Chapter Ten

Jassy had had more palatable meals in her lifetime. As it was, she was barely able to choke down any of Miss Sadie's succulent roast chicken with oranges, and the flaky biscuits went untouched.

She didn't know what twisted her stomach the most. The sight of Mary-Louise, her bright eyes avid and completely guiltless as she surveyed the people who had been a second family to her. Or Lila's miserable expression and arch attempts at flirtation.

Maybe it was Harrison's barely repressed violence. Or the slightly glassy expression in Claire's eyes after she returned from an overlong trip to the bathroom that had to have included a detour by way of the vodka bottle. Maybe it was a combination of all those things.

But deep inside she knew better. She'd been through any number of meals with Claire getting quietly drunk, Harrison sulking and Lila overbright and miserable.

No, it was the presence of Caleb Spenser that was turning her life upside down along with her stomach. Of all the people at the formal dinner table, he was the only one who ate with unconcealed gusto, clearly enjoying the food and everyone's discomfort. Jassy could watch her fill, for the simple reason that Caleb had obviously forgotten she was there. She'd always suspected she was a means to an end, and tonight he was proving it. He was watching everyone but her. Subtly, but definitely, those clear, light eyes of his took in every nuance at the table. Except her reaction.

She told herself it was a great relief. She was a strong woman, one who could stand up to other women's abusive husbands, recalcitrant bureaucrats, Harrison when he sulked, and even hungry alligators when they wandered out of the shallow river onto the broad front lawn of Belle Rive. But she couldn't stand up to Caleb Spenser when he turned those cool, light eyes on her, put his hard, strong hands on her body. For some reason she was far more vulnerable to Caleb than she had been to any man in her entire life. She felt much safer when he was distracted.

Claire reached for the little silver bell on the table, missed it, and reached again. "The ladies will retire," she announced with great solemnity.

Lila and Mary-Louise glared at each other across the table. The thought of being trapped in a room with those two snarling cats, while Claire probably sank into a discreet stupor, was more than Jassy was willing to accept. "Don't be gothic, Mama," she said flatly. "I'm not going anywhere."

"Suit yourself," Harrison snapped, pushing back from the table. "But Spenser and I have business to discuss. And we don't need your help, little sister."

She turned questioning eyes to Caleb, but he didn't even glance her way, all his attention on Harrison. There was a combative light in his eyes, one that sent chills down Jassy's spine.

"It's past time," he said in his slow, deep voice, rising with insolent grace and following Harrison out of the room.

"They're going to kill each other," Jassy said flatly.

Mary-Louise shrugged. "Don't be ridiculous, Jassy. Why should they?"

"Didn't Harrison tell you?" Lila broke in, her voice icy with rage.

Mary-Louise's smug smile would have enraged a saint. Lila wasn't a saint. "Harrison doesn't do much talking."

The word Lila used was one that Jassy would have thought her demure sister-in-law didn't even know. Clearly the pampered Claire had never heard it, for she simply blinked, looking confused. "Come along, Jassy," she said. "The gentlemen have business to discuss."

Jassy rose promptly enough. Instead of following the quarrelsome women, however, she went after Caleb, trailing at his heels just like his disreputable dog, moving into the library behind the two men.

Harrison caught her arm, spun her around, and marched her right out again, his fingers digging in tightly. "This is none of your damned business, Jassy," he announced.

She cast a beseeching glance at Caleb, but he didn't even look in her direction, his eyes cold and focused on Harrison's back with something that couldn't be mistaken for anything other than hatred. And then the door was shut in her face, and locked, securely.

She waited a moment, wondering if she were going to hear the sounds of a scuffle. As far as she knew, Harrison didn't have any guns in the room, but that didn't mean they couldn't find other, more creative ways of killing each other. Putting her ear against the heavy cypress door, she listened. All she could hear was the muffled sound of conversation.

She considered banging on the door, kicking and fussing. Emotionally it was what she wanted to do; rationally she knew better. Besides, the night wasn't as stifling as it had been, and it had looked as if the French doors to the veranda were open. If she scooted around outside she could manage to hear most of their conversation, and if worse came to worst, she could leap through the door and fling herself between them. She certainly wasn't going to let her brother kill Caleb, much as he obviously wanted to. And she wasn't going to let Caleb commit another murder.

Lila was stalking up the stairs, her back straight with anger and hurt, when Jassy raced through the hallway. She could hear the soft murmur of voices in the drawing room, Mary-Louise and Claire probably discussing the church auction or something equally innocuous. Jassy slipped out onto the veranda, feeling the soft night air close down around her.

Some of the humidity of the day had dissipated, some but not all. The sky was dark, clouds scudding past the quarter moon in angry swirls. If only those clouds meant rain. But Jassy knew better than to count on false promises.

The doors to the office were open to the night air. She moved stealthily along the terrace, concentrating on the polite murmur of voices, as phrases and sentences reached her.

"...can't prove anything," Harrison was saying. "You couldn't...too much time..."

"...not enough money. I want more." Caleb sounded cold, implacable, not an ounce of his lazy charm in evidence.

"What? I can be reasonable. If it's not money you want, Spenser, what is it?"

"Revenge."

"I can't give you that."

"The hell you can't," Caleb shot back, his voice cold and savage. "I'm going to take everything you ever cared about."

"Can't we be reasonable about this? It all happened so long ago. We were both kids. Times change, we get older, we learn from our mistakes...."

"I'm taking you down, Turner. I'm taking your wife, your sister, your money and your reputation. And there's not a damned thing you can do to stop me. All the good old boys you can dig up can't lay a finger on me. You're going to have to watch me pick things off, one by one, until you're left with nothing."

"I'll see you dead first."

"You can try," Caleb said. "I have an advantage over you, Harrison. I spent three years in prison for murder. That's hard time, and I learned a lot more than you ever picked up at Princeton. I intend to put that expensive education to good use when it comes to you and your family. You're going to be sorry you were ever born."

"I can come up with fifty thousand dollars...."

"Chicken feed," Caleb scoffed.

"You don't want my wife." Harrison's voice was high-pitched with blustery bravado, and if it weren't for his words Jassy would have exploded with the need to protect and nurture him. "She's no good in bed, anyway, and she whines. If you're looking for entertainment you'd be better off with Mary-Louise. She's very inventive. Or my sister. I've seen you look at her, Spenser. She's not going to stand by while you bring me down. If you want a chance at her you're going to have to think twice about some crazy scheme for revenge."

"I don't give a damn about your sister," Caleb said flatly, and Jassy believed him. "She's a means to an end,

Turner, and you're that end. I'm going to have you by the short hairs, and you're going to be screaming for mercy.''

There was a long silence. "When?" Harrison asked hoarsely.

Jassy didn't have to see Caleb's smile to know what it looked like, wreathing his cold, handsome face with its double-dare mockery. "When you least expect it," he said.

The wind picked up, swirling the hot, damp air along the veranda, and the live oaks on the front lawn creaked noisily. A night bird swooped close, making a raucous noise, startling Jassy, and by the time she turned back the room was silent. She craned her neck forward, peering into the library, wondering whether she'd see one of the men stretched out on the floor, the other with his hands around his neck, when she felt his presence behind her.

"Learn anything interesting?"

She refused to move quickly. She could feel the flush mount her face, and hoped that if she climbed down from her precarious perch slowly enough it might fade before she had to face him. Not that it mattered. Even if the color had faded from her face when Caleb saw her, he'd still know it had been there. He knew far too much.

The veranda was dark except for the yellowish light coming from the French doors. The shadows danced fitfully around them both, but she could see the glitter of his pale eyes, the glint of the gold hoop in his ear. He looked like a pagan tonight, she thought. Savage, vengeful, totally without conscience or heart. He'd proved that tonight in his conversation. So why wasn't she running from him like he was the devil?

She brushed imaginary dirt off her hands, then ran them down her rumpled linen sheath. "Nothing I didn't already know," she said. "Harrison has some connection with Sherman Delano's death. You're here to exploit that connection, and you don't give a damn who you hurt in the bargain. Me included.''

That cold, dangerous expression lifted for a moment, as a trace of distant humor lit his eyes, curved the hard edges of his mouth. ''Now how could I possibly hurt you, Jassy?'' he said. ''You wouldn't let me get close enough to do you any harm. You have to care about someone to let them hurt you. And you sure as hell don't care about me, do you, sugar?''

She didn't say a word. There was no way she could refute him, short of making a declaration she wasn't ready to make. Something she wasn't ready or willing to face, and the longer she put it off, the better chance she had of avoiding it entirely.

''You don't let anyone care about you,'' she said finally.

It wiped the humor off his dark, saturnine face. For a moment he simply looked at her blankly, startled out of his usual cool self-possession. ''Well, I wouldn't want to start with you, honey. I'd tear you into little pieces without even trying.''

''I'm tougher than I look.''

''I know that. But I'm a hell of a lot meaner than I look.''

''I don't think so.''

She could see the perceptible relaxing of his shoulders. ''Honey, you're an innocent. Haven't you learned that the world is full of nasty people?''

''Yes. I'm just not convinced you're one of them.''

He shut his eyes for a moment, a parody of amused exasperation. ''Honey, I'm the baddest of the bad. A convicted murderer, and one of the meanest SOBs you'd ever hope to meet. I came to Turner's Landing with the express purpose of destroying your brother, and quite possibly your whole family besides, and you just overheard me tell your brother that you don't mean diddly squat to me. So how can you stand there and tell me there's salvation for me?''

"I didn't say there was salvation. I just don't think you're as evil as you want people to believe."

"I'm going to destroy your brother. If I'm in the mood for it, I'll take you down, too."

"And I won't have any say in the matter?"

"You'll be begging for it." There was no sensual threat in his voice. He sounded bleak.

But it was that bleakness that gave Jassy hope. If he were as cold and vicious as he pretended to be then he wouldn't have any scruples about destroying them all. And clearly he had scruples aplenty. For the first time in hours she smiled, her mouth curving upward in a gentler version of Caleb's mocking challenge. "Maybe," she said. "Or maybe it'll be you doing the begging."

She took him by surprise. The starkness washed out of his face as he laughed, a brief, startled sound of pure amusement. "Mermaids shouldn't swim with sharks," he said.

"I'm not . . ." She didn't have time to finish the sentence. He'd dragged her into his arms, holding her tightly against his hard body, and one hand caught her chin, holding her face still.

"I'm a dangerous man, Jassy," he muttered. "Haven't you realized that by now? I'm a danger to all you love and care about, and I wish to God you weren't here. Why don't you pack up and leave? Go down to Miami, fly up north, just go away for a while. When you come back it'll all be over and you can pick up the pieces. You're good at that, aren't you? Picking up the pieces of people's broken lives."

"Will there be anything left to mend?"

"Not of Harrison."

"Caleb..."

"Don't reason with me. Don't beg me, don't plead, don't bribe, and for God's sake, don't treat me like I have a conscience. I don't."

He was so close. His body was rock hard, and hot against hers. She could smell the warmth of his skin, the whiskey he'd had before dinner, the night air surrounding them. "Of course you do," she said.

"I guess I'm going to have to prove it." He pushed her back against the stucco wall of the house and his mouth covered hers with savage insistence. There was no tenderness in the hard mouth on hers, no seduction, no wooing, no sweet promise. It was demand, pure and simple, mixed with threat, and he allowed her no room to respond. She could simply hold still for the erotic assault of his kiss, his mouth wet and hungry on hers, his body already hard against hers.

She put her hands against his chest, pushing against him, but he was too strong. He was out to frighten her, part of her understood that, and she knew she should struggle. But if she struggled, he'd move away, and she knew if he did she'd die. Her arms slid around his waist, clinging tightly, and she shut her eyes, giving herself up to the overwhelming power of his kiss.

He moved his head a few inches away, staring down at her in confusion as his breath came rapidly. "You're supposed to fight," he said in a rough voice. "You're supposed to scream and slap me."

She managed a smile. "I try very hard not to do what I'm supposed to do," she said, her voice equally shaky.

"Why don't you kiss me again? This time a little softer. Maybe give me a chance to kiss you back."

He didn't move. She could see that telltale light of amusement break through his dark expression. "I'm trying to scare you."

"You aren't succeeding."

"I can see that." He released her, and it took all her considerable willpower not to cling. "You're a hell of a woman, Jassy. You deserve a good man to love you. Not a few hot sticky hours in bed with a no-good like me."

"I beg your pardon?" She leaned back against the stucco wall, welcoming the cool roughness, feeling a little faint at the image his words had produced.

He reached out and touched her flushed face, trailing his fingers down her neck, the front of her linen dress, the swell of her breast in a caress that was calculatedly erotic. She jerked away in sudden nervousness, and that mocking smile was back in full force, in no way belied by the dark desire in his eyes.

"Do I shock you, lady? You're used to your polite, starched gentlemen, taking you to fancy teas, holding doors for you. I bet you've never heard a harsh word in your life. I'm kinda direct, myself. Downright crude, sometimes. I want you, Miss Jassy. I want you real bad. But I want your brother even more. Now clearly he doesn't give a rat's behind whether I take you or not. If he thought it would save him he'd hand you over without a second thought. So I can't get to him through you. Anything we do together under the sheets will be simply for mutual pleasure. It won't stop me from going after him, you need to know that from the outset." He stepped back, his large body no longer intimidating her smaller one. "So what's the answer, Miss Jassy?"

She felt shaken, deep inside, but she managed to lift her head, to meet his dark, hot gaze fearlessly. "What's the question?"

He took her hand in his large one. His skin was rough, calloused from hard work, his fingers long and deft, curling around her small, softer one. He put her palm against his chest, where his shirt was open to the night air, and his skin was hot, hair roughened, faintly damp. She could feel the slow, steady beat of his heart through her own skin, and the sensation was intimate, erotic, disturbing. "If you don't know, Jassy," he said softly, "then we shouldn't even be having this conversation."

She took a deep breath, feeling it shake and tremble down her throat. "We probably shouldn't be," she whispered, her voice not strong enough for anything louder.

He smiled then, and moved her hand down, across his bare chest, past the buttons of the shirt, to the solid leather and brass of his belt. Her eyes looked into his, shocked, startled, as he moved her hand lower, to cover the thick, pulsing heat of him.

The veranda door slammed open, bouncing against the side of the house. "Jassy?" Harrison demanded. "Are you still out there?"

She tried to yank her hand away, but he held her still, his grip tight and inexorable. They were in the shadows, Harrison couldn't possibly see them, but she still felt suffused with embarrassment. "Answer him," Caleb said in a quiet voice. "Answer him, or he'll come and find you."

Somewhere she managed to find her voice. "I...I'll be right in."

Harrison stepped out on the porch, his large figure dwarfing the light. "Are you alone out there?"

She could feel the rough texture of the denim beneath her fingers. The metal of the zipper, the hot, turgid size of him. She could feel the blood pulsing through him, hot. For her.

"Answer him, Jassy," Caleb whispered, his voice low and insinuating. "The truth, or a lie. It's up to you."

She'd kept her hand flat in his grip. Now she let her fingertips move, tracing the length of him, and she saw his response in his flared nostrils, the darkening of his eyes, the sudden intake of breath.

"I'm alone," she called. "I'll be there in a minute."

Harrison didn't move from his spot in the doorway, waiting for her. Caleb's fingers covered hers, pressing her harder against him. "I bet you're a real hellcat when you're aroused," he whispered. "You just haven't met anyone who's man enough to rouse you."

Jassy stared at him. She felt wild, reckless, a gypsy stranger who'd taken over her prim body. And then common sense reasserted itself, and she yanked her hand away as if she were burned. She could feel shocked color flood her face, and she knew if she didn't get away, and fast, she might be totally southern belle enough to faint at the man's feet.

She ran across the slate terrace, not daring to look back, running as if all hell was at her heels. She knew Caleb would wait there in the shadows, not ready for his revenge. Not yet. He didn't make a sound, but she thought she could hear the soft note of his mocking laughter follow her as she caught up with her brother at the terrace door.

"What were you doing?" Harrison demanded grumpily.

It was too dark to see the flush of color on her face, the suspicious brightness in her eyes. Besides, Harrison was scarcely the most observant of men where his baby sister was concerned.

"Just having a breath of air."

"This air's too thick to breathe."

She was acutely aware of the man in the shadows, watching, listening. "Let's go in...."

"Not yet. I want to talk to you, Jassy, and I don't want anyone overhearing us." He put his hand on her arm, and for some reason it felt heavier, crueler than Caleb's imprisoning grip.

"I don't want to discuss it, Harrison. It's between you and Lila...."

"I'm not talking about that," he said impatiently. "I want to talk to you about Spenser."

She tried to yank away. "I'd really rather talk inside."

"Mary-Louise is inside, and you know as well as I do that she can't keep her mouth shut. She maneuvered this little scene tonight, just to see what would happen."

"If you feel that way about her, then why...?"

"I told you, I don't want to discuss it. It's none of your business."

"You've already told me that what's between you and Caleb Spenser is none of my business, either." It took all her concentration to keep from glancing over to the shadows, where Caleb was watching.

"That was before you chose to involve yourself. I know you, Jassy. I've known you all your life. I can't say I approve of your taste in men, but I know better than to interfere." His voice was expansive, indulgent, at odds with the restraining hand on her forearm.

She stared up at him. "What are you talking about?" She didn't want to hear what she knew was coming. And she most particularly didn't want Caleb to hear.

"If you want Caleb Spenser I won't interfere."

He laughed, that grating, unbelievable laugh, and she could hear the desperation, the real fear beneath it.

"You're an adult, he's an adult," he continued. "What you two do together hasn't got a thing to do with me. I'm giving you my blessing."

"You mean you're telling me it's okay to sleep with him? The man you've been treating like he's your mortal enemy?"

"I'm telling you to do whatever you like. If you're as attracted to him as you appear to be, then maybe it could be used to the family's advantage. Don't look at me like I'm expecting you to whore yourself. You're obviously infatuated with the man. I'm just saying you could serve the family and your own biological needs at the same time."

She wanted to throw up. The knowledge that Caleb was hearing Harrison's cold-blooded proposal made it even worse. "My love life has nothing to do with what the family does or doesn't need," she managed to say in a deceptively calm voice.

Harrison, self-absorbed as always, released her arm and patted her cheek. "Of course, Jassy. I just thought I'd mention it. Are you coming in?"

Clearly the subject had been dismissed. "Not quite yet," she said evenly. "I still need a little fresh air."

"Don't take too long. Mary-Louise was saying she hadn't seen enough of you recently."

She waited until he stepped back into the house. Wrapping her arms around her, she shivered in the humid air, wondering how she was going to face Caleb.

She needn't have worried. When she reached the stretch of terrace in the shadows outside the library, Caleb had vanished.

She could only wonder if he'd left before or after her brother encouraged her to sleep with him.

Chapter Eleven

Caleb drove home slowly, letting the old truck with its deceptively powerful engine make its way down the gravel roads to the Moon Palace at a leisurely pace. He was feeling restless, edgy, like the wind rushing through the live oaks overhead. He could hear the distant rumble of thunder over the quiet sound of the radio, and he shifted in the seat. People around Turner's Landing seemed to think that once it rained, people's tensions would ease.

Personally he didn't think it would be that simple. The rain wouldn't make any difference in his plans for revenge. The rain wouldn't make him less angry, less determined. Or less horny, for that matter.

Of course, there were any number of ways he could handle the last problem, beginning with Mary-Louise Albertson. Despite, or maybe because of her relationship with the very married Harrison Turner, she was obviously more than available. He could have offered to drive her home. He could drive back into town and wait outside her mother's house.

There were other women around who'd made sure he'd feel welcome. He'd been flattered by their offers, but not interested. He was interested tonight.

But he didn't want a bored housewife, a randy young professional, a lusty divorcée or a precocious teenager.

He wanted Jassy Turner.

He still didn't know why. Why an ordinary attraction would become an obsession, one that threatened to rival his desperate need for revenge. Sometimes at night he woke up in a sweat, thinking he was back in prison, thinking Harrison was smug, laughing at him, triumphant once more.

But nowadays, just as often, he'd wake up thinking about Jassy, hard and aching for her. And he'd lived long enough, had enough women to know that a substitute wasn't going to work. It might take the edge off his need, but it wouldn't obliterate it. It would take Jassy herself to ease him.

That was one reason he'd walked away tonight, after he'd heard her brother's charming suggestion. Not that he expected her to act on it. She was going through a period of intense disillusionment where her darling brother was concerned. As the man said, she ain't seen nothing yet.

But she was too damned distracting. If he'd pushed it, taken her back home with him, or even simply pulled her into the woods and stripped that stupid brown dress off her, he'd forget all about Harrison, at least for a while. And he couldn't afford to do that.

If he had any sense at all he'd play it safe and forget about Jassy Turner. There were other ways he could get to Harrison, more effective ways. He should concentrate on them, on Harrison's wife and mistress, both of whom were more vulnerable than Jassy and infinitely tougher. He couldn't break their hearts. He could smash Jassy's.

Of course if he were showing sense, interested in playing it safe, he wouldn't be in Turner's Landing, stirring up a can of worms. He'd be somewhere else, making good money, the past behind him.

But he couldn't put the past behind him until he'd dealt with it. Dealt with Harrison Turner. And if he couldn't talk Jassy into leaving, he was going to have to deal with her, too. One way or another.

The Moon Palace was dark and still when he drove in. Dog was standing in front of a parked van, a disgruntled expression on his face. Caleb parked the truck, sliding out of the front seat and approaching the van warily.

The window rolled down. "Can you call this damned dog off?" Bo demanded. "Stupid mutt can't remember a friend for more than a week."

"Serves you two right for bringing the new van," Caleb said, signaling Dog to relax. "Besides, we've had a little trouble."

"Trouble?" Ray echoed, climbing out of the van and giving both Dog and his owner a doubtful glance. "Is that why we're here?"

"Among other things. Maybe I just got lonesome," Caleb drawled.

Dog was busy slobbering over Bo's hamlike hand. "So now we're friends, you damned dog," Bo said grumpily, scratching Dog's huge head. "Can't you keep your master better company so he doesn't drag us out here into the back of beyond?"

"I figured you guys were having it too soft up in Atlanta," Caleb said. "Besides, I'm pulling the whole crew down here once I get a little personal matter settled."

Bo glanced over at the Moon Palace. He was a huge man, with shaggy blond hair and eyebrows, massive shoulders and the gentle spirit of a lamb. He didn't like to talk about the reasons for his six-year prison term, but one night, after a bottle of Jack Daniel's, he'd told Caleb about the man who'd molested his little brothers and gotten off with a suspended sentence. The man who wouldn't be hurting any more children.

Ray was smaller, more wiry, more sly. He'd been a car thief, probably still would be if he hadn't met Caleb inside. Caleb had no illusions about him. Their friendship kept them together, and kept Ray on the straight and narrow. If something happened to Caleb, Ray would be back on the streets in no time.

There were others, all ex-cons, who depended on him in one way or another. If something happened, if this mess with Harrison Turner backfired, it wouldn't be just his life down the toilet.

But he couldn't give it up. Not yet. Not now. Not until he'd extracted at least a measure of revenge.

"This place is going to need all of us," Bo said in his slow, deep voice that made people foolishly assume he wasn't as bright as he was. "Why the hell did you pick such a spot?"

"Personal reasons. You'll meet them later. Besides, it's in a lot better shape than it looks."

"It better be," Ray said. "I don't fancy spending the next year in the boonies."

"Did you bring any beer?" Caleb started toward the house, Dog bounding along like an innocent puppy, batting his head against Bo's big hand.

"Is the Pope catholic?" Ray countered.

"This damned dog," Bo grumbled cheerfully. "You wouldn't believe that ten minutes ago he was ready to tear out my throat if I stepped out of the van."

"I believe it. Dog doesn't accept anyone totally, except for me. And maybe..." He shut up, too late, not wanting to explain Jassy Turner to his friends. At least, not until they'd gone through a six-pack or more.

Despite Bo's slow-moving demeanor he was right on top of things. "Maybe who?"

Caleb smiled wryly. "All in good time, my friend. She's one of the reasons you're here."

"She?" Ray echoed. "Since when did you start changing plans for any 'she'? I thought you were Spenser the untouchable."

"Still am."

Bo's snort of disbelief made Dog whoof sharply. "I've known you for eleven years, man. You can't con me. Something's got your tail in a twitter, and it ain't Harrison Turner. You've lived with that for a long time, made your plans clear years ago. So what's messed things up?"

He should have known he couldn't pull anything over on men who knew him better than he knew himself. "His sister," he said glumly.

"Oh, hell," Bo said with heartfelt sympathy.

"You got it right the first time," Spenser said. "Oh, hell indeed."

JASSY SHIFTED, burying her head beneath the thin pillow and moaning. Something was pounding, clanging, inside her head, rattling her teeth, trying to drag her from sleep with angry claws, and she struggled, desperate for a few more minutes, a few more hours. If she had to wake, why did it have to be in the midst of the most erotic dream she'd had in memory?

She burrowed deeper into the lumpy mattress, but there was no respite. No bringing back the delicious feeling of his hands on her body, no bringing back the taste of his mouth. Flopping over onto her back, she opened her eyes and stared up at the water-stained ceiling, and she slowly remembered why she wasn't in her own bed, and why she was so desperately tired. And tried to forget who was with her in her dream.

She sat up, the concave cot sagging beneath her. She was in the back room of the women's shelter, trying to catch a few minutes' sleep before driving back to Belle Rive. Pushing her tangled hair out of her face, she frowned, trying to place the banging, clanging sound that was coming from her office.

It might very well be Leroy Philips. When Faith had first called the emergency number Jassy had had a hard time recognizing her voice through the muffled tears. Her first sight of Faith's swollen, bruised face and mouth had explained that. She and little Tommy Lee had huddled in the secure back rooms of the shelter while Jassy had made hot chocolate and coffee, soothed and comforted and made absolutely no suggestions. She'd learned long ago that you couldn't tell a woman to leave. She had to make that decision on her own.

This was Faith and Tommy's fifth visit to the shelter in the past year. It was all Jassy could do to control her whoop of joy when Faith announced it was her last. She and Tommy were heading north, to her aunt's house in Boston, and she was never going to hold still for Leroy's brutal fists again.

Jassy let her make all the plans. Faith needed to learn she could rely on herself, not on someone else to rescue her. It was her need to be rescued that had made her turn to a handsome bully like Leroy Philips when she was sixteen. She was a smart, attractive woman who could take care of herself and her son just fine, if she only realized it. She was finally beginning to.

They shopped for new clothes from the closets full of donations in the shelter. Jassy wrote Faith a glowing recommendation for her considerable clerical skills while

Tommy slept the sleep of exhaustion in the back room. And at quarter of six in the morning she emptied out the emergency fund, drove them to Clearwater for the bus, and saw the two of them off on their new life.

They were going to make it, she told herself as she drove back. She'd seen enough to know which ones would make the break, which ones would succeed. Faith would make it, through her brains and talent and determination. Not to mention her considerable love for her son. She'd put up with the abuse when it had only affected her. When it started spilling over onto Tommy she'd finally had enough.

Jassy had been too tired to make it out to the house. She'd gone back to lock up the shelter, then decided to try to catch just a few moments' sleep before driving back. She peered at her digital watch, the cheap model that had replaced the Rolex her daddy had given her on her eighteenth birthday. She'd sold that and plowed the funds into the shelter, and she doubted if Harrison had ever forgiven her. It was quarter past ten, and whoever was pounding in her front office sounded more determined than enraged. It couldn't be Leroy.

The man in her office didn't hear her when she opened the door. It was no wonder. The tall, shaggy giant had her recalcitrant air conditioner torn apart, pieces all over a greasy scrap of cloth, while he hammered away at a small metal piece, whistling underneath his breath.

She cleared her throat, but he didn't hear. She slammed the door behind her, and he jumped up, banging his head on the overhanging air conditioner and cursing fluently.

"I didn't know anyone was here," he said, looking sheepish, and some of Jassy's initial panic faded.

"How did you get in? For that matter, who are you and what are you doing here?" She moved into the room, shutting off the shelter from his curious eyes, and she felt a little more self-assured. This large stranger didn't have a lick of meanness in his face.

"That's a lot of questions," he said, looking her up and down in frank curiosity. "I'm fixing your air conditioner. My name's Bo, and I'm a friend of Caleb Spenser. He sent me here, along with a donation." He nodded toward the desk, and Jassy could see a green check lying there. She let out a tiny sigh of relief. She'd had to float a check from the shelter account to cover the rest of Tommy and Faith's bus fare, and she had strong doubts about Harrison's willingness to cover it. At least a token contribution might help.

"That still doesn't explain how you got in."

"The door just opened."

"It was locked."

"Not to me," Bo said sweetly, and Jassy didn't bother arguing. She went over to the desk for lack of something better to do and picked up the check.

She dropped it as if it burned her fingers. "Is this real?" she gasped.

Bo looked up. "I didn't look real close. Why wouldn't it be?"

"It's for so much!"

Bo shrugged. "You do good work around here. Besides, Caleb's got money to spare. He lives pretty sparsely."

She picked the check up again with trembling hands, folding it in half and putting it into her pocket carefully. "You said you're a friend of his?"

"I've known him for a long time. I work for him."

"Oh," Jassy said blankly.

"That's right, I'm an ex-con," Bo said cheerfully. "And you must be Harrison Turner's sister."

"What do you know about Harrison?"

"Just what I hear from Caleb."

"And what's that?"

"Ask..."

"Don't tell me," she interrupted him. "Ask Caleb, right?"

"Or your brother."

"The next person who says that to me is going to wish he hadn't," Jassy said between clenched teeth. "Are you going to be able to fix the air conditioner?"

"Probably. She's all gunked up with oil, but she's still basically sound. If I can't, Caleb told me to go out and buy you a new one."

"Just like that?"

"Just like that."

"Sounds like the man has a guilty conscience."

Bo looked at her in confusion for a moment, then he laughed. "You mean you think he hits women? Not likely. Caleb can be downright nasty on occasion, but he doesn't take it out on anyone or anything that can't handle it. I guess you don't know him very well, ma'am."

"I guess not. Are you going to help him with the Moon Palace?"

Bo nodded. "Me and Ray drove down from Atlanta last night. I guess one motel's as good as another, and I sort of like that old place. Don't know how Caleb thinks he can turn a profit from it, but if anybody can, he's the one. He's got a magic touch with things like that."

"You're staying at the motel? I would have thought he'd want you out at the Palace."

"Caleb likes his solitude, and it's not really set up for more than one person. Besides, it doesn't take long to drive. Is there any reason why we should be out there?" he asked with sudden shrewdness.

"Ask Caleb," she said sweetly. "Or ask my brother. See if you get any further than I did."

Bo laughed. "I'll do that, ma'am."

In the end it was absurdly easy, so easy that she wondered why she'd never attempted it before. While Bo worked on the air conditioner, Jassy took a cup of instant coffee into the back room and went to work on the telephone. Within half an hour she'd managed to get a helpful clerk at the *St. Florence Register* to read her the account of Sherman Delano's murder some thirteen years ago in that small coastal town.

A drifter named Caleb Spenser, age twenty-one, was arrested for the murder of a local citizen, Sherman Delano of Wayfield Drive. Apparently they'd been involved in a high-stakes gambling game, one man accused the other of cheating, and Spenser pulled a knife. There was a witness, one Billy Ray Smith, and it was an open-and-shut case. They ended up plea bargaining, and the case never even went to trial.

The clerk had promised to send copies of all the pertinent newspaper articles. Jassy thanked her profusely, knowing that she'd already heard enough. It all jibed with the little Caleb had told her. What the newspaper articles didn't explain was her brother's connection.

"Find out anything interesting?"

Jassy looked up, startled, at the sound of Caleb's voice. She hadn't heard him come in, hadn't bothered to lock the secure back door into the dormitory-style room. "What are you doing here, Caleb?" she asked evenly, controlling her urge to leap off the sagging cot where she was sitting, cross-legged, a pad of paper in her lap.

"I thought I'd come to see how Bo was doing. He's got the air conditioner fixed." The room was dimly lit. It was an overcast, muggy day, and the light filtering in through curtained windows was diffuse, shadowy. Caleb was leaning against the open door, his chambray work shirt open halfway down his chest, his gold hoop glittering against the darker gold of his long hair. "You didn't answer my question."

"I don't remember what it was."

His faint smile told her he recognized a lie when he heard it. "I asked if you learned anything interesting. I figure you were checking up on me."

"Isn't that egocentric of you? Maybe I have other concerns."

He shook his head, moving into the room. "Maybe you do. But right now the risk I pose to your family's got you in a swivet. Not to mention the risk I pose to you, personally."

"I wasn't aware you were any particular risk to me."

Dare you, his smile said. He moved closer, glancing down at her scribbled notes, verifying his suspicions. "Did you ask about your brother?"

She didn't bother denying it. "I didn't ask anyone questions. I just had someone read me the newspaper articles concerning Sherman Delano's death."

"Learn anything new?"

"Not really."

Caleb nodded, more to himself, and then dropped onto the cot beside her. She pulled her legs away from him, but he merely smiled at her skittishness. "You look worn-out, lady," he murmured. "What have you been doing all night?"

"Helping someone."

"Who?"

"None of your business."

"Honey, this is a small town, and even a newcomer hears everything sooner or later. There's no such thing as professional discretion around here."

She knew he was right. "Faith and Tommy Lee Philips," she said. "I've lost count of how many times they've come to the shelter in the past year. Leroy's getting meaner and meaner, and he was no sweetheart to begin with. Thank God she finally decided she'd had enough. I put the two of them on a bus for... for parts north," she amended hastily. "She looked like she'd been hit by a Mack truck."

"Someone needs to have a conversation with Leroy," Caleb said in a diffident tone of voice.

Jassy wasn't fooled for a minute. "Please don't," she begged. "More violence won't help matters. Faith and Tommy Lee are safe, and there's no one for him to turn his fists on. He'll have to find some other way to beat out his frustrations, and I'd rather they weren't on you."

"Why?"

"For one thing, he's about half a foot taller than you are and maybe fifty pounds heavier. Bo out there might stand a chance against him, you wouldn't."

Caleb smiled, not bothering to deny it. "So you don't want me turned into hamburger? Why not? It would put me out of commission for a while, keep me away from your precious brother."

"Violence never solves anything," she stated flatly, knowing she sounded priggish, believing it anyway.

"Now there you're wrong," Caleb said, leaning against the white-painted walls. "Violence, directed at someone who sure as hell deserves it and is man enough to take it, can solve a whole lot of problems."

"I don't think I'm going to be trying it."

He turned his head to look at her. "Admit it, Miss Jassy. Wouldn't you just love to haul off and slap me sometimes? Wipe that grin off my face?"

Her hand was already itching, she didn't bother to deny it. "That's different."

"No," he said, "it's not. It's a matter of degree. And I know perfectly well that no matter how mad you get, no matter how tempted, you'd never hit anything smaller or weaker than you are."

"Of course not," she said indignantly.

"The same holds true for me. Remember that."

She looked at him out of steady eyes. "There's more than one kind of violence. What you're planning to do to my brother is going to hurt Lila, hurt my mother, hurt me. We're all smaller and weaker than you are."

"I wouldn't count on it," he muttered under his breath. "The three of you are a hell of a lot tougher than you think."

"Maybe I am, but..."

He shook his head. "You're the most vulnerable. You think you have to take care of everyone else, particularly your family, when if you just let them be you'd find they were perfectly capable of handling their own problems. I'm not so sure you are."

"You don't think I'm capable of handling my problems?" She was incensed.

But Caleb refused to be drawn. He shook his head. "I'm your biggest problem, Jassy. Think you can handle me?"

"With one hand tied behind my back." It was a mistake the moment she said it. His light eyes suddenly darkened with intent, and she knew he could lean across that concave cot, cover her smaller body with his, and show her just how incapable she was of handling him.

And as inevitable as that moment was, she wasn't certain she was ready to deal with it right now.

The banging from the front room grew suddenly louder, and that slumberous, intent expression vanished from Caleb's face, to be replaced with a wary one. "That's not Bo," he said. "I sent him out for coffee."

She was about to protest the ramifications of that when the door slammed open again, a huge figure filling it. Larger than the hulking Bo, and far more dangerous.

"Bitch," Leroy Philips spat, his furious dark eyes focusing on Jassy and ignoring the man beside her. "What the hell have you done with my wife?"

Chapter Twelve

Caleb began to uncurl himself from the cot with slow, dangerous deliberation. Jassy moved faster, jumping up and moving toward Leroy with a heedless unconcern for her own safety. Caleb grabbed for her, but he was too late, and he watched with mingled horror and pride as she confronted the vicious-looking man in the doorway, not a trace of fear in her slim, straight body.

"She's gone, Leroy," she said flatly. "She took Tommy Lee and went west, and she's never coming back."

The word Leroy roared was almost unintelligible, except that Caleb had experience with words like that. His meaty fist slammed out, almost connecting with Jassy's fragile jaw, but this time Caleb was lightning fast, shoving her out of the way and catching Leroy's blow on his shoulder.

It was a solid one, and the thought of all that force slamming into Jassy wiped out whatever compunctions Caleb had. He stood his ground, facing the furious man, his fists ready.

"Who the hell are you?" Leroy bellowed.

"Someone who's going to teach you a lesson, Leroy," he said in a low, mean voice. "One you're not likely to soon forget."

Leroy looked down at him, and spat. "You and who else?" he demanded. And then he charged, like a maddened bull.

In the distance Caleb heard Jassy scream, "No!" He paid her no mind. He waited till the last minute, then moved in, under Leroy's furious bulk, hitting him hard in his soft gut. Leroy doubled over, and Caleb slammed his fist down on the back of his neck, hard. Leroy went down fast, and his eyes glazed over for a moment, but Caleb wasn't fooled. Someone as mad as Leroy didn't fold that easily.

Reaching down, he grabbed a handful of Leroy's greasy hair and hauled his head up. "You don't hit women," he said between gritted teeth. "You hear, boy? You don't hit kids, either, or kick dogs, or pull the wings off butterflies. If you want to hit someone, try to hit me."

With a roar Leroy surged upward, batting Caleb backward as if he were nothing more than a rag doll. His fist connected with Caleb's mouth, and he went soaring through the air, landing on one of the narrow beds and collapsing it with his weight. "You got it, boy," he said, advancing on Caleb as he lay in a tangle against one broken cot. "I'm gonna teach you a lesson you ain't never gonna forget."

Caleb heard Jassy's scream of horror when she saw the knife glinting in Leroy's meaty fist, and he felt his own frisson of panic sweep over him. Not because he had any doubts as to his ability to deal with Leroy's little pigsticker. But because he was afraid Jassy would do something foolish like try to protect him.

Sure enough, she was getting ready to move when Caleb leaped to his feet. The thought of her putting her body between the two of them, being on the receiving end of Leroy's knife, wiped out any trace of conscious thought.

Rage swept over him, a killing rage, and he flew at Leroy with a guttural cry.

The last thing he noticed was the expression of primal fear on Leroy's thick, stupid face as he leaped at him. And then it was over, too quickly. The knife went skittering across the old pine floor, and Leroy was down, unconscious, blood pouring from his broken nose.

Caleb leaned down to check his pulse. It was slow, steady, like an ox. He hadn't killed the man, he'd simply put him out of action for a while. He considered breaking a few bones, just to ensure that Leroy stayed out of the way for a while longer, and then he looked up at Jassy and thought better of the notion.

She was staring at him in utter, complete horror, her face white, her soft mouth crumpled with fear. She'd been pampered and protected all her life, he knew that. For all her concern about battered women, she'd never seen violence up close, nasty and bloody and dangerous. Even the night when Harrison's good old boys had jumped him had been fogged in shadows.

He rose, still breathing deeply from his exertions. His back ached where it had slammed against the broken cot, his shirt was torn half off, and he was angry, sweaty and ready for a confrontation. She was looking at him out of frightened eyes as if he was a devil straight out of hell, and it riled him, pure and simple.

He stepped over Leroy's body, crossed the room to stand in front of her. Without even thinking about it he put his hand behind Jassy's neck, underneath her thick fall of hair, and pulled her up to him, setting his bruised mouth on hers with a hot, hungry kiss.

She tried to push against him for a moment, but he ignored her struggles, and after only a moment they weren't struggles at all. She put her arms around his waist, be-

neath the ripped shirt, and opened her mouth for him. She
didn't bother trying to kiss him back. He wasn't in the
mood to be kissed. He was in the mood to claim, and
that's what he did, kissing her with a hard, possessive fury
that swept over his entire body and then began to cover
hers. He felt her shake in his arms, felt the edgy, tremu-
lous beginnings of surrender; it was all he could do to rip
himself away.

But that was exactly what he did, pulling himself out of
her arms as his body screamed in protest. She had blood
on her mouth, his blood, and her eyes were wide, dark,
shocky.

That kiss hadn't slowed his breathing any, but now was
hardly the time or place to make love to her, much as he
wanted to. He wasn't going to have her on a narrow cot
with an unconscious bully lying on the floor and Bo ready
to walk in at any moment. When he took her to bed he
was going to have plenty of time to do it right.

He took a deep, shaky breath. "I'll have Bo get rid of
this garbage," he said in a deceptively even voice. "You
better go home."

She looked dazed, confused, staring at him as if she'd
seen a ghost. "Go home?" she echoed.

"Unless you want to come home with me?"

Slowly his question penetrated her confusion, and she
shook her head. He reached out, and she tried to flinch
away. He cursed, caught her shoulder, and with his other
hand touched her mouth, bringing his blood away on his
hand. "Go home," he said again. "When you want me
you know where to find me."

There was no question as to his meaning, to either of
them. She squirmed away, and he released her this time,
walking away from her. He knew her eyes were following

him, but he didn't look back. If he looked back, he might not leave her.

Bo was coming in the front door, two cups of coffee in his hands. "Job for you in there," Caleb said laconically. "See that he gets the message."

Bo let out a long, low whistle as he surveyed Caleb's bruised mouth. "Is there anything left for me to clean up, boss?"

"Enough. See that Jassy gets home."

"Shouldn't that be your job?"

"It should," Caleb agreed. "But it's not." And he slammed the door behind him as he headed out into the thick, humid heat of the late morning.

THERE WAS BLOOD on her mouth. His blood. Jassy stared in the mirror, remembering that he'd wiped some of it off. Some remained on her swollen lower lip. He'd marked her, and she thought of fox hunting, how the novice would be marked with the blood of the first kill. Stained by some rite of passage.

She took a washcloth and began to scrub her face, trying to scrub away the blood. But she couldn't wash away the feel of him, his mouth on hers, angry, possessive, his hard, hot body pressed against her, the strength and power in his hands. Hands that hadn't hurt her. Wouldn't hurt her. But hands that had almost killed a man. Hands that had killed a man in years past.

Leaning down, she splashed cold water on her face, again and again. She must be out of her mind. Try as she might, she couldn't wipe the memory from her. The sheer possession on his face when he'd risen from the man on the floor and looked at her. It had been primitive, sexual, and if he'd wanted she would have stripped off her clothes and lain with him on the bare wood floor. She would have done anything he wanted.

It was disgusting, she told herself, splashing more water on her face. Vile and base and degrading and absolutely awful. She was a civilized woman, from generations of civilized women, and her reaction to his savagery had been primal, basic and... and...

She could still feel it, thrumming through her body. The longing for him, a longing that was physical and something more, something even more disturbing. It was a need for him that had grown to unmanageable proportions, one of mind and soul as well as body, and she didn't know how much longer she could fight it. To give in to it would mean her destruction. To fight it was tearing her apart.

The only way she could keep her sanity was to ask his help. He didn't really want her, she was sure of that. He'd flirted with her as he'd flirted with every female, impartially, as naturally as breathing. If his attention had focused on her at all, then it was only as a temporary distraction. No one mattered to him, only whatever lay between him and Harrison. And she wasn't going to be a victim of that tangled history.

She could ask him. Beneath his cynical exterior there was some kernel of decency, she knew that. The shockingly large donation was a sign of it, the repaired air conditioner, his enraged, oddly gallant defense of her were all further proof. If she went to him, asked him to leave her alone, he would.

She shivered, looking at her reflection in the mirror again. Beneath the drops of water her face was pale, her eyes large and haunted, the feel of his mouth still lingering on hers. He'd agree, he'd have to. And Jassy didn't know if that mercy she counted on would be her salvation.

Or her despair.

"DAMNED WOMAN," Caleb said, draining his glass of whiskey.

"Haven't you had enough?" Ray inquired lazily, snagging the bottle from his hand and pouring himself a generous portion. Bo shook his head when he offered it to him, content with beer, as the three men sat in the kitchen of the old bordello.

"I know when I've had enough," Caleb snarled. "I don't need you to tell me."

"No, I suppose you don't," Ray said cheerfully enough. "What are you going to do about her?"

"Not a damned thing. You sure you took care of Leroy, Bo?"

Bo nodded. "I told you before, Caleb, he's resting peacefully in the county jail. A man on parole isn't allowed to carry a gun, and he was found smelling like a brewery with a pistol tucked in his pants pocket. I don't think they're gonna let him out for a good long time."

"Lucky for him," Caleb said in a sour voice. "I still wish I'd broken his arm."

"You break too many arms, Caleb. You can't save the world."

Caleb laughed without humor. "That's what I told Jassy."

"Maybe you two have something in common."

"Don't count on it. She looked at me like I was a monster from outer space after I gallantly defended her honor."

"You mean after you squashed Leroy like a June bug?" Bo countered. "So she's not used to the rough side of life. She's tough enough, she'll survive."

"She's not as tough as she looks."

"She's tougher," Bo asserted.

"You've seen her for maybe ten minutes. I've been around her for a hell of a lot longer. What makes you an expert?"

"Maybe because my glands aren't involved," Bo said.

Caleb's response was brief and obscene and he poured himself his third drink. Thunder rumbled overhead, a long, low grumble in the evening air, but he ignored it.

"At least we'll get some rain," Ray said from his spot in the corner of the old kitchen. "This place is like a sweat box."

"Don't count on it. That's heat lightning. There hasn't been a decent rain in months, the way I hear it. Not that anyone's worried about it—there's enough water in this damned swamphole to keep things going for twenty years."

"Place could do with a real thunder-boomer," Bo said. "It might clear the air."

"Nothing'll clear the air," Caleb said morosely. "The sooner I get things taken care of and we get the hell out of here, the better we'll be."

"What things taken care of, boss?" Bo asked. "The renovations on this old place? Or your business with Harrison Turner?"

"I'm sorry as hell I ever told you about Turner," Caleb muttered.

"Why?" Ray asked lazily. "You afraid we're gonna horn in on your fun? You should know we'll let you fight your own battles, until you call on us. We're here if you need us, but we're not going to interfere."

Caleb tipped back in the chair, running a hand through his hair. "I know. This place is driving me nuts. This place, and the people in it."

"Which people?" Bo asked with just a trace of too much innocence.

Caleb glared at him. "Don't go jumping to conclusions. The only person I'm concerned with is Harrison Turner."

"Uh-huh," Bo agreed, and Caleb knew him well enough to recognize that he hadn't fooled him for a minute. "You want us to bed down out here tonight?"

"There's no need. Leroy's out of action, and Harrison's not about to make his move. You might as well have a decent bed. I don't think Dog's managed to dispose of all the rats in this place yet, and I know how you two feel about rats."

Ray shuddered. "I'll take the motel. Besides, there's a waitress at the local tavern with the cutest little . . ."

"You're gonna get in trouble one of these days," Bo rumbled.

"And you're gonna die a saint," Ray said.

"Hey, I'm saving myself for true love," Bo said placidly. "That doesn't mean I won't drink with you."

"Thank heaven for small favors. But keep your eyes off the waitress. I saw her first."

Caleb stood in the doorway, watching them drive away, and that restless edge was still there. "Maybe I should have gone with them, Dog," he said to his companion. "Maybe Ray's waitress was just what I needed."

Dog whoofed with canine contempt. "No, you're right," Caleb said, turning back into the house, shutting the new screen door against the teeming mosquitoes. "Ray's waitress wouldn't do me any good. I know what I want, and if it's eating a hole in my gut I can damned well ignore it. She's not what I need.''

Dog sank his huge body down where he stood, lying crossways across the hallway and panting lightly. Caleb looked at him in disgust for a moment, then stepped over him. "I'm taking a shower," he told him. "A cold shower. Why don't you make yourself scarce? Go outside and guard the place. Catch a few rats. Make yourself useful.''

Dog lumbered to his paws, giving Caleb a hurt, soulful look before he padded out the door, pushing the screen with his huge head. Caleb watched him go, feeling ridiculously guilty. He was getting in rough shape, when he started worrying about a dog's feelings. Maybe he better stop pussyfooting around, finish up with Harrison Turner, and get the hell out of there.

The shower didn't do much toward improving his mood, or lessening the tension that crept along his muscles. He pulled on a clean pair of jeans, zipped but didn't bother to snap them, and was reaching for a T-shirt when he heard the car drive in.

He held himself very still, waiting for the sound of Dog as he terrorized whoever dared show up at that hour, unannounced. There wasn't a sound. Which meant only one person could have driven down the long, winding road to the Moon Palace.

He dropped the shirt back on the chair and headed toward the front door, watching, unseen behind the screen, as Jassy Turner made her way across the scarred and weedy path to the front door, while Dog did his best to overwhelm her with love and approval.

He almost called Dog off. He was big enough to knock her over, but Jassy seemed capable of dealing with his slobbering affection, and Caleb simply watched.

He wondered what that thick, curly mane of dark hair would look like if she loosened it. It was already curling around her face, ignoring her efforts to control it, and he found himself smiling faintly in the darkness, wondering if the rest of her body was the same. Fighting when she tried to repress its natural urges.

She was wearing a baggy shirt and skirt, as usual, and he couldn't begin to guess what kind of body she had underneath. He didn't really care. Plump or skinny, he wanted her, wanted her so badly he ached with it. She could be flat-chested or voluptuous, soft or muscled. None of it mattered. She'd managed to become an obsession, one he didn't want, didn't need, but one that haunted him when he least expected it.

She had a determined expression on her face, only softened for a moment as she rubbed Dog's huge head. She wasn't coming out to the Moon Palace at a quarter to ten at night for a social call, he thought. Or for a roll in the hay. She was coming with a purpose, and he probably wasn't going to like it. And he probably wasn't going to pay a lick of attention to it, either.

He pushed the screen door open, startling her. She looked up at him, for a moment completely vulnerable, and if he'd been a few inches closer and Dog hadn't been in the way he would have grabbed her then and there.

But as quickly as that look had passed over her features it was gone again, and her brown eyes were cool, determined, her soft mouth set in her face.

He realized then that he thought she was beautiful. He knew she wasn't—her mouth was too wide, her nose a little too short, her chin too vulnerable, her forehead too broad. None of that mattered. Her face mesmerized him, even set in its current, stern expression.

"Little late for a social call," he said, leaning against the open doorway.

"This isn't a social call," she said, concentrating on his shoulder.

"Did you come for sex?"

That jerked her head up, wiping that detached expression from her face, replacing it with rage and shock. "I did not! Is that all you ever think about?"

"Whenever you're around," he muttered beneath his breath, opening the door further, still not moving. "So why did you come?"

"I need to talk to you."

"We talk too much."

"May I come in?"

"I'm not stopping you." He still didn't move. She'd have to brush past him to step inside the dimly lit house, and he wanted that. He wanted the feel of her body, her clothes, brushing against him. He wanted her to know the feel, the warmth, of him.

She pulled her skirts close against her as she stepped inside, but the faint, flowery fragrance of her perfume danced around him. "Stay," he ordered Dog, slamming the screen in his face. Dog made a low, aggrieved sound, and then sank onto the front doorstep, ready to guard his master's privacy.

"We can talk in the kitchen," Caleb said behind her as she paused in the hallway, "or my bedroom. It's up to you."

"The kitchen," she said flatly, and Caleb forced himself to release some of his pent-up breath. He wasn't going to make it through the night, he knew that with sudden clarity. If he didn't put his hands on her he was going to die. Pure and simple.

By the time he reached the kitchen she'd already seated herself on the stool that Ray had recently vacated. She looked prim and proper, that big shirt done up almost to her throat, her legs tucked under her, close together, her knees touching. She was wearing sandals again, ignoring the danger of swamp creatures. She had wonderful toes.

"Beer or whiskey?" he asked.

"This isn't a social call, Mr. Spenser."

He poured her a whiskey. "We dispensed with Mr. Spenser a long time ago, Jassy. Drink up."

She wouldn't have, except she was nervous, her eyes shifting everywhere but at him, her hands needing something to do. He'd poured the whiskey neat, and she coughed slightly, frowning at the glass.

He took the chair opposite her, turning it around and straddling it. He liked looking up at her. He knew the change in position bothered her, and he liked bothering her.

"You can imagine why I'm here," she began in a voice unlike her own, high-pitched, nervous, as her hand fiddled with the top button of her shirt. He only hoped she'd fiddle enough to unfasten it.

"No, I can't," he drawled. "Unless you're making a personal visit to thank me for the donation to the women's shelter."

That threw her off for a moment, and real warmth lit her brown eyes. "That was so generous of you," she said. "Are you certain you can afford it? We surely do need it, but..."

"I can afford it," he said flatly. "If that's not why you came out here, why don't you get it over with?"

She hesitated, her eyes skittering over him once more. "Do you suppose you could put on a shirt?"

He'd had enough. "What the hell do you have against a man's body? I'd like to know what's riled you so. I just took a shower, I know for sure I don't smell. So what's got you in such a taking?"

She shut her eyes for a moment, steeling herself. "I want you to leave me alone."

He just looked at her. "That's not what your brother wants."

"You heard that, did you? I thought you might have. That's not the way Harrison usually is. You've pushed him, frightened him. Otherwise he never would have suggested such a thing."

"Hell, I thought it was the smartest thing I ever heard him say," Caleb drawled.

She came off her stool, fast, leaning over the table that stood between them. "It's not. You don't want me, Caleb, not really. You want to use me to get to Harrison. I know you're not really a mean person. You don't want to hurt anyone. I don't think you even want to hurt me. Please, Caleb," she said, her eyes huge and beseeching, her mouth soft and vulnerable.

He didn't move. "Please, what?"

"Let me go. You're only going to break my heart, and I don't need that. I don't want a man like you. I want someone who respects me, who's tender, sweet and gentle. Someone who'll consider my needs, my feelings, before his own. Someone who..."

"You want a gentleman," he said savagely, rising and kicking his chair out of the way. "You want a sweet, pale-skinned, soft-handed little gentleman to do your bidding and never say a harsh word to you. Well, honey, I'm not a gentleman. I'm not going to be what you think you want. But I sure as hell am going to be what you need."

"Caleb..." She was off the stool, backing away from him, but he wasn't going to let her go. He'd waited long enough, and so had she, whether she recognized that fact or not.

"Your friend said you're a semi-virgin," he said, advancing on her, smooth and steady, his intentions clear. "That you tried sex and didn't like it. You just didn't try it with the right man, sugar."

Her back was up against the door. He saw a flash of real fear in her dark eyes, and he stopped, every nerve in his body on fire. "Caleb," she said, her voice low and husky, "what if I say no?"

His need for her was so intense he thought he might explode from it. He'd never wanted a woman so much in his entire life, even after he'd spent three years locked away from them. He didn't smile. "Then I'll let you go," he said. "This time. And the next. And each time. Until you say yes."

He watched as a little shiver washed over her body, and her eyes were wide, full of sexual awareness. "How about maybe?" she whispered.

"Maybe's good enough." And he crossed the distance between them, knocking the table out of the way, and put his hands on her.

Chapter Thirteen

Jassy could feel the hardness of the door behind her back, the strength of his hard hands on her shoulders. He was close, too close, the smooth-skinned chest tantalizingly near to her mouth, and she was afraid. Afraid of him, of what he wanted of her. Afraid he'd be disappointed. Afraid she'd be disappointed. Afraid of staying with him. Afraid of running.

She forced herself to look up into his eyes, those clear, light eyes that saw too much. He could see through her right now, her indecision, her longing, her fears. Even fully dressed, she was more naked with him than she'd ever been in her life.

"Made up your mind yet?" His voice was soft, low, insinuating, and the gold hoop glinted in the shadow light.

She searched for her voice, but it had vanished. She swallowed, wondering if she dared change her mind. Wondering whether there really would be another chance.

She was going to be just as frightened, later. He was a frightening man. Or maybe it was the intensity of her confused feelings that frightened her. That turned her safe, reliable world on end, upsetting everything she thought she could trust and believe in.

"No," she said in a whisper.

"No?" he echoed, his mouth brushing her ear, his voice only a breath of sound, as soft as her strangled answer. "No, you don't want this? Or no, you're not sure?" His teeth caught her earlobe, gently, a tiny little pressure that sent shivers through her body.

She couldn't answer, couldn't bring herself to form the words, particularly since she didn't know what those words were. She let out a deep, shaken breath, one of surrender, and his hard hands slid down her arms, pulling her against him.

His skin was hot, blazing hot, burning her fingertips as she pressed against him. His mouth was hot, hot and wet as it closed over hers, and the fierce hunger of his kiss filled some deep, long-hidden need she never knew existed.

He put his hands on either side of her face, pushing her against the door, his hips holding her, his hands holding her, as he kissed her, long and hard and deep, allowing no shyness, no hesitation, no second thoughts. Tendrils of panic danced through her brain, entwined with a desire that was rapidly wiping out all conscious thought. She could feel his arousal against her stomach, and she wanted it, wanted him, so completely that everything else was receding. Common sense, family loyalty, age-old fears. When he pulled his mouth away from hers he was breathing deeply, and his eyes glittered in the shadowy kitchen. He tasted like whiskey, and love.

"Last chance," he said in a whisper. "No more maybes. Run now, little girl."

She didn't move. She couldn't move. Trapped between his strong body and the closed door, she couldn't have walked away if her life depended on it. She knew with sudden clarity that he'd let her. All she had to do was push, gently, against his chest, and he'd move away. And he was lying about it being her last chance. At no point was he going to force her to do anything she didn't want to do. He was going to seduce her into it, and if she had any sense at all she'd get out, now, before she lost her mind and her soul.

But she had no sense. She closed her eyes for a moment, unable to meet his too-knowing gaze. "No more maybes," she agreed. "But Caleb... be gentle with me." Silence, and she opened her eyes again.

"Honey, you don't need another night of sex that you can pretend didn't happen. When I get through with you you're going to know you've been taken care of. Well and thoroughly." His long fingers stroked the side of her neck, and she lifted her head to stare at him. "Think you can handle that?"

No, the last remnants of fear and sanity cried out. "Yes," she said, her voice shaky and uncertain.

There was no mocking quality to his smile, no double-dare-you grin. Just the light of pure satisfaction, tinged with an anticipation that both scared and aroused her.

A moment later she was in his arms, scooped up effortlessly and held high against his hard, hot chest as he kicked the door open behind her. The room was dark, but in the center she could see a pool table, covered with a mattress.

He dropped her onto the hard surface, and she stared around her wildly. "You're not going to make love to me on a pool table," she said flatly.

"Honey, it's that or the floor. Take your pick." He didn't wait for her answer, following her down on the mattress, covering her with his strong, hard body.

She expected it fast. She expected it rough. When he reached between their bodies for the buttons of her shirt he ripped it open, buttons flying everywhere. But when his hands touched her they were gentle, unfastening the front hook of her bra with deliberation, touching her skin with the rough texture of his work-hardened fingers like an artist discovering the beauty inside a blank canvas, an unworked lump of clay. He covered her bare breasts with his hands, and she arched upward, a wordless little sound escaping her lips as his thumbs brushed the rapidly hardening peaks into exquisite sensibility.

"You know how much I want you?" he whispered in her ear, his voice soft and mesmerizing as his hand swept down to the waistband of her skirt, yanking it open. "Every night I lie in this bed and think about you. About sweet little Miss Jassy, with her baggy clothes and her shy eyes, and I get so hard I think I'm going to explode. And the damnable thing is, no one else will do. Your buddy Mary-Louise would have been on her back in a flash if I'd let her. There are any number of bored women in Turner's Landing who'd be real happy to lay down for me. But I haven't wanted them. I've wanted you. And in the past week I've built up a powerful hunger."

He pulled the skirt down her legs and tossed it over the side of the pool table, leaving her wearing nothing but a modest pair of white cotton bikinis and her opened shirt and bra. He put his hand between her legs, against the soft white cotton, caressing her, and she jerked, startled, automatically raising her hips for him without realizing why.

Her body had taken over. Any protective instincts had vanished, overwhelmed by her need for this man, this moment. She made no protest when he pulled the rest of her clothes from her, so that she lay naked and vulnerable beneath him. She made no protest when he took her hand and placed it against the straining zipper of his faded jeans. Instead, her fingers caressed him, with a boldness that should have shocked her, but somehow felt right.

"That's it, sugar," he murmured, low in his throat. "You've been making me crazy ever since I saw you, all starched up and pretty at that stupid garden party. Let me see you sweat, lady. Let me hear you cry for me." His mouth covered hers, his tongue thrusting inside, and she kissed him back, completely, holding nothing in reserve, as he covered her body with his, the rough denim against the heat and dampness of her flesh.

She bucked against him, needing him, wanting him, wanting him inside her. He broke the kiss, staring down at her, and his light eyes were wild, glittering in the darkness as he watched her. Wild, possessive, determined. "You still want to run away?" His voice was husky.

"I don't know," she said, her voice equally raw.

"You're about to find out." He rolled off her, and with a deft movement stripped off his jeans, leaving him hot and naked and more aroused than any man she'd ever seen in her life.

Now was the time for panic. Now was the time to run away, let self-preservation and common sense reassert themselves. She tried to summon up even a trace of sanity, and then he touched her, his hand between her legs, stroking her, readying her, and all she could do was bite back the cries of complete surrender as she arched up to meet his hand, opening to him, her head flung back against the pillow as sensations began to shimmer through her body, shimmer and slide and soar and crash and she was sobbing his name, weeping, as her body convulsed against him.

He didn't give her time to recover, or even catch her breath. Before the last shock wave had died away he was over her, pulling her legs around his hips, pressing against her as she still trembled with response. "The running's over, lady," he said. And he sank into her, heavy and hard and deep, filling her with his massive strength, stretching her until she thought she couldn't handle any more, and then showing her that she could. She clutched his shoulders, slippery with sweat, and he pulled her legs around him, locking them behind his hips, as he pushed into her, slamming her against the mattress, and his mouth claimed hers, his tongue moving in the same demanding rhythm as his body, as he filled her, again and again and again.

Darkness swirled around her, thick and rich and dizzying, as she reached for that place she'd just been. He took her hands from his shoulders and shoved them down on the mattress, covering them with his larger, harder ones, his fingers entwined with hers, his body entwined with hers, as they rode the whirlwind that threatened to destroy them.

He lifted his head, and for a brief moment she opened her eyes in the darkness to see the expression of sheer wonder cross his face. And then her own body convulsed, shattered beneath him, dissolved into a million particles of sensation, until there was nothing left but the core of her, panting, sweating, barely breathing, as he lay on top of her, his heavy body pinning her down against the pool table, his arms cradling her head.

It was a long time before some form of sanity returned. She could feel him shudder against her, as he struggled to regulate his breathing. He was crushing her, but for some reason she didn't mind. A strange, delicious lassitude had warmed her body, accompanied by a sense of absolute wonder. This was what she'd been missing. She slid her arms around his waist, holding him for a moment, and her mouth opened against his sweat-slick shoulder, kissing him, tasting him, in a lazy aftermath of sensual delight.

"Don't do that," he said gruffly, rolling off her with a suddenness that left her feeling bereft. And then his words penetrated, and some of that rosy glow began to fade in the face of such blatant rejection. She sat up, reaching blindly for her discarded clothes, wanting to run, when his strong arm snaked around her, pulling her back down against him, curling into the side of his body.

"Don't do that," he whispered again, his mouth brushing hers, "or I won't answer for the consequences."

He was burning hot, and she was cold, so cold. She let him move her closer, pressed up against his body on the hard mattress, and she felt shaken, disoriented. "Consequences?" she echoed in a whisper.

"You're not ready for them," he murmured, stroking her hair away from her face and pressing it against his damp shoulder. "Even if I am."

She tilted her head to look up at him. "You are?"

"You forget—I've been wanting you for too long. It's going to take a hell of a lot to make up for weeks of abstinence."

She shouldn't feel safe in his arms, not when he frightened her. She shouldn't feel secure, when he was the one man most likely to shatter the tenuous security of her life. She shouldn't be feeling the slow, burning tendrils of arousal blazing in her belly again, not after she had just experienced the most physically satisfying moment of her life. But she felt all those things, sensible or not.

She slid her hands down his chest, over his flat belly until she reached his unwavering arousal. He groaned, deep in his throat, and she found she could smile.

"I've been wanting you all my life," she said, ignoring the foolishness of such a rash statement. "It's going to take a hell of a lot to make up for a lifetime of abstinence.''

He smiled then. A smile of pure, sensual joy, that lightened his dark face and chased away the shadows. Before she realized what he intended he'd flipped over on his back, taking her with him, so that she was straddling his hard body. "Sugar," he said, "I'm the man to do it." And taking her hips in his big, rough hands, he lifted her up and over him, pulling her down onto him, filling her.

For a moment she was motionless with shock. And then the sensations began to shimmer outward, as he arched up into her, and she put her hands on his shoulders, leaning forward to brace herself, her thick curly hair falling around them like a curtain, as he thrust into her.

She thought she was doing this for him. She'd misjudged her capacities. One moment she was concentrating on his almost agonized expression as he surged up into her, the next she'd shattered once again, lost in the darkness of the sultry night, found in the haven of his strong body.

She wasn't even aware of collapsing on top of him. Nor did she notice when he put her aside with surprising tenderness, tucking her once more against the shelter of his big body. She was dazed, shell-shocked, beyond coherent thought or speech. She opened her eyes for a moment, and it was dark all around. In the distance she could hear the rumble of thunder, and against the wall she could see the reflected crackle of the heat lightning. And then she slept.

CALEB WONDERED if it was going to storm. Part of him felt as if the promise of heat lightning had already been fulfilled. The fine edge of tension that had clawed at the back of his neck, prickled his spine, burned in his belly had, for the moment, abated.

He knew why, and he knew it wouldn't last. Much as he wanted to, he couldn't spend the rest of his life making love to Jassy Turner. Sooner or later he was going to have to climb down off this makeshift bed and get on with his life, his quest. And once he did that, it would signal the end to his involvement with Jassy.

She wasn't worth changing more than a decade's worth of plans. She wasn't worth forgetting that a part of his life had been thrown away, and the rest of it changed forever, because of a spoiled rich boy and his powerful father. She wasn't worth it. But damn, he was tempted.

She looked young and vulnerable, curled up against him in sleep, her tangled, curly hair twined around both of them. He knew it was no illusion. She *was* young and vulnerable, despite her thirty-one years. He doubted he'd ever been that innocent, that trusting. He certainly never would be again.

The sullen daylight was spearing into the room, a murky green light that presaged another muggy day. She was going to wake up soon, and he knew what would happen next. She'd blink, confused and disorientated for a moment. Then her hazel eyes would focus, on the room, on the bed, on him, and horror and regret would wash over her. Her creamy skin would turn pink with embarrassment, and she'd struggle to sit up. She'd probably attempt a casual conversation, and she'd give it up, running away from her night of indiscriminate sex with the poor trash who was out to destroy her brother.

He could let her go, secure in the knowledge that she'd never show up at his place again, looking for something she didn't know she wanted or needed. He'd be able to concentrate on Harrison, get on with the reason he came here, without the distraction of Jassy Turner.

Or he could pull her back down on the bed, stop her nervous babbling with his mouth, and kiss her into temporary acquiescence. Until the next time she came to her senses.

She stirred, tucking her hand under her chin, and he knew he didn't have much time to make up his mind. And then suddenly his time was up, as her eyes flew open, meeting his.

He was lying on his side, watching her, a light sheet pulled up around them. He held very still as her eyes widened in remembered astonishment, and he waited for the panic, the embarrassment, the rejection.

It started in her eyes, warming with memory, and traveled to her mouth, curving in a lazy, happy smile, reaching her arms, as they slid around him. She wiggled her body closer across the hard mattress, burying her face against his chest, pressing her cool body up against his, and she let out a sigh of complete trust and satisfaction.

He wrapped his arms around her instinctively, as his mind tried to deal with the shock. He wasn't used to being mistaken, particularly about women. But then, he already knew this wasn't just any woman. Jassy Turner had the potential of being his total downfall if he didn't watch it, all the more so because she was so obviously unaware of it. He had defenses against women who had designs on him. He had no defenses at all against trust.

He felt her lips against his throat, and he wanted to take those lips, that mouth of hers, and show her what mouths could do. His body was hard with wanting her, something she couldn't escape noticing, but he wasn't going to have her. The dark of night, when hormones and tensions ran high, was one thing. The hot, murky light of day was another.

She had an expression of such warmth and happiness on her face that he felt gut-punched. No one had ever smiled at him like that in his entire life. And then to top it off she kissed him, her mouth soft and damp and delightful.

He had to kiss her back. If he didn't he'd die. Pushing her back on the mattress, he cradled her head with his arms and kissed her, with all the passion and desperation that were at war in his body. When he lifted his head to look down at her, her smile had faded somewhat.

"Why did that taste like goodbye?" she asked softly.

He kept underestimating her. Pulling out of her arms, he sat up, swinging his legs over the side of the bed and reaching for his jeans. "You want some coffee?" he asked, not replying to her astute question.

Silence, but he couldn't turn and look at her. He had to give her time to pull her own defenses back around her. He owed her pride at least. "Sure," she said finally, her voice flat, devoid of emotion. "And then I'd better get home."

"Yeah," he said, zipping his jeans with difficulty as he kept his back to her. "Big brother's gonna be out for blood."

"Harrison doesn't interfere with my private life," she said. "Last night didn't have anything to do with him." There was a pause. "Did it?" Her voice cracked, almost imperceptibly, and never, in a life of feeling like a worthless heel, had Caleb Spenser ever felt worse.

But he didn't answer. Didn't reassure her, just walked to the door without looking back. "There's a bathroom and shower off to the left. I've only got one set of towels—you'll have to make do."

"Did it?" she persisted, her voice calmer.

He turned then, expecting despair or hatred. She was sitting in the bed, the sheet pulled up around her, a cloud of tangled brown curls rippling down her back. Her face was calm, and he knew she wasn't going to throw a fit. Only the darkness of her eyes reflected any of the pain she was feeling.

"You figure it out," he said flatly.

The string of names he called himself was long and inventive, obscene and colorful, as he heard her move around in the other room, the noise of the newly installed shower running full blast. He made a pot of the strongest coffee he could, his mind preoccupied. It was after seven—Ray and Bo would be showing up in a little while for work. He'd prefer it if they didn't see Jassy. It was the only thing he could do to protect her. All the other pain was a necessary part of his plan. Wasn't it? Damn it, wasn't it?

He didn't hear her come up behind him. "Coffee ready yet?" she asked in a calm voice.

He turned to look at her. Her hair was damp, fastened behind her head with a strip of material. She'd tied the shirt around her waist—he must have torn the buttons off last night, and her feet were bare. She looked calm, accepting, as if the night he'd passed between her long, lithe legs had never existed. Except for the fact that her eyes were red from weeping, no one would ever have guessed that he'd done his best to break her heart.

He poured her a mug, and his fingers brushed hers as she took it. She jerked, startled, and the coffee slopped over both their hands, burning them, splashing down on the stained floor between their bare feet.

"Sorry," she said briefly, moving away to the stool where she'd sat last night. "I'll be out of here in a moment. I can't move without caffeine."

He didn't believe her. She was still holding out a ray of hope, and he needed to smash that hope, quickly, before it grew to unmanageable proportions. For both of them.

"I didn't kill Sherman Delano," he said.

She'd arranged herself on the stool like a demure schoolgirl, her long skirt tucked over her legs, her ripped blouse pulled together. She looked up at him, suddenly wary. "I wondered about that," she said finally. "I don't think you're a killer."

"Now that's where you're wrong. I didn't kill Sherman Delano, even though I was framed and spent three years of my life in prison for a crime I didn't commit. But I have every intention of killing the man who did it. After I make him suffer."

The wariness was full-fledged panic. "Don't say it," she begged.

"Your brother," Caleb said, his voice flat, emotionless. "Harrison Turner killed Sherman Delano, and then he and your daddy made me take the fall for it. And I'm going to kill him."

Chapter Fourteen

Caleb waited for her reaction. He knew exactly what it would be. Shock, disbelief, rage. That innocent, hurt expression in her huge eyes would turn to anger, and she'd leave, calling him every name in the book, up to and including murderer.

He waited, and once more she was the one to shock him. "You're wrong," she said flatly. "I believe you when you said you didn't do it. But you're mistaken about my brother. I've known him all my life. He couldn't kill someone and then make someone else pay for it...." Her voice trailed off as her eyes clouded, and he could imagine the unwelcome memories that were forcing their way into her consciousness.

"Oh, yeah?" he drawled, leaning back against the counter and warming his hands around the mug of coffee. It was a hot, muggy day, like every day had been since he'd come to this benighted section of Florida, but he felt cold, chilled to the bone. "You mean he never made you take the rap for something he did?"

He struck home, as he expected. She flushed. "Silly things," she said. "Childish things. A broken window. A scraped fender. A few hundred dollars..." Her voice trailed off with the damning indictment.

He took a sip of coffee, giving her time to deal with it. "I'm not talking about conjecture, Jassy," he said, keeping his voice cold and uninvolved, even as his eyes took in the shocked misery in her eyes. "I'm talking about an eyewitness."

"They might have lied...."

"Me, Jassy. I'm talking about me. In the wrong place at the wrong time, as usual. I was just a kid, too wild for my own good and with half the brains I thought I had. I was doing some work for a small-time crook in Jacksonville, and I was running the high-stakes poker game where Sherman Delano brought his college buddy. They were drinking too much, they both got belligerent, and one of them was cheating. I couldn't tell which, and I didn't care. I kicked them both out of the game, but they weren't about to listen to some white trash kid who was younger than them to begin with. They kept quarreling, and the next thing I knew Delano was on the floor with a knife in his throat."

Jassy swallowed nervously. "It must have been self-defense...."

"The knife belonged to your brother. Delano was unarmed."

"But..."

"Unfortunately everyone else had cleared out when they realized trouble was brewing. The three of us were the only ones in the room. Your brother very calmly offered me a thousand dollars if I just got the hell out of there and never said anything to anybody. Since that was exactly what I was intending to do, it seemed reasonable enough to me. So he reached down and took the money from Delano's body." He shuddered slightly at the memory, a memory that had haunted him for years.

"But why didn't you go to the police?"

"The poker game was illegal, and I'd been on my own since I was fifteen, long enough to learn that the police were the last people you could trust. I didn't want to have anything to do with the whole stinking mess, I just wanted to get the hell away from there. I didn't get very far.

"Your brother waited until I left and then he called the cops. By that time the murder weapon had disappeared, so there was no problem with fingerprints. Your brother never even had to testify, so I never found out his real name. My court-appointed public defender talked me into plea-bargaining, and it seemed the smartest thing to do, considering that Florida was implementing the death penalty. So I did my time, and there wasn't a minute, a second of those three years that I didn't think about what I was going to do to that rich, spoiled kid and his daddy when I found them."

"His daddy?"

"Who do you think masterminded the whole thing?" Caleb said. "Harrison couldn't even do that much for himself. He called his daddy, and his daddy came running to bail him out. I saw him, just once, when I was going in for sentencing. A fine, upstanding southern gentleman, with his starched collar and his soft manicured hands. He looked right through me, like I wasn't even there, and kept on talking to your brother. That was when I decided I was going to kill him first."

"You were too late," she said, her voice dull and lifeless. "He died three years ago."

"I know. I can only hope it was slow and painful." Caleb was cold, savage, implacable.

"Cancer usually is," she said flatly. "So what happens when you kill Harrison? You got off lightly the first time, whether you did it or not. If it's premeditated you're far more likely to get the death penalty."

"It'll be self-defense."

"I beg your pardon?"

"I'm going to push him so hard he has to turn and fight. He'll make the first move."

"You don't know Harrison as well as I do. He's a physical coward. He'll send someone after you, rather than face you himself."

"He's tried that already and he didn't get very far. I'm not weak like Harrison. I'm patient. I've waited thirteen years. I can wait a few days, a few weeks longer."

She hadn't touched the coffee she'd professed to need, but he could see her hands were trembling as she held on to the mug. "So was I part of your master plan? If so, you miscalculated. Harrison wouldn't care if you slept with me—he wouldn't care if you'd slept with Lila even. He'd use anything to keep you away from him. But then, you knew that, didn't you? You overheard him suggesting I offer you a virgin sacrifice."

"Not quite virgin," he drawled, watching the flush mount her unnaturally pale cheeks.

"So I imagine my abasement was the only way you could get back at my father from beyond the grave."

It was like a punch in the gut, one he refused to react to. "Abasement?" he drawled. "Now I don't know if I would have put it quite that way. You didn't look abased as you writhed on top of me last night. But maybe I was misunderstanding your reactions. Maybe that was disgust that made you make those hot, hungry little sounds when I filled you. Maybe it was degradation that made you dig your nails into my back when you came. Maybe it was . . ."

"Maybe it was this morning, when you made me feel cheap and unwanted and in the way," she said, the color in her cheeks even brighter. "Maybe it was the way you made me fall in love with you, come to need you so much that I forgot about sanity, reality, family loyalty.''

"Love?" he mocked. "Don't be a fool! What the hell does love have to do with one helluva good roll in the hay? And what do you know about it?"

"What do you know about love?" she countered, her voice raw with emotion.

"Enough to know it doesn't exist," he said flatly.

She shook her head, and her thick mane of hair loosened around her face. "Then you're the one who's the fool," she said, her voice as calm as his.

They both heard the noise of the vehicle as it drove up to the house. For a moment neither of them moved, listening to the sound of male voices, the slam of a car door. Caleb leaned back against the counter, forcing the noticeable tension from the set of his shoulders. There was no way he could rid himself of the intensity eating at his gut, but he didn't need to advertise it.

"Maybe it's your brother, come to defend your honor," he said in a lazy drawl.

But she was beyond rising to his bait. Her face was pale, troubled, ignoring his taunt. "Something's not right," she said.

"You just discover that?"

She ignored him. "Why is it so quiet? Where is . . . ?"

At that moment Bo and Ray came into the kitchen, their huge, boisterous presence drowning out her words. "Hey, old man, you sleep late or something?" Ray demanded, not noticing the other occupant of the room. "You should have come to the bar with us last night. The women were hot and hungry. Not that Bo took advantage of the situation, but I sure as hell made up for him. You should have joined us."

"I don't think he needed to," Bo said quietly, looking at Jassy.

Ray turned to stare at him, and Caleb saw the calculating expression in the smaller man's eyes. Ray had always fancied himself a ladies' man, and any female was considered worthy prey. In the past Caleb had never objected—he wasn't the kind of man who put claims on the women he'd slept with. He wasn't going to put any claims on Jassy Turner, either. He was simply going to break Ray's teeth if he so much as touched her.

"Guess we should have knocked," Ray said. "You want us to make ourselves scarce?"

"No need," Caleb said, wishing them on the other side of the world. "Jassy was just getting ready to leave."

This time she didn't react, that troubled expression still in her eyes. "Caleb, where's Dog?"

Bo looked up from his shy perusal of the floor. "I was just about to ask the same thing. Where's the Hound from Hell? He usually keeps us penned in the truck until you call him off. You been giving him tranquilizers or something?"

"Hell," Caleb said, quiet and controlled. And he took off out the hallway at a dead run.

JASSY WAS THE ONE who found him. He was lying down by the stream, his eyes glazed and glassy, his huge, shaggy sides barely moving even as he struggled for breath. She screamed for Caleb, sinking beside the animal with a complete disregard for her own safety.

Bo was there first. "Don't touch him, Miss Turner. When a dog's hurt he'll turn on his best friend, and this one's always had an uncertain temperament."

Jassy ignored the warning, putting her hands on Dog's big head. For a moment he tried to lift it, and he focused on her, just barely managing a panting, doggy smile, before he sank back again, all his energy concentrated on breathing.

She put her body over him, listening for a heartbeat, hugging him in a useless effort to warm his ominously cool body. "Get Caleb," she said over her shoulder. "We've got to get him to a vet."

A moment later Caleb was on his knees in the muck beside her, his strong hands gentle as they pried Dog's clenched jaws apart. "Has he been shot?"

She sat up, tears blurring her vision. "Not that I can tell. I think—" Her voice broke, but she forced herself to say it, "I think he's been poisoned."

Caleb's light eyes were blank as they looked into hers. Both of them knew perfectly well who would have poisoned Dog—there was no need to say a word.

"Go start the van," Caleb said over his shoulder. "I'll carry Dog."

"Need any help?" Bo offered. "He's sure a handful."

"He'd still bite your hand off," Caleb said, scooping up the massive weight with seeming effortlessness. Only Jassy was close enough to see the strain in his muscle, feel the tension rippling through him. She trailed along after him to the van, preparing to climb in after them when Caleb managed to get Dog's limp body into the back, when his words forestalled her.

"Where do you think you're going?" he demanded. "Hasn't your family done enough? We don't need you."

"The hell you don't, turkey! Dog won't let anyone else near him, and he's too damned big for you to keep hold of all by yourself. And none of you know where the vet is. So shut your mouth and let me in."

She expected more of an argument. She never thought she'd see the light of grudging respect that might, in other circumstances, have held a trace of amusement. "Then don't waste your time talking," he said. "I don't know how much time he's got left."

The drive to the Roberts Veterinary Hospital was grim, fast and silent, broken only by Dog's labored breathing. Caleb didn't say a word, his face blank, emotionless, chilling. Even when Dog made a sudden, heartrending yelp of pain he didn't react, but Jassy watched his big hand clench in Dog's shaggy fur, almost involuntarily.

Jim Roberts was standing beside his truck, about to go out on his morning rounds, when they skidded into the yard. He started toward them, his earnest young face creased with concern, when he caught sight of Caleb Spenser struggling with his heavy burden.

"We think he's been poisoned," Jassy said, scrambling out after them. "We don't know how long ago—it may have happened last night. His breathing is steady but weak, so we brought him straight in...." Her voice trailed off as Jim made no move to come forward. Normally she would have expected all speed and efficiency from him, leading the way into the examining room and setting right to work. But he didn't move.

"I'm sorry," he said, his voice guilty and miserable.

Caleb stood still, shifting his heavy burden in his arms, and his face was cold. He glanced at Jassy. "He's not going to help us. Where's the nearest vet?"

"Don't be ridiculous," she snapped. "Of course he's going to help us. He's not going to ignore an animal in pain...." She looked back at Jim. She'd known him since grade school, a decent, bright, well-meaning boy. He still hadn't moved.

"Jassy, I can't!" he said, his voice pleading for understanding. "Your daddy got me into Cornell, he paid my way, damn it! I can't go against your family. Don't ask it of me."

Caleb had turned, heading for the van, his face grim and murderous. She reached out, grabbed his arm and held. "Wait right here," she said.

Releasing him, she crossed the dusty yard, ignoring the swelter of heat as it pressed down around her, ignoring her own mud-stained, ripped clothing. Reaching out, she took the lapels of Jim Roberts's jumpsuit in her strong hands and yanked, hauling his face down even with hers. "You're going to open up your examining room," she said fiercely, "and you're going to save that dog's life, and you're going to do it right quick. I don't give a damn how much my father did for you—you don't owe him your honor and decency. And if you're worried about loyalty, remember that I'm the colonel's child just as much as Harrison is. If you don't get your butt in gear I'm going to report you to the state veterinary board, or whoever it is who grants licenses, and you're going to be answering a lot of uncomfortable questions. You hear me, Jim Roberts?" She was shouting in his face, rage and frustration exploding out of her as she'd never allowed it to before. Jim was staring at her in absolute shock, and she jerked him one more time, just for good measure.

Then he nodded. "Bring him right in," he said, detaching himself from Jassy's fierce grip and heading for the infirmary.

Caleb hesitated, not moving. Jassy turned on him, still brimming with fury. "Get the hell in there. You can't afford to be picky. The nearest vet is a good forty miles away, and he's a drunk. Jim may be a wimp but he's a damned good doctor."

Caleb didn't wait any longer. Jim had already opened the doors, and Dog's huge weight couldn't have been an easy load. He walked past Jassy, carrying him effort-lessly, not bothering to look back at her.

Jassy watched them disappear into the examining room, and the sheer force of will vanished, leaving her trembling with reaction. She wanted to burst into tears, but that was hardly feasible, not with Ray and Bo staring at her with unabashed fascination. "You okay?" Bo asked, moving toward her.

"Sure," she said, her eyes bright with unshed tears. "I just need some coffee. I forgot to drink mine."

"I got a thermos in the van," Ray offered, his earlier leer forgotten. "I imagine we've got a bit of a wait."

He'd understated the matter. The three of them camped out in the waiting room, sharing the too-sweet coffee, barely talking, as the minutes, then hours, went by. There was no sign of Caleb, no sign of Jim or Dog. All they could do was sit and wait.

At one point Jassy tried to start a conversation, her years with Claire reminding her to practice her social graces, but neither men were in the mood to talk. Nor, for that matter, was she. She simply asked the question that mattered most. "What will happen if Dog doesn't recover?"

Ray stretched back and lit a cigarette in defiance of the No Smoking notice posted on the faux-paneled walls. "Now that all depends. Caleb might not make a fuss at all. He's always said that dog is a pain in the butt, and he's never been one for responsibilities and commitments. Dog was about all the commitment he cared to make, and I imagine he'd be just as happy to be free of it."

"If you believe that you're an idiot," Bo said flatly. "You shouldn't take Caleb at face value. He and Dog have been together a long time. I wouldn't like to be the man who poisoned him if he doesn't recover."

Jassy stretched her legs out in front of her. She'd managed to slip on her sandals before she'd run out to look for Dog, but tramping through the marshy land around the Moon Palace had liberally splattered her legs with mud. She wanted a hot bath, she wanted a drink, she wanted peace of mind. She'd get the first two. The last was a luxury she doubted she'd enjoy again for a long, long time.

"I've done everything I can do." Jim Roberts was standing in the doorway, exhaustion on his face. His jumpsuit was stained with blood, and he was alone.

"Is he dead?" Bo asked bluntly.

"Not yet. He's a tough old mutt, he might still make it. He's a fighter, but he was out there a long time before anyone found him. My guess is he...ate something tainted around midnight. That gave the stuff a hell of a long time to work in his system, and it's anybody's guess how bad the damage is."

Jassy closed her eyes in silent pain. While she and Caleb had been lying on the pool table, Dog had been alone and in pain. If Caleb didn't hate her before, he certainly did by now.

"I'm just going to have to keep a watch and see. The next few hours will make the difference. You might as well go home." Jim couldn't quite meet Jassy's eyes, and she knew the guilt he was feeling. Guilt, he more than deserved.

"Where's Caleb?" Bo demanded, lumbering to his feet.

Jassy expected Jim to say he was staying by Dog's side until the crisis passed. But Jim nodded his head in the direction of the yard. "He said he'd wait for you in the van. You want me to give you a ride home, Jassy?"

For a moment she considered it. Caleb probably didn't want to see her, and she wasn't positive she was in the mood to face his despair and anger. But she'd never been a coward in her life, and now wasn't the time to start. "Caleb can give me a ride home. I imagine you don't feel like facing Harrison right now." She kept the contempt out of her voice with an effort. In the end he had done everything he could to save Dog. It was up to fate to see whether it had been enough.

"That's a fact. Besides, I ought to stay here until my assistant shows up."

"Don't worry, little lady," Ray said, taking her arm. "I'll protect you from Caleb's temper."

"I wouldn't do that if I were you," Bo said mildly as they headed out into the blistering heat.

"Do what?"

"Put your hands on Caleb's lady."

"He's never been possessive before," Ray said in a defensive voice.

"There's a first time for everything."

Ray glanced toward the van. "Spoilsport," he said in an aggrieved tone, releasing her arm.

Caleb was sitting in the driver's seat, staring straight ahead, his hands draped loosely, casually over the steering wheel. He glanced up as they climbed into the van, his expression impassive. "We'd better get a move on," he said, his slow, deep voice devoid of feeling. "We've already wasted half the day."

Jassy stared at him. She'd had no choice but to climb into the front seat beside him—Bo and Ray had scrambled for the back. There was no sign whatsoever that Dog's eventual fate mattered to him, he merely looked impatient. "Would you mind dropping me off at Belle Rive on your way?"

"What about your car?" he asked with excruciating politeness.

"I can pick it up later."

"I'm not sure that's a good idea."

"Tough," she said, hoping to jar a reaction from him. It failed. He simply shrugged, started the van, and took off down the road, at a far more sedate pace then their headlong dash for help.

He stopped at the end of Belle Rive's long, curving driveway. "You'll forgive us if we don't drive you up to the front door," he said with exaggerated courtesy. "We're already behind on our work."

She sat there and stared at him for a moment, searching for signs of pain, of sorrow, of remorse, of caring in his bronzed, distant face. Not a trace. He wasn't even human, except that she knew differently. Every square inch of her body knew differently.

"You don't fool me," she said, reaching for the door handle.

"I hadn't intended to," he murmured in a bored voice. "You might be better off picking up your car before dark. We'll be off at a work site until then."

"But how will you get word about Dog?"

He shrugged again. "I'll find out sooner or later. Either he'll live or he'll die. There's nothing I can do about it, so I may as well get on with things. There's no room in this life for sentiment."

"Where will you be working? I can come out with word..."

"Goodbye, Jassy," he said, his tone of voice final.

She wasn't sure what she wanted to do. Scream at him. Cry. Or haul off and hit him. She sat there, motionless, silent, as she considered the possibilities, then decided against doing anything at all.

The two men were watching and listening with far too much interest. And if she hit him she was afraid of the consequences. Not that he'd hit her back. She had not the slightest trace of doubt that that was the last thing he'd do.

But that he'd kiss her. And that would do far more damage.

"Later, Caleb," she said firmly. And without another word she slid out of the van, slamming the door behind her.

Chapter Fifteen

Belle Rive was still and silent when Jassy let herself in the front door. The huge old grandfather clock in the front hall was just chiming the hour. Eleven o'clock. Jassy blinked at it in disbelief. It seemed days since they'd raced to the animal hospital, hours and hours and hours that they waited for word. She couldn't believe it was still before noon.

It explained why the house was empty, which suited Jassy just fine. She wasn't in the mood for a confrontation with Harrison, not yet. Not till she had time to absorb all the shocking things Caleb had said, not until she could decide what might have a kernel of truth to it. Not that she thought Caleb was lying to her. Whatever his faults, and they were legion, she didn't think he was a liar.

But he had to be mistaken. There had to be a reasonable explanation for the things he said. And the fact that Dog was struggling for life at Jim Roberts's place was a coincidence. He was obviously poisoned, but it had to be something like tainted meat, a wild mushroom, even a snake bite. No one could have deliberately set out to hurt a helpless animal.

Not that Dog was necessarily helpless. He was a big, oofy baby, but she could take other people's word for it that he could turn chillingly fierce when his loved ones were affected. If someone wanted to sabotage the Moon Palace, if someone wanted to sneak up on Caleb without warning him, then disposing of his guard dog was an effective first strike.

No, her mind screamed. It had to be a coincidence. She couldn't have spent all her life believing in her family, only to find her life of security was built on a foundation of lies. There had to be a reasonable explanation...there had to be.

She was heading up the stairs when she heard the insistent buzz of the telephone. She considered ignoring it. At that hour Claire would be sleeping off the effects of the previous evening, her shades drawn, her telephone extension turned off. Harrison would be in town, Lila had one of her never-ending doctor's appointments in her quest for pregnancy, and even Miss Sadie would be doing the morning shopping.

She could wait for the answering machine, but it might be Jim. Without another moment's hesitation she raced across the floor, grabbing the phone just as the answering machine clicked in.

"Mrs. Turner?" the voice at the other end was feminine, efficient, and Jassy didn't bother correcting her. "This is Dr. Bertram's office. The doctor asked me to call you and tell you there's really no need to repeat your husband's fertility test. His vasectomy was judged to be one hundred percent successful when it was performed five years ago. Unless he's interested in reversing the process there's no point in retesting."

"Five years ago?" Jassy said weakly. Harrison and Lila had been married for three years, had ostensibly been trying to get pregnant for the last two.

"Your husband made it clear that reversal was not something that he would consider. Has he changed his mind?"

Jassy sank onto the satin-covered chair by the phone. "I . . . I don't think so," she said numbly.

"Well," the woman said briskly, "if there's any way we can be of service please don't hesitate to call."

Jassy heard the platitude numbly. She made the only logical response. "Have a good day," she murmured in a faint voice, putting the receiver down.

Lies. Lies, and more lies. She'd spent hours holding Lila's hand while Lila wept over the bitterness of a fate that had made her barren with no discernible cause. And all the time there had been a very obvious cause. Harrison's selfishness, and Harrison's lies.

He'd never liked children, she'd always known that. And he'd never liked to share the center of attention. He was used to being cosseted and petted by the doting women of his family, his idiot sister included. The colonel had bailed him out of more trouble than Jassy could even begin to know about, and he'd always winked and smiled and said boys will be boys.

If Harrison could lie about something as elemental as this, if he could stand by and watch Lila go through a battery of painful, useless tests, if he could be sympathetic and patient, all the time knowing what was behind it and never say a word, then he was capable of anything. Possibly including murdering another boy in a blind rage and then letting someone else take the blame for it.

"You look like you've seen a ghost." Claire stood silhouetted in the garden doorway, the bright sunlight behind her.

Jassy swallowed her panicked shriek of surprise. "I didn't think you'd be up."

Claire stepped into the hallway, where Jassy could get a good look at her. Her silvery hair was neatly coiffed, there was a faint, healthy glow of color on her papery cheeks, and her eyes were clear. "I slept well for a change," she said with a careless shrug. "I thought I might do a bit on the garden. The men do their best, but they don't really understand roses."

"No, they don't," Jassy said lamely, knowing no such thing. One thing was clear; for once her mother had foregone her nightly tippling. Maybe in the face of family disaster there was a ray of hope after all. "Do you know where Harrison and Lila are?"

"Lila's at the doctor's again. She's been after Harrison to go in for more tests, but he's refusing. I understand his point. After all, he's been proven to be healthy. The problem is obviously with Lila, and she just can't admit it. The sooner she does, the sooner they can decide about adoption. Not that Harrison would ever agree," she said with a sigh. "He's a great believer in bloodlines. Personally I think our bloodlines could do with a fresh transfusion. But you know you can't reason with your brother."

"No," Jassy said flatly.

"I would like grandchildren," Claire went on in her mild voice. "If Harrison and Lila aren't able to provide me with any, you might consider paying attention to your own biological clock. You have any number of suitable beaux. Don't you think you might consider making your choice?"

Jassy closed her eyes for a moment, picturing a most unsuitable beau, someone wild and dangerous who'd already gone out of his way to reject her that morning. "I'm afraid I already have. For what good it will do me."

Claire looked at her, not saying a word, and Jassy had the odd notion that perhaps her mother knew her better than she'd ever imagined. "Things have a habit of working out for the best," she murmured, stripping off her gardening gloves and laying them on a side table.

"I don't know about that. I think disaster has a habit of crashing down." She stared out into the blazing sunlight, wishing it matched her gloomy mood.

"Perhaps," Claire agreed. "But it doesn't do any good to sit and wait for it. Will you join me in a glass of iced tea?"

For a moment Jassy didn't answer, distracted by the sudden memory of Caleb's hands on her body. Then she shook herself, forcibly banishing the rush of emotion. "After I change out of these muddy clothes." She started for the stairs, then paused. "Aren't you going to ask me where I was last night?"

"I have a fairly good idea."

"I'm in love with him," she said, shocking herself with the bald statement, hoping to shock her mother.

Claire simply smiled. "I know."

The front door swung open, and Jassy jumped nervously, wishing she'd had time to make it upstairs, to figure out how she was going to deal with the unwelcome information that had just come her way, when Lila and Harrison walked in the door. Lila was laughing, and her slender arm was tucked in Harrison's elegantly suited one. He was looking indulgent, handsome, even downright noble. And for the first time in her life Jassy hated her brother.

She didn't move, and for a moment they didn't see her, paused halfway up the winding stairs. Claire greeted them with calm affection. "What are you two so cheerful about?" she asked.

"We've decided to go on a cruise," Lila said. "Just go off for a couple of weeks and forget about babies and money and worries. Who knows, I might even come back pregnant."

Harrison patted her hand affectionately, and Jassy wanted to scream. Instead she gripped the smooth cypress stair rail, and the slight movement caught their attention. "When are you going?" she forced herself to ask.

"Day after tomorrow," Harrison replied, his eyes narrowing as he saw far too much in her rigid stance. "As soon as they can make the arrangements. I figured it might be good for both of us to get away from here."

Get away from Caleb Spenser's revenge, more likely, she thought. Or maybe provide himself with an alibi while another set of hired thugs tried to drive him away. "Sounds good to me," she said evenly. She started back up the stairs, paused, and turned around. "Oh, Harrison?"

"Yes, Jassy?"

"I had a long talk with the nurse at Dr. Bertram's office," she said in her sweetest, most innocent voice. "They thought you ought to come in for a recheck."

It wasn't Harrison's expression that frightened her. It was the absolute lack of it, as Lila let out a whoop of excitement, that sent a sudden tendril of dread down her spine. His handsome mouth curved in a polite smile, as his eyes were blank and chilly. "I appreciate that, Jassy," he said, his voice smooth and mellifluous. And suddenly Jassy was more frightened than she'd ever been around Caleb Spenser.

She dismissed the notion as absurd. Tossing her head, she gave him an equally phony smile. "Just thought I'd mention it," she said. "I'm going for a shower and a nap. I'll talk to you later."

"Yes," said Harrison grimly, ignoring the happy chattering of his wife and mother, "you will."

THE MOON PALACE was dark and deserted when Caleb drove up that evening. He'd ignored Bo's and Ray's offers of companionship, their invitations to come drinking, to play poker, to shoot the breeze and wait for word of Dog. He didn't need their heavy-handed sympathy. Hell, Dog was only a dog. A worthless mutt who'd lived off his generosity for a long time. The two of them rubbed along pretty well together, but that didn't mean he was going to go into some kind of decline if he didn't make it. Dogs didn't live as long as humans did. If you had a dog, you were bound to watch him die. He'd learned that as a kid, when the worthless crossbreed he'd bought for a dollar at the county fair had been killed. Dollar had been the first living creature he'd loved who'd loved him back unconditionally. When his father had shot him he'd learned about unconditional hatred.

He never should have fed Dog in the first place. Taken him in, fixed up his sores and bruises, taken him to a vet. Hell, there were always strays—he couldn't save the world. He told Jassy Turner that, when he should have been reminding himself.

He cursed then as he stepped into the empty house, suddenly remembering the hurt in her wide hazel eyes. He'd always been partial to blue eyes and blond hair. He'd never realized how beguiling, how downright hypnotizing that greeny brown shade could be. He had the uneasy feeling that he'd never like blue eyes again.

More sentimental crap, he told himself briskly, heading for the kitchen and a long-necked bottle of beer. He didn't need Jassy Turner, he didn't need Dog, he didn't need anybody. All he needed was a cold beer, and lukewarm shower, and something to eat, and he'd be as happy as a clam.

The shower didn't do much to ease his aching muscles. He'd spent too many days on his butt and not enough working. He'd worked today, worked so hard he'd hoped to blot everything out of his mind. Unfortunately things didn't work that way. But tomorrow he'd do it again. And again. Work his tail off, while he finished up with Harrison Turner. And then get the hell out of this steamy, godforsaken town and into a place with air-conditioning or at least a breeze.

He heard the distant rumble of thunder as he peered into his refrigerator, and he cast a sour look out into the gathering gloom. "You don't fool me," he said out loud. "Just more of a tease. Heat lightning, and nothing but." The contents of his refrigerator weren't encouraging. Dried-up cheese, moldy bread, several ancient casseroles. He slammed it again.

"The cupboard's bare," he said out loud, not thinking. "Sorry, Dog, you'll have to..." The words trailed off as he realized he was alone in the kitchen. Alone, as he'd always been.

He leaned his hands on the counter, and dropped his head down, staring at the cracked linoleum on the floor, staring as it fuzzed and faded, as inexplicable drops of wetness landed on his bare feet. He stood without moving for a long, long time, his muscles clenched with the need not to feel.

He almost didn't hear her come in. He didn't hear her car, or the front door open. He just knew. He looked up, and saw her, standing silhouetted in the doorway.

It was too dark to see her face, but her body was tense, wary, and he knew what she'd come to tell him. "He's dead," Caleb said flatly, no emotion in his voice whatsoever. He managed to sound bored by the whole thing, something he told himself he could be proud of.

She shook her head. "Jim says he's going to be fine. We can pick him up tomorrow morning."

For a moment Caleb didn't move. He tried a careless shrug, but it didn't work. Suddenly he felt like a ten-year-old kid again, tears streaming down his dirt-streaked face as he knelt in a dusty road and howled out his rage over the cruel injustices of life.

"Damn," he said, and his voice broke. "Damn."

In a moment she was there beside him, her arms wrapped around his waist, tight, her face pressed against his back. She held him, and for the first time since he was that ten-year-old kid he let the rage and grief out, shaking with it, as she held on for dear life.

When the first storm of emotion passed he turned in her arms, seeking her mouth blindly as he pulled her tight against him. She went willingly, and her own face was wet with tears. And suddenly he had to have her, now, immediately, not to blot out his feelings, but to celebrate them, feel them, feel them all.

He lifted her, moving her backward to the solid oak table, shoving the dishes off it onto the floor and pushing her back. He yanked at her clothes, and she helped him, ripping off her loose T-shirt as he stripped off her panties beneath the full skirt. By the time he unfastened his jeans he was fully aroused and ready for her, beyond ready. Pulling her legs around his hips, he sank into her wet, sleek warmth, feeling her shudder with pleasure as her hands reached up and caught his arms as he braced himself on the table. Her fingers dug into his skin as her eyes closed, and he watched her face as he drove into her, hard, watched the pleasure ripple through her skin, until her huge hazel eyes opened with a kind of shocked surprise, and she made a funny little catching sound in the back of her throat that could have been his name, and then he felt the unmistakable convulsions around him, convulsions his own body answered, as he pulsed and exploded within her.

It was all he could do to keep standing at the edge of the table. His body was trembling, his muscles weak, and he felt like crawling on top of the heavy maple and sinking onto her. But she was trembling, too, her eyes open now with shock and maybe self-consciousness, and he didn't want her to be self-conscious. He wanted to make love to her in every place, every way, until she forgot to be embarrassed and shy.

Carefully he pulled away, catching her hands as she tried to pull her skirt down. "Don't be ridiculous," he said in a husky voice, as he unfastened the side button with slightly trembling fingers. She let him, too bemused to stop him, as he stripped the rest of her clothes off, then stepped out of the jeans that had been shoved halfway down his legs, kicking them across the kitchen floor.

He reached down for her, lifting her into his arms, and she was shivering in the steamy heat of the kitchen. Outside heat lightning snaked across the landscape, followed by a distant rumble of thunder, and he held her close against him, letting his heat sink into her. He carried her into the bedroom without a word, putting her down on the mattress and following her down, drawing her into his arms and telling himself she needed reassurance, comfort. Knowing he needed them just as much.

Slowly her shivering stopped. She reached up to touch his face, her fingers smoothing the dampness away, and she managed a tentative smile. "It's all right to feel things, you know," she said, her voice not much more than a whisper. "It's all right to hurt."

He wanted to deny it, but it would have been a waste of time. He rolled onto his back, taking her with him, tucking her head against his shoulder. She sighed, as the last bit of tension left her body, and she was warm and pliant against him, completely trusting. "I don't want to," he said, his voice rusty in the shadowy room.

"I know."

He considered that. "You shouldn't be here," he said finally, keeping his arm around her, keeping her tucked at his side. Not that she was making any effort to leave.

"Why not?"

"Because I'm trash. I may not be a murderer, but there's not much else I haven't done, or wouldn't do. I was born bad—my daddy told me that from as early as I can remember, and I did my best to live up to it."

"Nice father," Jassy said. "What made him such an authority?"

"Hell, my daddy knew everything about right and wrong. He was a preacher man, an old-fashioned, Bible-thumping, scripture-quoting, devil-wrestling man of God. He knew a spawn of the devil when he saw one."

"If he was your father then you must have been his spawn."

"Exactly," Caleb said, exhaling, forcing some of the tension from his body. "My daddy warned me I was born to raise hell, and he did his best to beat repentance into me. It took me a while to realize he was trying to beat repentance into himself, and I was just a convenient outlet. He was shot by a jealous parishioner who found him in his wife's bed, and I took off. But I've got his gift. A sweet-talking ladies' man, just like my old man, and worth about as much."

"Caleb..."

"Don't try to convince me of my essential goodness, Jassy," he said, shoving a hand through his hair as he stared up at the old tin ceiling. "Don't try to tell me my father was full of crap. I know that. And I know I'm just as bad. I don't have any illusions about this life or myself."

"Then maybe you need some." She sat up, her thick, curly hair hanging around her, for once completely unselfconscious about her nude body. "You're a good man, Caleb Spenser. You hate to admit it, but no matter how hard you try to be a no-good waster you end up doing the right thing."

"You think coming here to kill your brother out of revenge is the right thing? You think going after you as part of my grand scheme, no matter how much it hurt you, was the right thing?"

She didn't move, as her body seemed to absorb the blow, considering whether it was fatal or not. And then she lifted her head. "You went to bed with me last night as a way to get back at my brother?" She sounded frankly skeptical.

He considered lying. In the long run it might be the kindest thing to do for her, but right then he wasn't feeling kind and self-sacrificing. Right then he needed her, needed her too badly to be noble. "No. I took you to bed because I couldn't stand to be without you for another moment."

She smiled then, a sweet upturning of her mouth, and without thinking he pulled her down to him, tasting that mouth, feeling it soften against his while his body hardened against hers. When she pulled back a moment she reached out and pushed his long, damp hair away from his face. "You're not going to kill my brother," she said, her voice soft and certain. "You're not going to break my heart, either. There's a lot more possibilities in this life than you're even considering. There are happy endings."

"Not for me."

"Sorry," she said firmly. "But I don't intend to settle for less. And it's come to the point where my happy ending is dependent on yours. So you're going to have to accept it."

"You can't go around saving lost souls," he said.

"I can if I love them enough."

"You don't love me. We have good sex together. Hell, we have terrific sex together. The best. But that's not love."

Nothing was going to dent her certainly. He could probably shove her off the makeshift bed and she'd simply climb back on. "The best?" she asked, looking pleased. "I didn't have much to compare it to but it certainly was astonishing to me. I figured maybe that was the way it was supposed to be."

He didn't know whether to shake her or kiss her. To laugh or to cry. "It's supposed to be that way," he said, "but it seldom is. Life would be a lot less complicated if it were. Fewer divorces."

"Fewer divorces? Is that a proposal?"

"Jassy," he said with a warning sigh.

"Never mind, Caleb. I don't want to argue with you. There are a lot of better things we can do."

He looked at her warily. He didn't know when an uptight, semi-virgin suddenly became such a threat to his plans and his well-being. If he'd had any notion she was going to turn his life upside down he would have kept his distance. If he could have. "Like what?" he said.

She levered forward, her hair hanging around them, her lips brushing his, as her small, perfect breasts brushed his chest. "Use your imagination," she whispered. "We've got all night."

"Shameless," he murmured against her mouth, as he reached for her. "Completely, wonderfully shameless." He cupped her face, pushing her back for a moment, denying himself the distraction of her increasingly inventive mouth. "And what happens in the morning?"

"I turn back into a pumpkin," she said. "And you turn back into a rat."

He didn't move. "God help me," he murmured. And he kissed her, hard, and there were no more words.

Chapter Sixteen

"I need to go home," Jassy murmured, her face buried against Caleb's shoulder.

"Um-hmm," he agreed, not moving.

It was morning. How early, Jassy had no idea. All she knew was she didn't want to move. She wanted to spend the rest of her life wrapped around Caleb Spenser. If she got up and went home she'd have to face Harrison.

She couldn't pretend as if nothing had happened. She needed to hear Harrison's side of the story—she owed him that at least. It would most likely be a pack of self-serving lies, ones he probably didn't realize weren't the truth. That was the way people's minds worked. Few people did wicked things and reveled in their evil. They somehow worked out a justification for it all, to a point where they no longer realized they'd done anything wrong. She'd known Harrison all her life, had helped bail him out of trouble since she was old enough to lie for him. She could practically write the scenario herself.

"I don't want to talk to Harrison," she said out loud. Caleb's muscles tensed beneath her, but his hand didn't stop stroking her arm.

"Then don't. What do you expect to accomplish? Do you expect to find out the truth?"

"I don't think my brother knows what the truth is anymore. But I need to tell him why I'm leaving."

This time the stroking of her arm halted. "Leaving?" he echoed, his voice flat. "Where are you going?"

She sat up then, and he made no move to stop her. His face was remote again, unreadable in the early-morning light. "With you?"

He didn't say a word. It took all her self-control to be patient, to wait for him to say something. She wanted to scream at him, to beat on him with her fists, but she waited.

Slowly he shook his head. "It won't work."

"Why not?"

"There's too much between us. Don't look like I kicked your dog, Jassy, you know I'm right. It doesn't matter how good we are together. The fact remains that I spent three years in prison for a crime I didn't commit, and I was put there by your brother's lies. It doesn't matter how much I care about you. I'm still going to destroy your brother."

"And then you'll go back to jail, maybe to the electric chair. They kill people for premeditated murder in this state, Caleb. And you've certainly made it clear to any number of witnesses that you're out for Harrison's blood."

"I have no intention of killing your brother," he said wearily. "Much as the thought gives me a certain satisfaction. There's more than one way to destroy someone. You can take their money, their reputation, their family from them, so that they have nothing left. Then they might as well be dead, and maybe they'll take care of it themselves. Either way, I'll have my revenge."

"And revenge is more important than me?" She knew she shouldn't ask him. She was forcing him to choose, and she wasn't going to be able to live with that choice.

"Yes," he said flatly, and she couldn't be certain if there was doubt in his clear, light eyes or whether she was just clinging to a vain thread of hope.

But she couldn't beg. Couldn't weep and plead, bargain or argue. She climbed off the high bed, for once unselfconscious in her nudity. "Then there's nothing more I can do," she said. She walked into the kitchen, picking up her scattered clothes from the floor and pulling them over her. At least this time he hadn't torn them off her, she thought, fastening the button of her loose skirt. When she walked back into the bedroom he hadn't moved. He lay on the mattress, the white sheet pulled up to his hips, his face as cool and calm as the day was hot and windy.

She waited for him to ask her not to leave, to reach out his strong, tanned hand for hers, and she would have climbed right back up on that absurd bed with him. But he didn't. He didn't say a word, just continued to watch her out of distant, hungry eyes.

"How long do you think this is going to take?" she asked.

She'd managed to startle him. "How long is what going to take?"

"Your grand scheme of revenge. How long will it take you to ruin my brother?"

She'd asked the question in a calm enough voice, and he answered her in the same way, sitting up in the bed and watching her. "He's already managed to bring himself to the brink of financial ruin, with his gambling and his other women. One stiff breeze and it'll topple like a house of cards."

"All the family money is tied up together, including mother's and mine. Does that mean that we're going to be paupers as well?"

"Yes."

She nodded, refusing to flinch at the brutal news. After all, that wasn't his fault, it was Harrison's, and theirs, for trusting him. "What about the rest? What about his friends? What about his family?"

"His friends will drop him when they learn he's lost his money, his home, through dishonest dealings. It's too late to prove anything that happened thirteen years ago, but I have friends in the press who just love to muckrake, and they don't need a whole lot of concrete evidence if they're convinced of the facts."

"And his family?"

"His wife has been turning a blind eye to his extracurricular activities. She won't be able to do that once it's published. And Claire's more interested in the bottle than she is in Harrison."

"So that leaves me."

"That leaves you," he agreed. "The loyal, self-sacrificing sister, who does everything for everybody. Are you going to stand by him, hold his hand as he faces ruin?"

She moved to the edge of the bed, close enough for him to touch if he reached out his hand. Close enough to reach him if he gave her any sign. "Do I have anyplace else to go?" she asked quietly.

He closed his eyes for a moment, as pain washed over his face. "What do you want from me, Jassy? I can't be the kind of man you deserve. I can't give you what you need."

"You already have."

"We're not talking about sex, damn it, we're talking about life!"

"You are my life," she said desperately. "You're the air that I breath, the blood in my veins. I existed before you, existed on a diet of good works and doing for others. You showed me what it was like to be alive. You gave me a taste of a feast, and I don't want to go back to the way it was before. Weak tea and cucumber sandwiches and bridge parties, and people with ice water in their veins. I want to live, Caleb. I want to live with you."

She didn't wait for his answer. She was too afraid of what it might be. She turned and ran.

She'd managed to stop crying by the time she turned into the long, winding driveway to Belle Rive. The dashboard clock read a surprising 11:15. The day was dark, overcast and stiflingly warm at that hour in the morning, and the breeze that riffled through the live oaks was a hot, angry one. A storm wind, she thought as she parked the car haphazardly. Maybe a hell of a storm, to blow away all the misery and lies that festered in Turner's Landing.

She heard the sound of voices as she let herself in the front door, and she paused there, silent, still. Harrison was home in the middle of the day, not that unlikely an occurrence, but still something she hadn't counted on. For a moment she was tempted to sneak upstairs, lock her bedroom door until she was ready for the confrontation she knew was inevitable. She could hear Claire's plaintive tones, that faint whine in her voice that was tinged with a slur, and a sudden foreboding filled her. Ignoring her original intention, she turned and walked into the living room, in time to see Harrison handing Claire a tall glass of clear iced liquid. One that certainly wasn't ice water.

"Isn't it a little early for vodka?" she asked abruptly.

Claire jumped, startled, a guilty expression on her pale face. "Jassy, you frightened me," she said, placing a trembling hand against her narrow chest.

"Did I?" Jassy walked into the room, past her brother. "You don't need a drink at this hour."

"How dare you talk to me like that?" Claire said in a weak attempt at bravado. "And you know perfectly well I don't drink anything more than a little light wine. That's ice water...Jassy!" she shrieked as Jassy took the glass out of her hand and took a swallow.

The vodka hit her like a taste of liquid fire. He hadn't even bothered to water it down, and the two ice cubes were more for decoration. Jassy looked down at the glass, wanting to hurl it through the French doors in sudden rage. Except that her rage and hurt were for Caleb, not her mother.

She set the glass back down on the table beside her mother with a quiet little click, as she pulled her emotions back tightly around her. "I can't stop you from drinking," she said quietly. "It's your life, and your body. But you ought to think twice before you let Harrison bring you down."

She walked from the room, not bothering to look at her, her contempt and dislike too overwhelming.

He caught up with her at the top of the stairs, and his hands were hard, painful on her arm. Why hadn't she noticed what a bully he was before, she wondered, tugging uselessly at her arm.

"What the hell did you mean by that crack?" he demanded, and she could see the slight bulge of vein at his temple, the fury in his eyes. "Mama's drinking problem isn't my fault."

"She's been sober the past few days. You were the one handing her a tall glass of vodka, Harrison."

"You're a fine one to pass judgment. Where the hell were you all night? You come home looking like a slut, smelling of sex, and you dare to act like I'm the bad guy."

The pain in her arm was intense, shockingly so. For a moment she wondered whether he might actually break her arm. "I was sleeping with Caleb Spenser. That's what you told me to do, isn't it? Aren't I the obedient little sister, always ready to do my best for you?"

He shook her, hard, and she half expected to hear the bone crack. "What's he been saying to you? It's all lies, you know that. Who are you going to believe, a convicted murderer or your own brother?"

"I don't know who to believe anymore," she said coolly, trying to ignore the faintness that was closing in around her. She stopped trying to pull free, hoping he'd loosen his vicious grip. "And you forget, I've talked to more people than Caleb. What about Dr. Bertram's office?"

He looked dark, wary and very dangerous. "What about Dr. Bertram's office?" he asked in a cold, evil voice.

"You had a vasectomy five years ago, a little fact that you failed to mention to your wife as she's gone through extensive fertility testing. There's no problem with Lila's fertility. Just in her choice of husbands."

They both heard the gasp of horror. Lila was standing in her doorway, her face pale, eyes red and swollen from earlier tears.

It happened so fast Jassy couldn't be clear. Harrison uttered a filthy word beneath his breath, and finally released her arm. Released it as he shoved her, as hard as he could, toward the deadly marble floor at the bottom of the long flight of winding stairs.

Someone screamed, Jassy, or Lila, or maybe Claire, who'd come out into the hallway during the last few moments. The world tilted as Jassy fell, floating, dizzy, flying through the air toward certain death.

She slammed up against the railing and it took a few breathless, hysterical moments to realize that she'd managed to grab the banister and break her fall. Struggling for breath, she looked up to the top of the stairs, to see Harrison backhand Lila across the face. And watched, as Lila took it with nothing more than a resigned whimper.

The bedroom door slammed behind them, and through her struggles for breath Jassy could hear the sound of Lila's quiet weeping. A moment later Claire was standing over her, her hands gently removing Jassy's death clutch on the banister. "You shouldn't have riled him," she said quietly. "You've always underestimated Harrison. He's got a streak of meanness that shouldn't be tampered with." She surveyed her daughter critically. "You're all right, aren't you?"

Jassy stood up, her knees trembling, her hands shaking. "In one piece." Both women heard a thud, and Jassy started up the stairs purposefully, when Claire caught her arm, holding her back.

"Don't do it," she said quietly. "You'll only make it worse."

"I'm not going to sit by and let my own brother beat his wife," she said savagely.

"She's used to it. If you interfere she won't thank you. She knows best how to calm him down."

"You can't be defending him...."

"I'm not. I just know the best way out of these things," Claire said quietly. "The less fuss you make, the sooner these things blow over. Harrison's a good husband in other ways, a good son. These little incidences don't happen that often.''

"Little incidences?" Suddenly Jassy wanted to throw up. There was quiet from the room upstairs, just the muffled sound of voices as the violence passed. "Go back to your vodka, Mother," she said coldly. "I'm getting out of here." She pushed past her, starting back down the stairs.

"Where are you going?"

For a moment she thought of the Moon Palace, of Caleb Spenser's bleak face and beautiful body, then dismissed that notion as effectively as he'd dismissed her. "I'm not sure. Just away from here."

SHE WASN'T USED TO running away. She wasn't used to backing down from abusive husbands or sticky situations. But that hot August day things suddenly became too much for her. She ran, driving her little Ford Escort as fast as she could, away from Turner's Landing. Away from love, and betrayal, and pain that she simply wasn't ready to face, ran until the gray, stormy day turned into darkness, and she found herself at the edge of the swamp road.

She'd stopped at the women's shelter long enough to take a shower and grab a change of clothing from the neat closet full of donations. She took a couple of moth-eaten blankets, a lumpy pillow and a little bit of food, and then struck out for Rowdy's cabin. The darkness of the afternoon sent little tendrils of unease through her, and the intermittent streaks of lightning made her jump, but she forced herself to ignore them. The storm was nothing but a lie, an empty promise of rain that would never come. The rumble of thunder was another lie, and she'd had enough of lies.

The path through the swamp was trampled down, more than she'd remembered, and she wondered if hunters had been out there, using Rowdy's makeshift cabin. For a moment she was tempted to turn back. She wasn't in the mood to face interlopers at this point, or to stake her claim to a shack that was falling into the swamp. And then she stiffened her back. She'd accepted defeat too many times in one day. She wasn't giving up the last thing that mattered to her.

The air was thick with humidity and a dark, shadowy mist was rising from the swamp. The rumble of thunder had become a steady companion by the time she reached the clearing at the edge of the water, and it took her a moment to focus, another to believe what she was seeing.

The fresh lumber was piled beside the cabin, and the smell of freshly sawn pine mingled with the scent of damp vegetation. The roof was already replaced, the door rehung, the rotten boards on the porch now white and shiny new. The building still sagged precariously, but some of the thick posts that lay in the pile of lumber must be intended for shoring it up. He was going to save it for her, even when he'd told her it was a lost cause.

She wanted to cry, but she'd cried too much that day, and there were no more tears left. Besides, she was no longer sure what her tears would be for. There was no reason for him to work on her hopeless cabin. Except that he cared for her, much as he tried to deny it.

She was tired, so tired, that she just tossed her bedding onto the rickety old cot and collapsed on top of it, ignoring the food she'd brought, ignoring the gathering storm outside. With the new roof and door she'd be safe if miracles still occurred and they actually got some rain. She didn't need to worry.

She had no idea what time it was. She hadn't bothered to bring matches or a flashlight, and the darkness was growing thick and heavy around her. She hadn't had much sleep in the last forty-eight hours, and she was so tired she thought she could sleep forever. Her last thought, as she closed her eyes and let exhaustion take over, was that it was far too dark for five o'clock in the afternoon.

SHE DREAMED of violence. Of blood and death and anger, of rage so deep that the world shook and roared. When she opened her eyes finally she discovered it was no dream. All hell had broken loose.

The rain had come, finally. And not just rain. A violent, soaking downpour that was pounding against the new roof, soaking through the thin pine walls, puddling on the floor as it seeped underneath the door. The lightning was coming at regular, breathless intervals, barely moments apart, lighting up the blackness with eerie brightness. Jassy scuttled back on the cot, fighting the panic that beat down around her, as she listened to the storm scream in fury.

She'd never felt so alone in all her life. A few miles away her mother would be quietly drinking herself into a stupor, or maybe she'd already passed out. Harrison and Lila were probably in the honeymoon stage that inevitably followed an episode of violence. He'd promise all sorts of things, and she'd believe him, because she wanted to so desperately.

As for Caleb, he'd dismissed her from his mind. He was probably sitting in the kitchen of the Moon Palace, drinking beer and planning his vengeance. If he thought of her at all it might be with regret that it was the wrong time and place. But he'd shrug and accept it. And then forget it, as he concentrated on what was important to him.

God, what a pitiful mess she was, she thought. Sitting huddled in a decrepit shack, feeling sorry for herself. She needed to get off that cot and figure out how she was going to get out of the situation she'd gotten herself into. And then she'd figure out how she was going to fix everything else. She wasn't one to accept defeat easily. She was tired and emotional now, but it wouldn't last. If she couldn't have Caleb Spenser, she could at least see what she could do about the rest of her family.

No, damn it. Maybe she'd better see what she could do about her own life, and let the rest of her family figure out their own problems. She couldn't fix everything, hadn't Caleb told her that time and time again? Right now she wasn't even sure she could fix the unpleasant situation she was currently in.

The water was ankle deep on the cabin floor when she climbed off the cot. The door was stuck, and she struggled with it for a moment, only to have it jerked out of her hands by the furious wind. It slammed against the side of the cabin, and splintered, half of it hanging on the newly replaced hinges, the other half floating into the swamp.

Jassy backed into the cabin in panic at the fury of the storm. As she watched, a huge live oak toppled over with a great rending sound, missing the roof of the cabin by no more than a few feet. This was no ordinary storm raging. This was something of biblical proportions, and Jassy was trapped, with no ark in sight.

Her shoes were floating away in the murky light, and she dived for them, slipping and falling on her knees in the water. There were creatures around her, frightened inhabitants of the swamp struggling to find safety in a storm that had uprooted their lives along with the tree, and Jassy scrambled to her feet in panic, remembering the alligators, the cottonmouths that usually kept away from their natural enemy, man.

She had two choices. She could stay huddled in the flooded cabin and hope the storm would pass. Or she could strike out in the darkness, trying to find the path that would now be several inches deep in water, and hope she didn't stumble deeper into the swamp.

She didn't like either choice. At that moment something slithered by her leg in the deepening water, and she screamed, jumping onto the rickety table and pulling her legs under her.

The table wasn't made for a hundred-plus pounds of frightened female. It creaked and shifted beneath her, and she knew it was going to collapse without much help from her. She moaned, a frightened little sound, but the noise of the wind swept the noise away. She sat there on the table, huddled in the darkness, and wondered what in God's name was going to happen to her.

She heard the curses first. Rich, inventive profanity over the howl of the wind as his shadow filled the broken doorway. A flashlight swept the room, finally landing on her as she crouched on the table, and his cursing increased.

"What the hell are you doing out here?" Caleb shouted furiously, wading through the water that was now calf deep. "Don't you listen to the radio? Don't you pay any attention to the weather? For God's sake, you've lived here all your life, don't you know there are hurricanes this time of year?" He took her shoulders in his hands, and she knew he wanted to shake some sense into her. Instead he pulled her into his arms, and she could feel the faint tremor in his iron-hard muscles, and knew that imperceptible weakness came from relief.

She buried her face in his neck, against the cool wetness of his rain poncho, and clung tightly, so tightly she thought she'd never let go. He held her just as fiercely as another tree thundered down into the swamp nearby.

"We've got to get the hell out of here," he said thickly. "This cabin isn't going to last much longer in this kind of wind."

"But the work you've done . . ."

"I told you it would be a waste of time." He held her away for a moment, and the movement made the precarious table collapse underneath her, sending her tumbling into the water. He caught her, of course, swearing again. "You don't have any shoes?"

"They floated away."

"Then I'll have to carry you."

"Caleb . . ."

"Don't argue with me, Jassy. We don't have time." He bent down in the water. "Climb on my back."

She didn't say a word. She climbed on, wishing she hadn't eaten cheesecake last week, wishing, if she were going to die, that at least she'd die in bed with Caleb. He started out into the rain. "Keep your head down," he shouted, and the wind took his voice and hurled it into the darkness. "And say your prayers."

And he started out into the raging hell of the hurricane.

Chapter Seventeen

Jassy couldn't see, couldn't hear, couldn't breathe in the raging turmoil of the storm. She buried her face against Caleb's back and held on, shuddering as the thunder and lightning crashed around them. He moved steadily, surely, his body buffeted by the fierce winds but seemingly untroubled by her weight as the rain poured down over their heads.

Over the shriek of the winds she heard a loud, rending sound, and she lifted her head, jerking around and almost throwing Caleb off balance. Through the sheets of rain she could see the collapsed shell of the cabin as it floated on the rising waters of the flood.

"Hold still!" he shouted, though she could only guess what he was saying through the noise of the storm. She put her head down, clinging tighter, and wept as the only thing that had ever been hers and hers alone was washed away.

It took centuries to cross the water-filled pathway back to the cars. She was convinced he must have set out in the wrong direction, that they were heading out into the middle of the swamp and certain death, and she was unsure whether she minded or not. As long as she was wrapped tightly around him, the insanity of nature couldn't frighten her.

And then he stopped, sliding her down onto solid ground, and she staggered, falling against the solid wet metal of his pickup. Yanking the door open, he pushed her inside, then waded around to the driver's side.

For a moment the comparative silence was deafening. Even with the roar of the wind outside the truck, the grinding energy of the engine as he turned the key, his muttered, continuous cursing under his breath, it felt suddenly peaceful. She leaned back, closing her eyes, and let out a long, shaky breath of relief.

"You'd better hold on," he muttered. "This isn't going to be an easy ride."

That was, if anything, an understatement. She barely had time to appreciate the consummate, desperate skill in his driving as he dodged floating tree trunks, debris, even the corpse of a dead deer, as he raced through the rapidly deepening flood waters. The truck was built high, the water only coming partway up the wheels, but Jassy knew that area far too well. With the steady, deadly downpour, the waters could rise rapidly, as riverbanks overflowed and saturated land could no longer absorb the rainfall.

"Where are we going?" she shouted over the noise of the storm.

"My place," he muttered, not taking the time to even glance in her direction as he concentrated on the dangerous driving.

"But it's near the swamp. It'll be flooded...and it's old. It might not withstand these winds...."

"I wouldn't have bought it if it weren't as solid as a rock," Caleb shot back. "And it's set higher than it looks. Higher than Belle Rive, for that matter. You'll be safe enough there."

"My mother," Jassy said. "I've got to make sure she and Lila are all right. When I left ..."

"Harrison will take care of them."

"Harrison will take care of himself," she said bitterly. "If you won't take me there I'll walk."

"You mean you'll swim," he said bitterly, jerking the wheel of the truck to avoid a thick tree limb. The turnoff to the Moon Palace loomed up, and he slowed the truck. Then he cursed, stomped his foot on the accelerator, and shot past it. "You're a pain in the butt, you know that," he muttered. "I'm not in the lifesaving business. Your mother and sister-in-law can fend for themselves."

"Then why are you driving me to Belle Rive?"

"To get rid of you?" he suggested.

She pushed her sopping hair out of her face, wiping away some of the moisture. "Nope."

"Don't start with me, Jassy. This isn't the time or place to argue."

"I'm not arguing. I'm—" Her calm voice deteriorated into a panicked shriek as Caleb slammed on the brakes, throwing them both hard against the dashboard. One of the huge live oaks had come down across what Jassy could only assume was the driveway to Belle Rive. The rain was too heavy to be certain, but she thought she could see the pale bulk of the house in the distance.

Without hesitation she opened the truck door, ready to jump out, when Caleb hauled her back in. "You'll never make it," he said. "Stay put and let me go."

"Not on your life. It's my family, my responsibility, not yours," she shouted back, struggling.

She hadn't realized how strong he was, or how he'd held back when he'd touched her before. He wasn't holding back this time. There was no way she could break free of his grip, no way he couldn't overpower her.

"Your family can take care of itself," he said. "You don't need to risk your life for them."

She became very still. "You're right," she said in her calmest possible voice. "They're probably safe and sound in town somewhere."

Under normal circumstances he wouldn't have been fooled. But with the violence of the storm raging around them, he took her word and released her, putting the truck in reverse.

She was out in the rain before he'd even let up on the clutch. She heard his shout of rage follow her into the stormy night, and then nothing but the solid noise of the storm as she fought her way toward the house.

The house was pitch-dark when she staggered in the front door. "Lila!" she screamed. "Mother! Is anyone here?" Silence answered her, and she wondered if she'd been a crazy fool to risk her own life for a family that was more than capable of taking care of themselves. She called out again, prepared to head to the highest part of the house and wait out the storm, when she heard a noise. It sounded like a cat, a weak, mewling sound, coming from the living room. Except there were no cats at Belle Rive. Harrison wouldn't allow it.

She moved slowly across the marble floor, ignoring the puddles her soaking clothes were making, ignoring the thin layer of water that was seeping in from the terrace. The living room was full of dark, huddled shapes, until the lightning flashed once more, and she could see someone curled up in a corner.

It was Lila.

Jassy rushed to her side, stubbing her bare feet on the overturned furniture, and sank onto the floor beside her sister-in-law. "Lila, are you all right?" she asked urgently. She reached to put protective arms around her, but

Lila flinched away in terror, letting out that strange, miserable little cry. "Where's Claire, Lila?" she forced herself to ask calmly.

Through the almost constant flashes of lightning Jassy could see Lila fight to control herself. "I don't...know," she said finally, her voice muffled. "In her room..."

"We've got to get you out of here," Jassy said briskly. "It's flooding, and I don't know how strong the foundations are of this old place. Let me help you out to the car and then I'll go back for mother. There are some trees down, but if I drive across the lawn we should be able to make it."

"Harrison..."

"Is he here?"

"I don't know," Lila moaned.

"We won't worry about him. Harrison can take care of himself." She put her arms around Lila, feeling her shiver. "Stand up, Lila. We need to get you out of here." Slowly, carefully, she pulled her to her feet, and the lightning flashed again, illuminating her face.

Jassy sucked in her breath in shock, but the sound of the storm covered the noise. Lila staggered, then righted herself, wrapping an arm around her waist, and it took all of Jassy's concentration to ignore the rage that swept over her. Lila had been beaten, so badly she could scarcely see, scarcely stand, and there was no question at all as to who had done it.

They moved through the hallway toward the front door when a tall male figure loomed out of the shadows. Lila screamed then, a sound of such heartrending panic that Jassy almost screamed, too. And then the lightning flashed again, and she knew it was Caleb.

"Take her to the truck," he said tersely, making no move to touch her, understanding far too much without even being able to see. "Where's your mother?"

"Passed out upstairs, I think," Jassy said.

"I'll get her. What about Harrison?" Caleb said.

"I don't know."

"No," Lila said in a panic. "I can't go. He'll kill me. Don't, Jassy, please . . ."

Her babbling pleas made no sense at all. Jassy uttered soothing noises as she led her toward the storm. "Don't worry, Lila. Everything will be all right. You'll see. Just come with me. Caleb's truck is out there, and it's warm and dry and safe. We'll get out of here, and you'll be fine, just fine."

For a moment the fear left Lila. She stood still in the open doorway of the old house, silhouetted against the lightning-filled sky. "Don't you realize, Jassy," she said, "that it will never be all right again?"

Jassy cast a glance over her shoulder, but Caleb was already sprinting up the wide, curving stairs toward Claire's bedroom. She didn't bother wondering how he knew his way around the place—it was one of those things Caleb would know. She had to simply trust that he'd be able to find Claire in the darkness and get her out of there safely. Someone had to get Lila to the truck, and she wasn't in any shape to tolerate the help of a man.

The water was ankle deep by the time she got Lila safely stowed. They'd slipped, climbing over the massive trunk of the fallen oak tree, and the Spanish moss had tangled in their legs. "Stay put," Jassy shouted through the rain. "We'll be back in a moment."

"Harrison," Lila moaned, and Jassy wasn't sure whether she was afraid they wouldn't find him. Or afraid they would.

"Stay put," she said again, striking off back toward the house.

The sky was a little lighter as she looked toward the huge old house, illuminated against the angry sky, and she wondered whether the merciful eye of the storm might be approaching, allowing them enough time to get to safety before the next torrent hit. But there seemed no letup to the buckets of rain, and she realized with sudden horror that the brightness around Belle Rive was no longer the streaks of lightning but the bright glow of a burning building.

She started running. She stepped on something sharp and painful, fell face first into the rising waters, and then rose and ran again, ignoring the pain, ignoring everything in her desperation to reach the house, and Caleb, before the entire place went up in flames. The front door was open, and the glow of the fire spread out in a deceptively welcoming light. She raced through, shrieking his name, and then skidded to a halt in the water-filled front hallway as she looked up in horror.

Claire was standing there, her gray hair long and straggly, her robe pulled loosely around her weaving body. She was holding on to the banister, a dazed expression on her face, barely conscious of the confrontation a few feet away. Harrison and Caleb.

"For God's sake," Caleb said, his body rigid, "let me get your mother out of here. What's between us can wait."

He was backed against the wall at the top of the stairs, not moving. Things were no longer dark, they were illuminated by the blaze and crackle of the rapidly spreading fire, and even the downpour overhead seemed to have no effect on it.

Harrison stood silhouetted against that blaze, and his very calm was the most horrifying of all. He was perfectly dressed, even to the linen suit, his hair neat, his white suit spotless, his manicured hand holding the hunting knife as if it were a Cross pen.

"You've destroyed me," Harrison said in a calm, eerie voice. "You've wrecked my reputation, my business prospects, you've taken my wife from me. All because I saw you kill Sherman Delano."

Jassy didn't move, confusion sweeping over her. She believed Caleb; deep in her heart she'd never had any doubt. But how could Harrison stand there and lie?

"You know I didn't kill him, Harrison," Caleb said gently. "You know I haven't gone near your wife...."

"She told me!" Harrison's voice rose in a little scream. "I beat the truth out of her, until she couldn't lie anymore. She told me about all the times she slept with you. How she spent last night in your bed, making love, laughing at me."

Jassy moved forward, opening her mouth to protest, but a small, imperceptible movement of Caleb's hand waved her to silence. She hadn't even realized he knew she was there, but he was aware of everything. Including the acrid smoke and stench of the fire as it billowed through the hallway toward them.

"It's not your wife I've been sleeping with, Harrison," Caleb said. "It's your sister."

"That tramp. I'll deal with her after I'm finished with you. You've all betrayed me. I won't let you do it. I won't let you take everything away from me. It's mine, all of this, it's mine, and you can't touch it." He sounded like a spoiled child, an angry little boy who didn't want to share his toys.

"Fine. We'll go away. Let me help your mother...." He reached toward Claire's woozy figure, and Harrison slashed out with the knife.

"Leave my mother alone. She'd rather be dead than accept help from murdering trash like you." He moved a little closer, and Jassy saw with sudden horror that there was blood on the wicked-looking blade. He must have caught Caleb with that last flashing attack. "I'm going to kill you. I'm going to cut your heart out, and leave you here to the fire, and no one will ever know. Jassy won't say anything. She's loyal, beneath all her willfulness. And Claire wouldn't testify against me. After all, I'm just righting a wrong. You should have paid with your life for Sherman's death, you and I both know it."

"Harrison, you killed Sherman," Caleb said flatly. "You and I both know it."

"No!" he screamed in rage. "You did, you did, you did, you did, you...!"

Claire had lifted her head and staggered toward them in sudden, brief consciousness. Harrison reached out and slammed her out of the way, giving Caleb his chance. Caleb dived at him, ignoring the knife, and for a moment Jassy couldn't watch as the life-or-death battle raged above her.

A column of smoke billowed out, obscuring them. And then she heard the still, horrifying cry, as a body crashed through the cypress railing and tumbled down to the marble floor below.

Jassy didn't move. She could see her brother's white-suited body spread-eagled on the floor, and she knew without a doubt that he was dead. That he might have been dead before he fell, with that vicious-looking knife stuck in his chest.

Caleb emerged from the fire, Claire's comatose body held in his arms. He paused at the bottom of the stairs, to look at Harrison, to look at Jassy, and once more there was no expression in his light eyes. No grief, no regret, no triumph. Just a bleak emptiness.

CALEB DROVE with single-minded concentration, ignoring the three women squeezed into the front seat of his pickup. Harrison Turner's women. Belonging to the man he'd just killed.

His hand clenched around the steering wheel as he avoided a fallen tree trunk, and he barely noticed the pain. He'd never killed a man before. He'd thought about it, long and hard. In particular about killing that man. He didn't know when he'd finally given up the idea, when he'd let go of the need for vengeance in place of justice. For what good it had done him. In the end Harrison had won. Harrison had given him no choice at all, and with that act he'd sealed his own fate. He'd become what Harrison had made him.

The light that was Belle Rive was only a faint glow in the stormy, sullen sky. No one looked back as he'd driven away, no one had asked any questions. The questions would come later, from people like Clayton Sykes and the law-abiding citizens of the town. And the answers would come from the women in the truck.

He slammed on the brakes, cursing. "We can't make it into town," he announced to no one in particular. Harrison's wife was staring out the window, in some distant world, his mother was passed out. Only Jassy was listening.

"Why not?" She sounded unnaturally calm, polite, and he wanted to curse again.

"See for yourself. The road's flooded. We'll have to wait for the police to come to us."

If he'd hoped to startle some sort of reaction out of her, he failed. "They'll find us," she said evenly.

He half wished he were wrong about the Moon Palace. That it had collapsed in the storm like the flimsy little shack where he'd found Jassy hiding out. But it stood in a shallow pool of water, straight and tall and oddly welcoming.

"What the hell happened?" Bo waded out to the truck, opening the door as Lila tumbled out into his arms. She let out a panicked shriek, one Bo seemed to take in his stride. Somehow he was able to calm her, shepherding her into the old bordello with his usual gentleness as Jassy followed after them.

Claire was a dead weight. Her eyes had been open, though, and clear as she watched the struggle at the top of the landing. She'd provide a creditable enough witness if it came to that. He had no intention of letting it come to that.

He carried her into the house, settling her in the spare room where Ray and Bo had set up cots. The beds were unmade but warm and dry, and he doubted Claire was in any condition to be fussy. She was snoring slightly as he covered her up, and he wondered whether she might black out everything that happened. He could hardly count on it.

Jassy was standing in the door, watching him. The place was lit with a combination of candlelight and kerosene lanterns, and she looked like a drowned rat with her clothes plastered against her, her hair long and wet against her body. She'd never looked so desirable.

"She should sleep it off," he said.

"Yes," Jassy said, her voice cool.

"How's Lila?"

"Bo's taking care of her. She'll survive, I'd say. She's pretty shaken up, bruised and battered, but I don't think any bones are broken."

"What makes you so sure?"

"I'm used to seeing women who've been beaten by their husbands, remember? I know what broken bones look like."

"I guess you do." He started to move past her, but she didn't get out of his way.

"Where are you going?"

He grinned then, a sour, humorless smile. "Think I'm going to run away? The way I see it I've got two choices. I can get the hell out of here and start a new life someplace. I figure there's a good chance I could make it. The truck can go almost anyplace, and the police are going to have their hands full with the hurricane. They won't even know anything happened out at Belle Rive until I'm long gone. I don't have a telephone here, so you can't call them, and I've got the only vehicle that stands a chance of getting through high water."

"What's your other choice?" She sounded no more than casually interested.

"Wait for that sheriff of yours. Sykes, wasn't that his name? The one who lived in your brother's back pocket. I figure I stand a real good chance of getting lynched, if I'm lucky."

"Doesn't sound like much of a choice. You're going to run."

"Not likely," he said in a savage undertone. "I've had enough of running. I'm staying put. Don't you worry about me tarnishing the family reputation. You'll still be lily-white. I wouldn't expect anyone to believe me anyway, so why waste my breath? It all boils down to the fact that I came here for Harrison Turner, goaded him until he was beyond rational thought and ended up killing him. Those are the facts, and anything else is just extraneous."

"Extraneous," she echoed. "Like the fact that I love you?"

"Don't!" His voice was raw, anguished. "Don't even think it. I killed your brother, Jassy. He was right, I'm nothing but murdering trash, and if you ever let me put my hands on you again you'd end up despising yourself. Didn't you listen to him? He never admitted it. His last words were accusing me of killing Delano. How can you be foolish enough to believe me?"

"Because I *know* you. I know you're not a murderer, and never were. And Harrison was. I don't think he was lying at the end, I think he no longer knew the truth. He'd spent so many years covering up and rearranging the past to his own satisfaction that he no longer knew what was real."

"Jassy, it's hopeless. Let it go."

She didn't move. "All right," she said. "If you do."

"Do what?"

"Leave. Get out of here. You won't get a fair deal from Clayton, I know that as well as you do. Harrison had everyone fooled into thinking he was a hell of a nice guy, and they're going to think you're a cold-blooded killer. It won't matter if you tell them about Sherman Delano, it won't matter if they see Lila's face. They'll believe what they want to believe, and you won't stand a chance against them."

"Sorry," Caleb said. "I'm sick of running. I've been running since I was fifteen, and I'm not running anymore."

"Caleb . . ."

"I hate to interrupt anything." Ray appeared in the hallway beyond them. "But why are the police here?"

Caleb suddenly became utterly still. "That settles that," he said. "I guess there must be more than one way from town."

"The high road through Whitler," Jassy said. "I should have remembered. Caleb, please . . ."

"You heard the man, Jassy. It's too late. For both of us."

Chapter Eighteen

"Now we can do this the easy way or the hard way," Clayton Sykes said as he heaved his impressive bulk onto the kitchen stool. "I ought to take the bunch of you down to headquarters for your statements, but we got a bit of a problem with the roads. Not to mention that this damned hurricane doesn't seem to want to give up, and I've got other problems besides the Turners to deal with. So we're gonna try it this way, nice and easy, and if you give me any trouble we'll go into town come hell or high water, and it looks like we're having a taste of both outside. You ready to take down their statements, Orville?"

"Yes, sir." Orville, the lanky, red-faced deputy who trailed in Clayton's shadow had to content himself with leaning against the counter, steno pad propped on the new Formica.

"So who wants to go first? You think you're feeling up to it, Miz Claire?"

Claire nodded weakly. She'd been pumped full of coffee, and she'd managed to put her long gray hair in a semblance of order and straighten her old robe. Even so, for the first time in Jassy's memory she looked her age, and then some. "Certainly, Clayton . . ."

"I'll go first," Caleb said, his voice low, deep, authoritative.

Clayton didn't like anyone else sounding authoritative. "I'm the one who's gonna say who's going first," he said flatly. "You take your time, Miz Claire. I don't want to make this any harder on you than it is already. Maybe Miz Lila..."

"No," said Bo, not the slightest bit intimidated. "She's lying down, and she doesn't need to be bothered by a lot of upsetting questions."

"Who the hell are you, boy, to talk that way to me?" Clayton demanded. "You another one of Spenser's ex-cons?"

"You still can't talk to her," he said stubbornly,.

"Well, hell," Clayton snarled. "You all want to tell me when you're ready and I'll be glad to accommodate you...."

"I told you, Sheriff—" Caleb began, but Jassy interrupted, slipping past him and perching on the stool opposite Sykes before he could stop her.

"Ladies first," she said, trying to control the hammering in her heart. She saw Caleb subside, leaning against the doorway with that same shuttered expression on his face. She knew what he wanted—the one thing she couldn't give him. He wanted to be punished, and she figured he'd been punished enough.

"So what the hell happened, Jassy?" Clayton was demanding. "Belle Rive's an inferno—not even forty days and nights of flood could stop it. And where the hell is Harrison?"

"Inside," she said flatly. "He's dead, Clayton. I don't really know how to explain it. He... he's had some business losses lately."

"Hell, it's worse than that. He was facing bankruptcy. Criminal charges, too, for embezzlement. I'd been doing my best for him, but I was on my way out to arrest him when the storm hit. I'm real sorry, Jassy, but the money's gone."

She nodded. "He was a little crazy, Clayton. Caleb had driven me out there to see whether they needed help. He was helping Mother down the stairs when Harrison came at him with a knife. The house was already on fire, and he slipped and fell over the banister, landing on his knife."

Clayton just looked at her as silence filled the crowded kitchen, broken only by the steady drone of the rain against the windows. "That's the poorest excuse for a reasonable story that I've ever heard, Jassy," he said finally. "So damned poor, as a matter of fact, that I'm almost tempted to believe you."

"It's true, Clayton." Claire spoke up, her voice surprisingly clear. "I was a witness, as Jassy was. Harrison wasn't quite...rational. The floor was wet with rain, smoke was pouring out, and he fell."

"What do you say to that, Spenser?" Clayton barked at him.

Jassy held her breath. Throughout her brief testimony he'd said nothing, his face distant and unreadable, the gold hoop in his ear winking in the kerosene light. She was suddenly, terribly afraid he'd do something stupid like tell the truth. But after a moment he simply nodded. "I wouldn't contradict two ladies, Sheriff."

"No," Clayton said wearily. "Neither would I." He heaved his bulk off the stool. "Which I suppose means you're free to go. Which I suggest you do. As far away from here and as fast as the storm will let you. No later than tomorrow. You hear, boy?"

Caleb looked at him. "I hear."

"Miz Claire, why don't we drive you and Miz Lila into town? There are any number of people who'd be happy to take you in while you get things settled."

"No, thank you, Clayton," Claire said with dignity. "If Mr. Spenser doesn't mind, I think we'll just wait out the storm here."

"Stay as long as you like, Miz Turner," Caleb said. "I won't be back. The place is yours if you'd like."

"I couldn't possibly..."

"Go ahead, lady," Ray said. "He doesn't need it. We'll fix up the place for you, make it real homelike. Won't we, Caleb?"

Caleb nodded, his face remote, already miles away. And then he pushed away from the counter, following Sykes and his deputy out into the hallway without a backward glance.

"He couldn't mean it," Claire was saying with a fluttering nervousness.

"He means it," Jassy said abruptly. "You and Lila should be very comfortable here once it's finished."

"What do you mean, 'you and Lila'? Where will you be?"

Ray smiled, and his dark, ferretlike face brightened. "You better hurry," he offered.

"You're not leaving?" Claire demanded in a shriek. "Jassy, you can't abandon us. Not now! We need you. Our lives are in ruin. How can we...?"

Jassy leaned over and kissed Claire's withered cheek. "You'll have to do it by yourself, Mother," she said gently. "I'm gone."

The rain had slowed in the past few minutes, down to a quiet drizzling, and the heavy winds had let up. The lightning had passed, along with the thunder, and in the distance she could see a faint glow. This time it wasn't

Belle Rive. It was the astonishing approach of sunrise. Another day. A new life. An end to the old one.

Dog was already in the truck, his tongue lolling out as he greeted her happily. "You don't look any the worse for wear," she said, climbing in beside him. "Do you suppose he's in the market for another stray? Or do you think he'll kick me out?"

Dog tried to crawl onto her lap, an impossible feat for an almost-Newfoundland-size dog. She shoved him onto the floor with gentle hands, rubbing his huge head. "You'll have to bite him if he tries it," she told him. "I'm not sure if I've got any fight left in me."

"CAN'T TALK YOU into staying?" Ray asked, watching Caleb as he threw his clothes into a duffel bag.

"What's the use? You heard the man. I'm not welcome around here anymore. Which suits me fine—I've had enough of backwater Florida towns."

"Where are you going?"

"I don't know yet. I'll send word. Don't worry—you'll get your weekly paychecks."

"Don't insult me. I've never worried about getting paid with you, boss. I just don't like to see you heading out like this."

Caleb paused for a moment, feeling the heaviness press around his chest. His heart, as much as he hated to admit it. "It's for the best. You and Bo look after the women, Ray. Make sure they're okay, that they have what they need."

"I think Bo'll do just fine with his broken bird. He'll have her eating out of his hand in no time. And the old lady's tougher than she looks. She'll be okay."

"And Jassy," Caleb forced himself to say.

Ray grinned at him. "You want me to take care of her, boss? I'd be more than happy to, but I kind of thought..."

"Keep your hands off her," he growled, "or I'll cut your heart out. She deserves something better than you or me and, damn it, she's going to get it." He slung the duffel over his shoulder and started for the door. "I'll be in touch."

He kept his head down as he made his way across the soggy ground. He didn't notice her until he opened the driver's door and tossed the duffel bag behind the seat. He stood there in the light drizzle, staring at her.

"What the hell do you think you're doing?" he asked in a roughened voice.

"Coming with you."

He looked at the two of them. Dog, with his huge, doggy grin on his face. And Jassy, her long, thick hair curling wildly around her face as it dried, the same hopeful, determined look on her beautiful face.

"I killed your brother," he said flatly.

"Not in cold blood."

"There was too much smoke. It was dark. You couldn't see clearly."

"I *know*," she said. "I didn't have to see. You can haul me out of the truck but I'll just follow you. I'll turn up on your doorstep when you least expect it, I'll haunt you. You might as well accept it, Caleb. I'm your destiny. You're never going to get rid of me."

For all her bravado she was frightened. He could see it in the faint tremor of her lush red lips, in the shadow behind her eyes. She'd been crying, and he'd made her cry too much in the last twenty-four hours. He couldn't stand to make her cry again.

It was that fear that decided it for him. That melted his heart, destroyed his resolve and defeated him. He climbed into the truck beside her, slid his hand beneath her wet tangle of hair and pulled her against him, settling his mouth on hers.

When they finally moved apart the sun had broken through the twilight of early morning. "You'll regret this every day of your life," he said, his voice husky. "But I can't give you up."

"Why?"

He never thought he'd say it. In the end, it was inevitable, and simple, and right. "Because I love you."

Her smile was brighter than the sun. "Then there'll never be anything to regret."

She threaded her arm through his, leaning against him as he started the truck, and he found, to his absolute amazement, that he believed her.

The morning was cool and silent, the oppressive heat vanished in the face of the violent, cleansing storm. He could hear the distant sound of birds singing, and suddenly life seemed new, and full of hope, as together they drove off into the glorious colors of the sunrise. The storm was over. A new day had begun.

Following the success of WITH THIS RING, Harlequin cordially invites you to enjoy the romance of the wedding season with

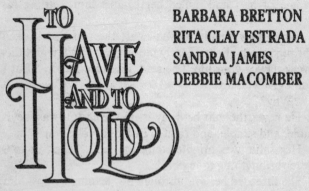

BARBARA BRETTON
RITA CLAY ESTRADA
SANDRA JAMES
DEBBIE MACOMBER

A collection of romantic stories that celebrate the joy, excitement, and mishaps of planning that special day by these four award-winning Harlequin authors.

Available in April at your favorite Harlequin retail outlets.

THTH

"GET AWAY FROM IT ALL" SWEEPSTAKES

HERE'S HOW THE SWEEPSTAKES WORKS

NO PURCHASE NECESSARY

To enter each drawing, complete the appropriate Official Entry Form or a 3" by 5" index card by hand-printing your name, address and phone number and the trip destination that the entry is being submitted for (i.e., Caneel Bay, Canyon Ranch or London and the English Countryside) and mailing it to: Get Away From It All Sweepstakes, P.O. Box 1397, Buffalo, New York 14269-1397.

No responsibility is assumed for lost, late or misdirected mail. Entries must be sent separately with first class postage affixed, and be received by: 4/15/92 for the Caneel Bay Vacation Drawing, 5/15/92 for the Canyon Ranch Vacation Drawing and 6/15/92 for the London and the English Countryside Vacation Drawing. Sweepstakes is open to residents of the U.S. (except Puerto Rico) and Canada, 21 years of age or older as of 5/31/92.

For complete rules send a self-addressed, stamped (WA residents need not affix return postage) envelope to: Get Away From It All Sweepstakes, P.O. Box 4892, Blair, NE 68009.

© 1992 HARLEQUIN ENTERPRISES LTD.   SWP-RLS

"GET AWAY FROM IT ALL" SWEEPSTAKES

HERE'S HOW THE SWEEPSTAKES WORKS

NO PURCHASE NECESSARY

To enter each drawing, complete the appropriate Official Entry Form or a 3" by 5" index card by hand-printing your name, address and phone number and the trip destination that the entry is being submitted for (i.e., Caneel Bay, Canyon Ranch or London and the English Countryside) and mailing it to: Get Away From It All Sweepstakes, P.O. Box 1397, Buffalo, New York 14269-1397.

No responsibility is assumed for lost, late or misdirected mail. Entries must be sent separately with first class postage affixed, and be received by: 4/15/92 for the Caneel Bay Vacation Drawing, 5/15/92 for the Canyon Ranch Vacation Drawing and 6/15/92 for the London and the English Countryside Vacation Drawing. Sweepstakes is open to residents of the U.S. (except Puerto Rico) and Canada, 21 years of age or older as of 5/31/92.

For complete rules send a self-addressed, stamped (WA residents need not affix return postage) envelope to: Get Away From It All Sweepstakes, P.O. Box 4892, Blair, NE 68009.

© 1992 HARLEQUIN ENTERPRISES LTD.   SWP-RLS

"GET AWAY FROM IT ALL"

Brand-new Subscribers-Only Sweepstakes

OFFICIAL ENTRY FORM

This entry must be received by: April 15, 1992
This month's winner will be notified by: April 30, 1992
Trip must be taken between: May 31, 1992—May 31, 1993

YES, I want to win the Caneel Bay Plantation vacation for two. I understand the prize includes round-trip airfare and the two additional prizes revealed in the BONUS PRIZES insert.

Name _____

Address _____

City _____

State/Prov._____ Zip/Postal Code_____

Daytime phone number_____
                                    (Area Code)

Return entries with invoice in envelope provided. Each book in this shipment has two
entry coupons — and the more coupons you enter, the better your chances of winning!
© 1992 HARLEQUIN ENTERPRISES LTD.   1M-CPN